Praise for the writing of Evangeline Anderson

Slave Boy

"*Slave Boy* is a wonderfully written and moving science fiction story set in a lushly detailed and believable world of the future. The plot and characters are as complex as the love of Haven and Wren is tender, caring and passionate."

—*Literary Nymph Reviews*

Eyes Like a Wolf

"Evangeline Anderson's *Eyes Like a Wolf* is dark, violent, extremely erotic, and definitely tests societal boundaries, but wow it is hard to put down. This book grabs readers from the get go and refuses to let them go. A steamier, more seductive or more controversial werewolf story would indeed be a challenge to find."

—Tammy, *Love Romances and More*

The Assignment

"*The Assignment* is an erotically romantic tale of two men and awakening feelings. It takes two close friends that have stood by each other through all the ups and downs of life and tells how they come to fall in love. Highly erotic and emotionally stirring, this story is to be highly recommended to the readers."

—Anita, *The Romance Studio*

Loose Id®

ISBN 10: 1-59632-754-5
ISBN 13: 978-1-59632-754-2
SLAVE BOY

Originally released in e-book format in July 2008

Cover Art by April Martinez

DISCLAIMER: Many of the acts described in our BDSM/fetish titles can be dangerous. Please do not try any new sexual practice, whether it be fire, rope, or whip play, without the guidance of an experienced practitioner. Neither Loose Id nor its authors will be responsible for any loss, harm, injury or death resulting from use of the information contained in any of its titles.

Printed in the U.S.A. by
Lightning Source, Inc.
1246 Heil Quaker Blvd
La Vergne TN 37086
www.lightningsource.com

SLAVE BOY

Evangeline Anderson

Chapter One

"Ah, Master Haven, I am so glad you are finally here." The Gowan ambassador bowed deeply, his furry head and bright turquoise eyes disappearing for a moment as he got out of view-screen range.

"I am but a Servant of the Light, but I am honored to be assisting in your peace negotiations." Master D'Lon Haven, the most respected mediator in The Order of the Light bowed deeply as well, until the tips of his blue-black hair nearly brushed the top of his space pod's control console.

The Order he represented was centuries old and its members were highly respected, both for their vast and amazing mental powers and their commitment to peace and the unity of the universe as a whole. The long apprenticeship and rigorous physical and mental training methods used in the Temple of the Light meant that not all who found sanctuary between its high stone walls were able to attain the title of master or mistress. But because the universe's most highly skilled mediators, healers, and scholars all came from the Order, there was never any shortage of applicants for the few coveted novice positions that came open each Earth-standard year.

Haven himself had been a Servant of the Light or Light Bringer, as they were sometimes called, for most of his life. He had been found on an aptitude search as a young child and started his training at the Temple in his tenth standard year and he was now around thirty-two. His broad shoulders and muscular form beneath the standard Order uniform of a flowing pale blue tunic over fitted black trousers was testimony to the fact that his training was not limited to diplomacy. Servants of the Light strove to bring peace and harmony wherever they went, but if physical action was necessary, they were willing and able to rise to the task.

As he exchanged pleasantries with the Gowan ambassador, Haven scanned the velvet blanket of stars outside his pod, looking for the fast approaching Tiberion warship. His deep blue eyes narrowed and his large hand tightened on the steering rod when he saw its vast, menacing bulk coming up fast on his starboard side. This wasn't just another negotiation for trading lanes or decreased tariffs on goods and services. This was a peace summit -- a last-ditch effort to avert a bloody and pointless war. The Tiberion emperor, Rudgez the Fourth was poised to wipe the peace-loving planet of Gow gi Nef off the face of the galaxy and commit genocide by killing every Gowan man, woman, and child. And all over some slight, real or imagined, that the Tiberion emperor had supposedly sustained during routine trade negotiations with the hapless Gowans.

"Master, I know we're almost in range but I wanted to…oh, excuse me." The light tenor voice behind him interrupted Haven's conversation. He turned to see his novice, Wren, standing behind him, obviously fresh from the sonic shower because he was dressed only in a towel.

Giving the young man a stern look, Haven turned back to his pod's view-screen and the fat, furry Gowan ambassador dressed in elaborate golden robes to make his apologies. "Please pardon the interruption, Ambassador," he said smoothly. "And continue what you were saying."

"Not at all, not at all." The ambassador peered through the view-screen, his attention momentarily focused on Wren's slender, athletic figure, the white towel draped low around his narrow hips and his pale golden skin still beaded with water droplets. "On the contrary, Master Haven, I am both pleased and relieved that you brought your slave with you."

"Excuse me?" Haven tapped his earpiece and frowned. "I'm sorry, Ambassador, what did you say? I think my universal translator must have a glitch in it."

"I said," the ambassador shouted, as though raising his voice would make his meaning clearer. "I am glad you have brought an appropriately desirable slave with you, just as I requested in my last transmission."

Haven stroked his neatly clipped black goatee and mustache thoughtfully with his thumb and forefinger. "It's possible that your transmission got garbled in the encrypter," he told the Gowan ambassador. "But my understanding was simply that you wanted me to bring a companion. Which I did -- this is Wren, my novice. He is an apprentice in the Order of the Light." He nodded at Wren, who bowed deeply, splattering cold droplets of water from his still-wet hair onto the back of Haven's neck with the motion.

"No, no, no!" The ambassador's pointed brown ears laid flat back against his round, furry skull in apparent agitation. "That is not what I said at all! I specifically requested that you bring a *slave* to service you during the negotiations. It is a matter of etiquette with the Tiberions! All persons of rank within their society have one, and to appear before Rudgez the Fourth without one would be the gravest offense."

"I assumed that you wanted me to bring a companion for state dinners and the like," Haven said smoothly, wiping the water droplets from the back of his neck with one hand. "But I understand the Tiberion emphasis on correct protocol and symbols of rank."

"Does your understanding encompass the fact that my entire planet will be obliterated if you offer the Tiberion emperor offense?" the ambassador spluttered. His large blue-green eyes narrowed to slits and his whiskers twitched in excitement. "Observe," he continued, stepping back so that the scope of the view-screen included a Gowan woman who was standing behind him. Like the Gowan ambassador, she had large jewel-toned eyes, pointed ears at the top of her head, and fur all over her body. But in her case, some of the fur had been shaved off in what Haven supposed were meant to be erotic patterns, outlining her small, firm breasts and the tender vee between her thighs.

"Your slave girl, I assume," he said neutrally as the Gowan ambassador came back into view.

"Naturally not!" The ambassador sounded huffy. "We Gowans do not condone the sale of other sentient species -- it is abhorrent to our nature. This is Ylla -- she is a courtesan trained in all the finest court manners and graces. She is accompanying me as my slave in order to satisfy the Tiberions' barbaric customs."

"Greetings, Servants of the Light." The erotically shaved courtesan/slave girl bowed demurely and smiled to show tiny, sharp white teeth.

"Well, this problem is easily solved, then." Wren smiled and placed a hand on Haven's broad shoulder. "I'll simply pretend to be your slave as Ylla there is pretending to be the ambassador's, Master."

"It may not be quite that simple." Haven frowned at him and shook his head. "*Don't offer to act until you understand the action you will be taking, Novice*," he sent through the private mind-link all masters and novices shared for the length of their partnership. But it was too late -- the Gowan ambassador had seized on the idea already.

"It seems a perfect solution to me." The ambassador was all smiles again, showing his own set of sharp white teeth as he nodded encouragingly.

Haven frowned. "Ambassador, if you would excuse us for a moment. I have a few matters to attend to and I will call you back when we are about to dock with the Tiberion ship."

"Of course, of course." The Gowan ambassador bowed deeply again, his rich robes rustling with the movement, and then the view-screen's picture folded to a small white dot in the center of the screen as Haven cut the transmission. Before he could say another word, Wren was standing in front of him, a look of determination in his wide-set, amber eyes.

"Master, I can handle this."

Haven sighed and ran a hand through his thick blue-black hair. "How do you know what you can handle, Novice, until you know what it is you are supposed to be handling?

How do you know what a slave's duties are according to Tiberion custom?"

Wren shrugged gracefully. He was never going to attain Haven's height or size, but he had a swimmer's build with lean, toned muscles and smooth, pale golden-tan skin that drew the eye with each easy movement. His hair was beginning to dry into its usual brownish-blond spikes, and he rubbed one hand through it as he talked.

"It's probably what you said, Master -- attending state dinners, waiting on you hand and foot." He grinned irrepressibly. "Nothing I'm not used to already."

"Worthless novice." Haven shook his head, smiling to take the sting out of his words. In the past he might have grabbed Wren and rubbed his large knuckles roughly through the golden brown spikes of his hair or slapped him on the rump. But lately, the casual contact that had been the hallmark of their partnership ever since he had taken Wren as his novice almost four years before and their friendship even before that seemed…dangerous somehow. Wrong. So he contented himself with returning the young man's grin, keeping his arms firmly crossed over his broad chest.

"I know what's at stake," Wren continued. "And I know you were against taking me on this mission in the first place because of the danger but, Master, you can't keep me a child forever. I'm nearly twenty-two standard years old -- the same age you were when you rescued me. When you bought me for ninety-five credits and a fresh loaf of dewberry bread. Remember?"

"Do I remember?" Haven sighed as he looked at the slender young man standing with hipshot grace before him and wondered how Wren had grown so fast. "How could I forget?"

* * *

It had been Haven's first real mission as a Servant of the Light. He'd passed his trials only the week before and his own master, Serin, had released him with his blessings. Being sent out alone into the universe to do the service of the living Light that surrounds and encompasses all things was a heady experience for a young man. But Haven had a serious, thoughtful nature which wasn't given to rash actions, and he'd had no intention of bending any rules or doing anything out of the ordinary. He had planned to go in and get his mission done speedily and by the book -- that was until he'd seen the ragged young slave boy hunched over a crippled bird in an alley of the common marketplace the Rigelian envoy was showing him.

Haven supposed they were in the market to get a bit of the local flavor. The air was full of exotic spices and the cries of vendors hawking their wares. In his hand was a fresh, hot loaf of the local dewberry bread with its crispy brown crust and the tender middle flecked with pale pink berries that he intended to have for lunch. The Rigelian double suns had been pounding against his uncovered head and he had welcomed the chance to duck into the shade of a nearby narrow alley.

But the narrow stone throat of the alley held more than a respite from the sunlight. Kneeling and leaning against the rough gray stones was an assortment of slaves -- mostly tired looking women with pain collars around their necks to keep them from escaping, not that any of them looked like they had the energy to try.

It wasn't the women that caught Haven's eyes. Down at the end of the alley was a single boy who looked to be around ten standard years of age although he could have been older and small for his size. There was something about him -- some pull that only Haven, with his years of training, could feel.

"There is nothing of interest to see here, Light Bringer," the envoy, a nervous older man with thinning gray hair murmured, attempting to move Haven along. But Haven resisted the polite tug on his long sleeve.

"I won't be a moment," he told the uncomfortable envoy who was obviously more used to the graceful pleasures of the Rigelian court than the dirty discomforts of the planet's underbelly.

Going to the end of the alley where the boy crouched, he watched the little scene that was playing out quietly. The boy, who was dressed in a ragged, oversized smock and had tangled golden brown hair, was so intent on watching the tiny, hurt bird that fluttered around in the dust that he didn't even notice Haven's presence. The bird had speckled brown feathers and a downy gray breast -- one of the Rigelian nesting wrens that were as common as dirt on the desert planet. One tiny wing -- its right -- was cocked at an awkward angle. Through the living Light, Haven could feel its pain like a needle piercing the skin of his own right arm, exactly where the bird was wounded.

"It's all right," the slave boy murmured. "It's all right, little bird." Reaching out carefully, he scooped the struggling bird into his small hands, making a shelter for it with his fingers.

To Haven's surprise, the bird stopped fluttering and held completely still in the slave boy's cupped hands. He held his breath, wondering what would come next. Most boys would have ended the creature's suffering, and probably not in a very humane way. But this slave boy was different, Haven could sense it, and as he watched, there was a ripple in the alley that only he could feel.

"I'll make it better," the slave boy whispered and then, to Haven's astonishment, the living Light poured through him, like sunbeams through a clear pane of glass. The surge of healing power was so pure and sweet he caught his breath at its sheer beauty. Biting his lip to keep from exclaiming, Haven watched as the boy carefully opened his fingers.

Sitting on the slave boy's palm peering at him with bright, expressive eyes, the wren looked like an entirely different bird. It cocked its head and flapped its wings experimentally, as though testing to see whether its wounded limb was really sound again. With the cessation of pain, Haven felt another emotion from the tiny creature -- joy as sharp and bright as a ray of sunshine on the sand. It pierced him with its brilliance and he gasped out loud as the wren spread its wings and took flight, cheeping happily as it flew toward the sky.

The boy turned at his sudden sound and looked up at him, shading his eyes to see all of the tall stranger bending over him.

"Hello, little one." Haven crouched beside him in the alley and gave him a friendly smile which the boy returned tentatively.

"Hello," he echoed. A metal pain collar circled his dirty neck and his eyes were the most extraordinary color Haven had ever seen. Their pale, amber shade reminded him of the golden oceans on Radiant, the world where the Temple of Light was located.

"I saw what you did for that bird," Haven told the slave boy. "Do you do that kind of thing a lot?"

The boy shrugged, the ragged, dirty white sleeves of his smock rising with the motion. "Dunno. Sometimes. It was hurting, you know?" He looked up at Haven appealingly. "I can't stand it when something is hurt. I have to help it if I can. But please don't tell Dungbar -- that's our owner over there." He lifted his chin and nodded at the slaver at the other end of the alley. "He gets mad and says it's a waste of time to bother with other creatures." He hunched his thin back and gave Haven a guilty look. "If he catches me at it, he beats me."

"It's never a waste of time to ease the suffering of others," Haven told him softly, looking at the boy approvingly. Feeling the pain of others was one of the early signs that a child was sensitive to the Light and would be able to use its power to make changes for good in the universe. "How old are you?" he asked the boy.

A shrug of the thin shoulders again. "Twelve standard years last name day. I only know because Dungbar says I'm almost old enough to sell now. Not just my mouth -- my ass too. He's got a special buyer lined up an' everything."

"I see." Haven fought to control the rush of anger that filled him at the boy's casual admission. "What's your name?" he asked, trying to keep his voice low and steady.

The matted golden-brown head shook sadly. "Don't have a name. Dungbar just calls me 'boy.'"

"Boy, hmm?" Haven frowned. "Do you know the name of that little bird you just healed?"

"Sure." The slave boy nodded eagerly. "It's a nesting wren. They're all over the marketplace." He sighed. "Sometimes I watch them and wish I could fly too -- fly away from here."

"Well, from now on, I'm going to call you Wren," Haven told the boy. "And you can fly away from here -- if you come with me. Would you like that?"

The boy looked at him warily. "Beggin' your pardon, sir, other customers have said the same thing to me. But after they use me, they all give me back."

Haven felt his heart swell at the pain in the slave boy's clear, amber eyes. "It's not going to be like that this time, Wren," he promised, reaching out to stroke the thin, dirty cheek. "I won't use you. But I will take you away from here to a place where you can be as free as that little bird you healed." Standing, he patted the boy on the head and went to face the slaver.

Dungbar, as Wren had called him, was a fat, bald man with an evil temper. He stood at the other end of the alley, picking his teeth with a sharpened bone and waiting for the double suns to set so he could ply his trade. Haven ignored the Rigelian envoy's look of horror and went up to the slaver directly.

"How much for the boy?" He nodded to the other end of the alley where the slave boy was still watching him with uncertain eyes.

Dungbar turned to him, his fat gut nearly brushing Haven's flat stomach in the narrow alley. "You c'n buy his mouth for five credits, *Light Bringer*," he said, his small black eyes flicking disdainfully over Haven's sleeve where the icon of the rising sun, the symbol of the Order of Light was stitched. "But his ass ain't for sale. I have a fine gentleman who wants a virgin just his age and he's willing to pay top credit for it."

"You don't understand." Haven felt the anger seething within him and worked hard to control it. He couldn't kill this man, as much as he might want to; the vows he had taken as a Servant of the Light forbade it. He could only bargain for the boy's life and trust in the Light to help him. "I don't want to, ah...rent any one part of him," he told the fat slaver. "I want to buy him outright. So how much?"

"Two hundred credits." But the greedy gleam in the small black eyes told Haven that this was just a starting bid.

"Fifty," he countered, crossing his arms over his chest and tightening his grip on the fresh loaf of dewberry bread he'd almost forgotten he was holding.

"One hundred," Dungbar said, his eyes now fastened on the bread instead of Haven. "He's worth at least that much -- I won't go a credit less."

Haven felt his heart drop. He only had ninety-five credits to his name and the money was supposed to buy him passage back to Radiant. Well, he could work for passage as well as buy it -- every ship's captain was always glad to have a Servant of the Light aboard because of their healing skills. He knew very well that the Council of Wisdom wouldn't be pleased to see him show up at the temple with a new recruit -- one that was technically too old to begin the training to enter the Order and who had no formal schooling of any kind. But Haven couldn't help himself -- he knew the ragged slave boy, Wren, was a true Servant of the Light -- and Haven would be damned before he'd leave him here to rot in this narrow stone alley on a backwater planet.

"Ninety-five credits," he said. And then, with sudden inspiration, "And I'll throw in this fresh loaf of dewberry bread, still hot from the ovens." He waved the loaf under the fat slaver's nose and watched as Dungbar's tiny eyes widened, then narrowed as he considered his options.

"Done!" the slaver growled at last. "Bring the boy here and I'll take off the collar. He was getting too old to sell, anyway."

* * *

And so for ninety-five credits and the loaf of bread that was to have been his lunch, Haven had bought a human being, the ragged slave boy named Wren and taken him back to the Temple of Light. As predicted, the Council of Wisdom wasn't happy to see a boy who was two years too old to begin the training and one that hadn't even been found on a formal search. But they couldn't deny that Wren was filled with the living Light and had enormous untapped abilities. When Haven told them about the bird the boy had healed, they had agreed to take him in on the condition that he would be Haven's novice when the time came.

Haven had agreed to the terms of the council readily -- by the time he and Wren had gotten back to Radiant they had already bonded. He had watched the boy's progress through the training program eagerly, tutoring him after hours when necessary, which wasn't often, as Wren proved to be highly intelligent and quick to learn. When Wren's eighteenth name day came and his formal training ended, Haven was proud to claim him as his novice. That was almost four years ago now and Wren was almost ready to undergo the trials himself, to move from novice to master. It was the only reason Haven had agreed to take him on this difficult and dangerous negotiation between the Gowans and the Tiberions in the first place, and now he was beginning to wonder if he might regret his decision.

Looking at his novice now, standing before him in the cramped confines of the space pod, Haven wondered where the ragged slave boy with wide uncertain eyes had gone. When had the fear in Wren's eyes turned to self-confidence, and how had the thin, dirty little boy Haven had rescued from the narrow stone alley on Rigel Six filled out into this slender young godling with pale golden skin?

Recently he had noticed the change in his novice, although he supposed he should have seen it before. He thought it probably had to do with the fact that the space pod they'd been crammed into for the last standard week was so tiny they were forced to share a room -- and a bunk. On the trip back from Rigel Six, Wren had slept beside him every night, his bony limbs curled around Haven's large, warm body for comfort and warmth. But that had been years ago, and now when Wren turned over in his sleep and draped an arm across his master's bare chest, Haven often found it necessary to get out of bed and meditate to purge his improper thoughts and urges.

He sometimes wondered if his novice had any idea of the feelings he engendered in his master and decided that he probably didn't. Wren was just young and careless, ignorant of the effect he had on a man almost ten years his senior. But even if the age difference between them hadn't been a factor, the fact that Haven was Wren's master would have discouraged any thought of a relationship between them. The Order of Light strictly forbade sexual contact between a master and novice for obvious reasons, and Haven absolutely agreed with the policy. It would be wrong -- a terrible abuse of his power and position -- to coerce his novice into a sexual relationship, no matter how alluring Wren looked standing there wearing only a towel with beads of water still shining on his smooth, tanned skin.

"*Master, what are you thinking?*"

Wren surprised him by using their private link instead of speaking aloud. Haven jumped at his novice's familiar soft mind-touch. Quickly, he shielded his thoughts and cleared his throat.

"Just that...you've really come into your own lately, Wren. You're not the ragged little slave boy I picked up on Rigel Six anymore."

"No, Master, I'm of age now and have been for several years." Wren's light tenor voice was dry with sarcasm. "Which is why I can handle this assignment -- no matter what it involves." He dropped suddenly to his knees before Haven, surprising him, and placed a hand pleadingly on his master's knee.

"Wren, I don't want to put you in danger." Haven sighed and ran a hand through his hair, trying to ignore the light touch on his leg. "Not only physically, but mentally and emotionally. Remember where I found you. Don't you think playing my slave will bring back some…traumatic memories?"

Wren shook his head firmly. "That's all behind me now -- that part of my life ended when you took me away from Rigel Six and put my feet on a new path." Then, using the link again, he pleaded, "*Please, Master, you know I can do this. I'll be the best slave the Tiberions have ever seen.*" The slender hand on Haven's thigh moved upward, lingering dangerously close to where his cock was suddenly swelling in his fitted black trousers. "*I know how to play the part -- how to be submissive,*" Wren added. He sent a quick image of himself kneeling completely naked with his head bowed and his arms bound behind his back through the mind-link.

"Gods!" Haven jumped up suddenly, feeling like his shaft was about to burst out of his pants.

"Master?" Wren looked up at him innocently, his amber eyes filled with confusion at Haven's sudden move. "Is there a problem?" he asked.

Yes, there's a problem. I find you entirely too damn desirable for comfort lately. Haven was careful not to send the thought through their link. There was no point in confusing and frightening his novice with his unwanted feelings. Abruptly, he made a decision.

"Fine." He frowned. "You can come and pretend to be my slave. But Light help us both if this negotiation doesn't go smoothly. The Tiberions are just looking for an excuse to blow the Gowans out of the sky."

"I know it's a serious situation, Master," Wren said gravely. "And I promise you can count on me to conduct myself in a manner befitting the Order in all things."

Haven felt his frown melting. Reaching down, he lifted his novice from the cold metal deck and gave him a brief, hard hug. "I know that, Wren. I'm proud of you and I want you to know I trust you. No matter how difficult these negotiations become, I know we'll come through them together. Now go get dressed." He nodded at the limp white towel wrapped around Wren's narrow waist which was sagging dangerously low.

"Yes, Master." Wren turned to do as he was told, exposing his back, crisscrossed with faint white lines. The scars were all that remained of his harsh childhood as a slave on Rigel Six. Troubled, Haven watched him go, wondering how returning to his roots would affect his young novice.

Chapter Two

Wren knew exactly how long he had been in love with his master -- for nine years, eleven months, and fourteen days. The exact period of time that he had known Haven. It had started the moment he looked up and saw the tall man with dark hair and kind deep blue eyes looking down at him in the narrow stone alley on Rigel Six. At first, Wren had been afraid that the man was just another customer, there to use his mouth like so many men before. Men who bought him for a few minutes of selfish pleasure and yanked his hair painfully, thrusting between his lips and spurting salty, bitter jets of cum down the back of his throat while Wren gagged and choked back tears of pain and humiliation.

But this time was different. The tall, broad-shouldered man had actually bought him from Dungbar for good and taken him away from the dirt and filth and degradation of his life as a slave boy in the back alleys of Rigel Six. Wren would never forget that first night he'd stayed in Haven's rooms at the Rigelian embassy…

* * *

"Come, Wren, you're safe here. Wouldn't you like a nice warm bath?" Haven's deep, calm voice was so coaxing that the newly named Wren was almost tempted to comply -- almost. He looked mistrustfully at the large marble tub filled to the brim with steaming water and then back at his new master, Haven, who called himself a "Servant of the Light." Haven sat on the lip of the tub, still clad in his pale blue tunic and fitted black pants, the look on his face one of infinite patience.

"I...I don't know," Wren faltered, watching Haven carefully to be certain his indecision wouldn't make the big man fly into a sudden rage. Bathing hadn't been high on his list of priorities in his meager existence on Rigel Six. Getting clean usually meant being drenched in one of the sudden and infrequent downpours that happened during the very short rainy season.

Haven wasn't angry at Wren's reluctance. Rather, he seemed to understand the boy's fear. Reaching into the tub, he pulled out a large warm, soapy sponge dripping with water and bubbles. "Let's take it slow, little one," he told Wren. "Just take off your shirt and we can start by washing your top half. How about that?"

"Take off your shirt" was a command that Wren understood. He knew what came next, too. Feeling relieved to be back on familiar ground, he shrugged out of his dirty white oversized smock and knelt on the floor at his new master's feet.

"Master," he murmured, pressing a kiss to the inside of Haven's thigh. "Do you want me to pleasure you with my mouth or my hands?"

"What?" Haven jerked back and nearly fell in the tub himself. "No, Wren," he protested when he caught his balance. "That's not what I meant at all. I meant...Light help me..." He sighed and sat up straighter. "Come here," he ordered, and Wren, who had scooted quickly away at his new master's sudden move, came reluctantly back to stand between Haven's legs.

"Yes, Master?" he asked, trying to keep his voice from trembling.

Haven cupped Wren's thin, dirty cheek in one large hand and looked into his eyes. "That part of your life is over from now on," he said softly. "I promise you here and now that you'll never have to do *that* ever again. All right?"

Wren looked at him doubtfully, wanting to believe, uncertain if he really could. "All right," he echoed at last.

"Good. Now turn around so I can wash your back," Haven directed.

Wren turned, but instead of feeling the wet sponge, he heard his new master utter a low curse. "Master?" He started to turn around again but the gentle hand on his shoulder stopped him.

"Who did this to your back?" Haven demanded and the controlled fury in his voice made Wren shiver, glad it wasn't directed against him. At first he wasn't sure what his new master meant, and then he remembered that he had gotten a beating from Dungbar that morning because a customer had complained. The large, hard leather belt of the slaver was nothing compared to the curving metal buckle that cut deep when Dungbar hit him with it, but such beatings were so commonplace that Wren had learned to tune them out. That was one reason he loved to heal the little hurt creatures that somehow seemed drawn to him -- it was easier not to think of his own misery when he was concentrating on easing the suffering of another.

"Dungbar beat me because a customer complained," he explained to Haven. "I-it's not as bad as it looks, Master. Not as bad as usual, even," he added, trying to downplay the pain he felt from the bruises and cuts that crisscrossed his narrow back.

Haven had made another low, angry noise, almost a growl in his deep chest, and then he took a breath and released it slowly. "All right," he said at last in a calmer tone. "Well, this part of your life is over now too. Never again will anyone beat or hit you for any reason if I can stop it." He stroked Wren's shoulders and suddenly some kind of warm, healing magic seemed to flow from his large palms. Wren gasped and quivered beneath the soft, soothing touch and wondered if the small animals he himself had healed had felt this way.

"Master?" he whispered, making the word a question. "What…?"

"Healing you," Haven's deep voice explained quietly. "I'm afraid I can't do anything about the scars, but your bruises and cuts will be better very soon, Wren."

"Yes, Master," Wren sighed. At that moment he surrendered himself completely to the man behind him. The man who promised never to hurt him, never to take him against his will or sell him to others for pain and humiliation. For the first time in his young life, Wren felt trust and kindness in the hands that were touching him. And something else as well -- he felt love in Haven's soothing touch. A deep and abiding emotion he somehow knew would follow him for years to come.

* * *

Just thinking of that first night, of the way Haven had healed him with his touch and taught him it was all right to trust again, made Wren feel warm inside. He glanced at his Master, who was sitting beside him piloting the space pod through the wide slit in the side of the Tiberion warship to reach the docking bay. Haven's face was serious and intent, the black brows pulled low over his deep blue eyes, one large hand gripping the steering rod firmly as he navigated.

So handsome, Wren thought longingly, being careful to shield the wayward emotion from his master. With his broad shoulders and large, well-built frame, Haven dominated any room he walked into. Long ago, Wren had given up the hope of ever growing as tall or as muscular as his master, but it was just as well, considering how small the space pod was. If both of them had been of Haven's massive build, they never would have fit into it. As it was, things were a tight fit, and Wren hadn't exactly been going out of his way to make things easier, either.

He thought of the long nights aboard the small pod when he and his master had shared the single narrow cot. For Wren, it was a golden opportunity to be close to Haven -- as close as he had been as a boy, although his intentions now that he was of age were considerably less pure.

Wren knew beyond the shadow of a doubt that there could never be any kind of sexual relationship between himself and his master. Even if Haven had been interested, such conduct was strictly forbidden between masters and their novices, and Wren knew his master was much too scrupulous to ever break the rules. But knowing that a relationship between himself and his master was impossible didn't keep Wren from wanting him. For years as the forbidden emotion grew in his heart, he had shielded his impure thoughts and desires carefully from his master. And because Haven was an affectionate master, quick to hug Wren or wrestle with him or simply tousle his hair, the young novice was able to keep his needs in check. But in the last couple of months or so, Haven had been withdrawn and not nearly as physically demonstrative as he had been when Wren was younger.

Wren supposed he was getting too old to wrestle with his master or to curl up against his side and put his head on Haven's broad chest when he felt lonely or insecure. But by the Light, he missed it so much! The gentle touches, the way his master had always healed every small injury with a touch or a kiss, the sound of his master's heart drumming in his ear and the feel of Haven's large, warm arm draped around his shoulders when they sat together at night -- he missed it all.

With no platonic touching to keep his desires in check, Wren found that his need had gone from a small flame to a blazing inferno -- raging out of control. Sometimes in the past week as he lay beside his master in the narrow cot it was all he could do not to lean over and kiss Haven's narrow but sensual lips. He wanted to run his hands all over the big, muscular body that lay beside him in the dark and to feel his master's warm hands exploring him, touching and stroking. Wanted to feel Haven's hot mouth licking and kissing and sucking him. He wanted to submit to his master utterly, to give Haven every part of his body completely and without reserve, just as he had given his heart from the first moment they met.

At such times, though Wren was careful to shield his innermost thoughts and desires, he was sure that some of the emotion he was feeling had leaked through the link he shared with Haven. Why else would his master suddenly find it necessary to get up and go into the other room to meditate? Wren was sorry he was making his master uncomfortable, and yet he couldn't seem to stop. Watching as Haven set the space pod down smoothly in the spot designated for their landing, he wondered if his master would be glad to stretch his long legs and make some room between himself and his troublesome novice, even if it was on the ship of a hostile faction.

The docking bay was a huge space, all gunmetal gray and large enough for thousands of spacecrafts the size of the pod they had traveled in for the past week. Wren watched in awe as the glittering translucent blue O2 barrier slid back into place after their pod passed through, allowing a breathable atmosphere to return after the vacuum of space. A loud alarm sounded to indicate that the atmosphere had normalized. As they disembarked from the pod, Wren saw a small figure already hurrying to meet them.

"Master Haven, I am Minister T'will. We are pleased to have you aboard." The Tiberion envoy who bustled up to them as they disembarked had a self-important air only minor officials seemed to possess. He also had glowing red eyes and the muddy green skin that made Tiberions look, in

Wren's opinion, much like oversized sand lizards from his home planet of Rigel Six. Otherwise, like the Gowan ambassador, the Tiberion envoy was mostly humanoid. A thin crest of purple skin that Wren supposed was the Tiberion version of hair ran along the length of his narrow, pointed head and waved excitedly when he talked.

"Minister T'will." Haven bowed and nodded. "I assume the Gowan ambassador is already aboard."

"Yes, he landed some time ago and has already been presented to the god-emperor Rudgez the Fourth, may he live forever." The sneering look on his flat face made it perfectly clear what Minister T'will thought of the Gowans. "But we have no time to stand and speak, Master Haven," he continued. "Not if you are to be presented to the god-emperor as well before his audience hours end for the day." He looked Haven up and down, his glowing red eyes flickering over the fitted black trousers and flowing blue tunic. "These clothes will never do! And where is your slave?"

"He is here," Haven said. "Wren, show yourself."

Wren stepped out from behind his master and bowed deeply. "May it please you, Minister T'will, I am Master Haven's personal slave."

The Tiberion envoy looked at him, his thin upper lip curling in disgust. "It most certainly does *not* please me. Is this some sort of joke, Light Bringer?" he demanded, turning to Haven. "Do you really expect me to believe that you allow your personal slave to go out and about dressed like *this*?"

Wren looked down at himself in confusion. He was wearing the pale green flowing tunic and fitted dark brown trousers of a novice of the Order of Light. The garments were simple and well made -- not flashy, but obviously of good quality, and no one had ever complained about them before. Like his master, he was wearing high black boots that came to his knee -- a Servant of the Light could never tell what kind of terrain he might find himself in and it was wise to be prepared for the worst.

"If I may inquire," Haven said icily. "What is wrong with my slave's attire?"

"What is wrong?" Minister T'will threw up his hands, which had webbing between the fingers. "You might as well ask, 'what is right?' I cannot even begin to tell you how inappropriate it is to allow a slave to dress in so similar a manner to his master." His red eyes narrowed. "In fact, such similarity of dress begs the question, is this person really your slave at all?"

Wren knew exactly what he had to do. He dropped gracefully to the floor at his master's feet just as Haven was answering the accusation.

"I assure you, he is in fact and indeed --" Haven began indignantly, but he stopped abruptly when Wren leaned forward and kissed the tops of his high black boots. "Wren?" he said, his deep voice coming out a bit strangled.

"I serve my master in all things," Wren said softly, shifting position so that he was sitting between Haven's widely spread legs. "He bought me when I was a child and he has owned my heart ever since."

"Wren, that is…enough." Haven reached down and brushed his fingertips through Wren's short, spiky golden brown hair, making him shiver.

Minister T'will looked at them for a long moment before nodding briefly. "Very well, I see my mistake. The boy has been with you for a number of years so you treat him more like a lover than a proper slave."

"I --" Haven began in a choked voice.

"Exactly," Wren said smoothly, cutting his master off. "But that doesn't mean I don't fulfill my master's every wish and desire, Minister T'will." Leaning to one side, he rubbed his cheek lovingly against the inside of Haven's thigh, causing his master to clear his throat and shift nervously.

"*Wren, enough*!" The command came loud and clear through their mind-link.

Wren looked up at him innocently. "*But, Master, I'm only playing a part -- the part of your submissive slave boy.*"

"Well, you must understand that we have strict protocol about how slaves must dress and act on Tiber," the Tiberion envoy continued, unaware of their silent communication. "And before you go before the god-emperor, may he live forever, you must both be properly attired." He shook his head, the purple fringe of skin swaying with the motion. "I only hope we have time before the god-emperor's audience hours end. Come!"

Chapter Three

"Are you quite certain this is necessary?" Haven looked down at the stiff golden brocade robe which hung open over the red silk shirt and tight black trousers he was currently wearing. The minister of the wardrobe, a smaller and even more irritating Tiberion than Minister T'will, had forced him into the outlandish outfit the moment he had gotten Haven into the dressing area, a small set of brightly colored rooms near the rear of the massive ship. Wren had been led to a different room, and Haven wondered if his novice was being made to wear anything half as uncomfortable as he was.

"Quite certain, quite certain!" the minister of the wardrobe twittered, circling Haven in the small dressing room and tugging at the hem of the brocade robe to be sure it was straight. "You cannot appear before the god-emperor, may he live forever, in anything less than court finery. It would be a terrible insult!"

Haven looked longingly at his discarded tunic, lying in a soft pile of pale blue fabric on the floor and shifted his broad shoulders in the confining golden robe. He sighed. "Well, I certainly wouldn't wish to give offense." *Especially not when it's so damn easy to do here*! he added silently to himself.

"Now then, I think you're almost ready," the minister of the wardrobe said, nodding rapidly. "If you'd only let me shave off that unsightly hair around your mouth…"

"I'm *not* shaving." Haven brought a hand to his mouth, covering his short, neatly clipped mustache and goatee protectively. "Unless it's a mortal offense to appear before the god-emperor with facial hair?"

"No," the minister of the wardrobe said reluctantly. "It's just my professional opinion that you would look much better without it, Master Haven. Body hair of any kind is so low, so *common*, and I --"

"Minister! Minister, please, come quickly." The door to the tiny dressing room slid open and another Tiberion bounced in.

The minister of the wardrobe gave the intruder an irritated look. "What is it, B'orl? Can't you see I'm trying to get Master Haven ready for his audience with the god-emperor, may he live forever?"

"But, Minister," his assistant squeaked. "It's Master Haven's slave! He's being most defiant. First he insisted on shaving himself, even though I explained to him that a slave is never to touch his own private areas. And then, once I managed to get the inhibitor manacles on him, he refused to let me prepare him for court!"

"What? But how…?" the minister of the wardrobe began, but Haven had already brushed past him, striding out of the small room to see what was being done to his novice. What he saw when he entered the slightly larger dressing chamber where Wren had been taken stopped him dead in his tracks.

Wren was kneeling with his arms bound behind his back and his legs spread wide on a waist-high, dark red platform. His head was bowed low in apparent submission, and his sides were heaving as though he had just run a race, but worst of all, he was completely naked.

"*What in the seven hells? Wren, are you all right?*" he sent anxiously through their link.

"*I'm sorry, Master.*" Wren looked up, his large golden eyes wide with fear. Haven could actually see the white showing all around their amber depths as though his novice were a frightened animal. Below his navel, he was completely smooth; the soft nest of brown curls that surrounded the base of his cock had been shaved away. The cock itself was curled against Wren's right inner thigh, completely soft, looking pink and terribly vulnerable.

"*Sorry about what? What have they done to you?*" Haven demanded.

But Wren only shook his head, his thoughts a chaotic jumble that Haven couldn't begin to make out. His protective instincts aroused, he strode quickly to his novice's side and stroked the pale forehead which was damp with sweat. Wren turned his face into his master's large palm, still breathing hard, obviously seeking comfort.

Haven felt his heart swell with emotion. He never should have allowed this to happen -- never should have let them separate him from Wren! He turned to the minister of the wardrobe and his assistant, who had just entered the room.

"What have you done to my slave?" he demanded, nodding at the naked Wren, who still kneeled submissively.

"Only gotten him ready for his court appearance -- or tried to!" The minister of the wardrobe sounded defensive. "Why, he isn't even dressed or oiled yet! And audience hours are almost over. Oh, Minister T'will will have my head if you aren't ready in time, and just look at this!" He gestured at Wren with agitation and then turned to his assistant. "B'orl, how could you allow this to happen?"

"Minister, I swear, I tried to get him ready but --"

"Enough!" Haven roared, cutting off the twittering argument. "Where are the clothes he needs to wear? I'll get him dressed myself."

"The harness is here." B'orl stepped forward, holding out a bewildering array of black leather straps. "But we didn't get as far as that, Master Haven, because your slave refuses to be oiled."

"Oiled, what in the seven hells are you talking about?" Haven demanded angrily. Court protocol or not, there was only so much foolishness he was willing to put up with.

"Oiled. *Prepared*," the minister of the wardrobe emphasized, raising his thin purple eyebrows suggestively. "In case you wish to make obeisance to the god-emperor, may he live forever." He frowned, gesturing with a long, thin vial of pale golden liquid that B'orl had handed him. "My understanding from Minister T'will was that you were quite fond of this slave, Master Haven. You don't want to injure him by taking him too roughly if the situation demands it, do you?"

"Taking him too…" Haven's voice died away as the meaning of the minister's words suddenly hit home.

"*Master, you know what he's talking about.*" Wren sent a sudden image of himself, kneeling naked on hands and knees with Haven behind him. Haven's long, thick cock was in his hand and he was pressing it deep into his novice's tight, virgin rosebud, filling him, fucking him, as Wren panted and moaned beneath his master, open and ready for his assault.

"*Enough, Wren! That isn't going to happen*!" Haven took a deep breath and pushed the deeply erotic image away from him with all his strength. He refused to think of such things, despite the way his cock was throbbing angrily in the too-tight trousers he had been forced to wear. "I don't plan to…to *take* my slave in that fashion," he explained carefully to the anxious minister of the wardrobe. "So there is no need for any, ah, oiling to take place."

"What? You would refuse the command of the god-emperor, may he live forever, if he orders you to honor him with your slave?" The minister of the wardrobe looked beyond shocked.

"Our customs differ from yours in that we do not perform intimate acts in public," Haven said firmly. "Surely the god-emperor will understand this."

"Most assuredly he will not!" B'orl protested. "This is the sort of thing that got the Gowan emissaries in trouble in the first place. First they refused to eat the meat that was placed before them at the Feast of Clemency -- claiming that they did not eat the flesh of other species. Imagine!" He snorted. "And then when it was time to make obeisance to the god-emperor, they had no slaves to service them. It was a dreadful scandal, to be sure."

"To be sure!" the minister of the wardrobe echoed his assistant. "Of course, it is by no means certain that the god-emperor will demand that you perform for him. But not to at least be ready is the height of offense. Your slave's shaft must be shining with oil, Light Bringer, if for no other reason than to show your respect for his majesty, Rudgez the Fourth." He frowned and handed the thin vial to his assistant. "Unfortunately, your slave refuses to allow B'orl here to oil him."

"It's true, even with the inhibitor manacles on he is most obstreperous." B'orl looked indignant. "He acts more like a free man than a proper slave. Why -- he doesn't even have a brand."

"A brand?" Haven frowned at them. "Are you serious?"

The minister of the wardrobe crossed his arms over his chest. "Of course. All slaves on Tiber are branded on the upper arm or pelvis. A slave can never truly escape if you burn your mark into his flesh." He looked thoughtful. "You know, Light Bringer, I could arrange for that if you like -- we Tiberions use the standard alphabet for our branding irons and I'm sure I could find one to match your initials."

"*Please, Master, don't let them*!" Wren looked up at Haven again, his beautiful eyes wide with fear.

"Gods, no!" Haven stepped in front of his novice, shielding Wren with his body. What the hell was wrong with these people? The thought of burning his name into another man's body was abhorrent, sickening -- yet the minister of the wardrobe spoke as though it was a matter of course. "I mean..." He cleared his throat, trying to keep the disgust from showing on his face. "I mean, my people do not brand their slaves."

The minister of the wardrobe shrugged his narrow, stooped shoulders. "You may suit yourself in this matter, Master Haven, but unfortunately, there is no question that your slave must still be oiled. Do you wish to do it yourself or should B'orl complete the task for you?"

"*Please, Master,*" Wren's inner voice came through their link again. "*If you do it, I can stand it. But please don't let anyone else put their hands on my body! Please*!"

"*Peace, little one.*" Haven leaned down to look in Wren's eyes and stroked his novice's cheek soothingly. "*No one will touch you but me, I swear it.*"

Inside he felt sick that he had allowed things to come to this. It was just as he had feared, being manhandled and put in this horribly submissive position was bringing back Wren's childhood trauma. If there were any way out of the situation, he would have taken his novice home to the Temple of Light on Radiant at once. But he still had to consider the negotiations between the Gowans and the easily offended Tiberions. He couldn't allow an entire planet to be obliterated, even for the sake of his beloved novice. No, there was no way around it, he would have to go on with the mission and simply try to shield Wren as best he could.

Haven sighed. "Give me the oil," he said, standing and holding out a hand for the thin vial of golden liquid. "I'll do it myself."

"Very well." B'orl sounded sulky as he handed over the vial. "Be certain that you oil his phallus as well as his anus,

Master Haven, so that it can be seen when the harness is put on."

"I..." Haven shook his head, unable to finish the sentence. He had been prepared to simply pour the vial of oil over his novice's crotch, but it was becoming apparent that he would have to handle Wren's body in a much more intimate fashion than that. His heart ached for the humiliation Wren would suffer as much as for the fact that he would be doing something with his novice that was expressly forbidden by the ruling council of the Order. But again, there was no help for it -- the survival of an entire planet was resting on his decisions. Abruptly, Haven made up his mind -- decisive action was best.

"*Forgive me, Wren,*" he sent through their link, pouring a palmful of oil into his hand to warm it. "*I'll do this as quickly as I can.*"

"*Master, as long as it's your hand on me and no other's, I'll submit to anything.*" Wren looked up at him, such perfect trust in his ocean-colored eyes that it nearly melted Haven's heart.

"*Very well. Try and relax and it will be over soon,*" he promised. Holding the palmful of oil carefully to avoid spilling it, he reached down and cupped his novice's slender shaft in one hand. Wren gasped and bit his lower lip, squeezing his eyes closed at the gentle touch.

"*Master...oh, Master, your hand on me...*" The thought was cut off abruptly, but Haven couldn't help noticing that his novice's cock, which had been so soft and vulnerable looking a moment before, was hardening rapidly in his hand as he attempted to spread the oil in a quick and businesslike fashion. Carefully, he stroked from the root of Wren's shaft up to the flaring head, swiping his thumb over the tender nugget of flesh where beads of pearly white precum were already forming. Could it be that it was his touch that was so arousing to Wren? Or was it simply the fact that his novice was young, with the sexual readiness of a young man to be excited by anything? Haven was sure it was the latter, and he pushed the desire he felt and the insistent throbbing of his own hardened cock to the back of his mind.

Pouring another handful of oil, he reached lower and cupped his novice's tender sac, cradling the egg-shaped balls in his palm until they were thoroughly coated. A long sigh fell out of Wren's full, panting lips and a sexual flush colored his high cheekbones.

"*Master,*" he sent. "*Your touch is so gentle…so warm.*" The tightly closed eyes opened for a moment, and Haven found himself lost in their depths as he stroked and fondled his novice's vulnerable balls for much longer than he had intended.

"*It feels good?*" he found himself sending without meaning to.

"*It feels wonderful, Master,*" Wren sent back honestly. "*Your hands on me always feel wonderful. So big and warm and kind.*"

"Ahem!" The minister of the wardrobe cleared his throat impatiently, breaking the spell Haven seemed to have somehow fallen under. "May I remind you, Master Haven," he said in his high, irritating voice, "That we are on a tight schedule? You must hurry and oil your slave's anus or we'll never get the harness fitted in time to make an audience with the god-emperor."

"Step back," Haven snapped, turning to give the minister and his assistant an angry glare. "You've already made my slave nervous enough for today. I'm well aware that we are under a time limit, but I require some privacy for this act."

Muttering angrily, the minister of the wardrobe and his assistant stepped back and began whispering together in the corner of the dressing area.

Haven took a deep breath and poured some more oil into his hand. This was going to be difficult. It was one thing to coat his novice's genitals with oil, to stroke Wren's cock and balls gently until he was hard and ready. But it was another thing entirely to invade his body, to stretch and open the tight, virgin rosebud until Wren was ready to take a cock in his ass. Not that it would come to that, Haven assured himself hastily. But in order for Tiberion court protocol to be met, it had to at least look that way.

"*Wren*," he sent softly, trying to keep his mental voice calm and soothing. "*Do you feel ready for this?*"

In answer, Wren spread his thighs wider and looked up to meet Haven's eyes once more. "*Master, I'm ready for anything you have to do to me*," he sent. "*Touch me, open me... I'm not afraid*."

Impulsively, Haven pressed a soft kiss to his novice's forehead. He could smell the sweet musk of Wren's skin, taste the slightly salty tang of his sweat. But most of all, through their mental link he could feel his novice's complete confidence in him. Wren was naked on his knees with his hands manacled behind his back, utterly helpless, but as long as Haven was there to take care of him, he wasn't afraid.

"*My Wren,*" Haven sent gently, and reached between his novice's legs to spread the rich golden oil over the tender opening of the young man's body. He circled the tight orifice gently at first, trying to loosen Wren a little and get him used to the idea of being opened. Then, when his novice didn't try to draw away or close his legs, he inserted just the tip of his middle finger into the tight opening, breaching the tense muscles guarding Wren's inner rosebud and working deeper and deeper, spreading the oil inward as he went.

Wren drew in his breath sharply and caught his bottom lip between his teeth as Haven's gently probing finger invaded his body, but he still made no move to try and get away from his master's hand. In fact, he spread his thighs even wider and threw back his head, his eyes squeezed closed again as he panted through pink, open lips, submitting utterly to Haven's touch.

Just the fact that Wren would trust him so absolutely, would open himself to such an invasion was almost too much for Haven to bear. He thought he had never seen anything so beautiful as his novice kneeling naked with his thighs spread, submitting to having his ass prepared to be fucked. It didn't matter that he was never actually going to fuck Wren, to fill Wren's tight ass with his cock. What mattered to Haven was the clear and distinct impression that he got through their mental link that even if he *had* wanted or needed to fuck his novice, Wren would have submitted in the exact same manner.

The thought of the slender, golden body lying beneath him, of Wren spreading his thighs and welcoming his master's weight on top of him, of begging for Haven's thick cock in his body filled his head and wouldn't go away. Haven withdrew briefly to get more oil and then added another finger, scissoring gently as he worked his way into Wren's virgin rosebud, as though he really were preparing the young man to be fucked.

At last his gently probing fingers seemed to touch something, some spot inside his novice's body that electrified Wren. Every muscle in his lean, beautiful form tensed suddenly, and the tendons in his neck stood out as he gasped. Through their link, Haven caught the impression of overwhelming pleasure as he rubbed carefully over the spot, watching the beautiful submission on his novice's face as though in a dream.

"Master, please, no more lest I shame myself!" Wren rasped in a low, agonized tone, breaking the trance Haven had somehow fallen into again.

Looking down, Haven saw what his novice was talking about. The long, slender shaft stood at stiff attention against Wren's flat belly, the broad, tender head an angry purple color broadcasting his need. Precum flowed in a river down the underside of his novice's cock and dripped from his tightly drawn balls to the platform below. Wren was literally seconds from orgasm, probably because Haven had been carelessly stimulating his prostate. How much greater would his humiliation be if he came helplessly all over his master's hand in the presence of two strangers?

What's wrong with me getting carried away like this? Feeling ashamed of his thoughtless lust, Haven carefully withdrew his fingers and sent calming thoughts and images to his novice through their link.

"*Relax, Wren, it's over now. Peace, little one. I'm sorry I went too far.*"

"*Too far or not far enough, Master?*" Wren looked up, a flash of the old teasing in his eyes, and Haven felt himself returning his novice's grin almost against his will. At least Wren's spirit hadn't been broken by the forced intimacy between them, for which he was supremely grateful. Yet he had a feeling that this was only the beginning of a long and difficult road that he and his novice would have to walk together. A feeling that was only strengthened when B'orl came forward with the bewildering array of black leather straps and suggested that since he was finished oiling his slave, he should now get him dressed for their audience with the god-emperor.

Chapter Four

The collection of straps, or harness, as B'orl and the minister of the wardrobe insisted on calling it, was nothing more than an elaborate cock ring that strapped around Wren's upper thighs and snapped together in the back. Wren held perfectly still, trying to slow the racing of his heart as his master fastened the apparatus onto him. His cock was still achingly hard from being so overstimulated only moments before, and he thought if he lived to be a thousand, he would never forget the deliciously erotic feeling of Haven stroking his cock and balls and opening his nether entrance as though he really intended to use Wren, to fuck him, instead of just playing a part.

Master, he thought, carefully shielding his thoughts. *Oh, Master, if only you really would*! He kept catching glimpses of thoughts -- images in which he was pinned beneath his master's muscular body, his legs spread, willing and able to take Haven's thick shaft deep into his ass. Was it wishful thinking on his part, or were some of these images leaking through from Haven's part of their link? It was crazy, wasn't it, to hope that his master had the same wishes, the same unfulfilled desires that Wren had?

Even if he did, it's not like he could act on them, Wren reminded himself sternly. After all, if the council back on Radiant had even an inkling that an improper relationship had started between Haven and his novice, the two of them could be separated and Haven could be barred from the Order. That was the last thing that Wren wanted -- the Order of the Light was his master's life, as it was his. But still, since they had been placed in this difficult situation together, a situation where his master had to touch him and Wren had to submit to his touch, was it really so wrong to hope that Haven was enjoying it as much as he was?

Wren's thoughts were wrenched back to the present as Haven finished settling the confusing collection of straps in place. There was a one inch thick leather band that was meant to encircle the base of Wren's still erect cock and keep it hard. Before he buckled it in place, Haven gently cleaned the trickle of precum that had leaked down the underside of his novice's throbbing shaft with a soft towel.

"*There,*" he sent when the cock ring was fastened in place. "*But I'm afraid they're not going to give you many more clothes than this. How do you feel about that, Wren?*"

Wren bowed his head. Submissive, he had to be submissive. He had been here before, years ago. Had done this so many times with so many different men. But never with one he loved as he loved Haven.

"*Master,*" he sent at last. "*As long as I'm by your side, I don't care what I wear or don't wear. Just...keep me near you.*"

"*Of course, Wren.*" Haven helped him stand, no easy task since his hands were still manacled behind his back and his legs were almost asleep from kneeling in the submissive posture for so long. Wren took a step, feeling awkward with his naked, hard cock sticking straight out in front of him.

"Are we finally ready?" The minister of the wardrobe hurried up, his red eyes glowing with anxiety.

"We will be, as soon as you uncuff his hands." Haven gestured angrily at the manacles that still bound Wren's hands behind his back.

"Very well, we can release his arms, but as long as you are aboard the ship he must still wear the inhibitor manacles," the minister of the wardrobe explained, producing a small electronic key and freeing Wren's hands.

"Why?" Haven demanded. "To show he's a slave? Isn't it obvious enough by the way you're forcing him to dress?"

The minister of the wardrobe clicked his tongue. "Not at all, Master Haven -- to keep him from touching his private areas. If he tries, the inhibitor manacles will deliver a strong and very unpleasant shock to his central nervous system. In this way, he will be completely dependent on you for gratification."

"But that's ridiculous -- and dangerous," Haven objected. "The manacles have to come off at some point -- what if he needs to bathe?"

"Oh, that's safe enough, Master Haven, never fear," the minister of the wardrobe assured him. "But I am sorry -- as long as you stay with us on Tiberion territory, your slave must keep the manacles on at all times. I could no more allow him to appear before the god-emperor without them than I could allow him to appear dressed in those hideous clothes he was wearing when you first arrived."

Haven opened his mouth to argue some more and then appeared to decide it was a losing battle. "*Sorry, Wren,*" he sent through their link, giving Wren an apologetic look.

"*That's all right, Master, maybe we can find a way to get them off when we get to our own room. If they give us a room,*" Wren sent back. But inside he tried to quell the rising tide of panic. Was he really going to be completely dependent on his master for sexual gratification? His cock was already so hard he was longing to come, longing to slip into the privacy of a bathroom somewhere and ease the ache his master's big hands had started in his body. He wondered how long he would be required to wear the damn cock ring harness and if there was any way out of the inhibitor manacles besides the key that the minister of the wardrobe had already put back in his pocket.

Suddenly the door to the dressing area slid open with a loud bang and Minister T'will stalked in, his red eyes blazing. "Well? Where are they? I expected them to be ready ages ago. The god-emperor, may he live forever, is only in the audience hall for ten more standard minutes."

"We're ready," Haven said, stepping in front of his novice to shield Wren's nakedness.

"Not quite!" B'orl suddenly appeared beside them holding a tray. "You have yet to choose a collar for your slave to wear, Master Haven," he said, pushing the tray under Haven's nose. From where he was standing, Wren could see that the collars were of three different colors -- pure white leather, brilliant scarlet, and pitch black. For some reason, looking at the black collar gave Wren a shiver of apprehension.

"What in the seven hells…?" Clearly, Haven was out of patience. "That one," he snapped, pointing to the scarlet collar. "Here, give it to me and I'll put it on him myself."

When the collar was in place, strapped securely but not chokingly around Wren's neck, Minister T'will led the way through a winding maze of corridors painted in pale pearlescent colors and carpeted in some kind of soft, springy silver-gray fur. Obviously, no expense had been spared anywhere in the vast ship, and everywhere they went there were Tiberion officials with half naked slaves.

Wren kept his chin high and tried not to feel horribly exposed. There was no doubt that this humiliating experience was bringing back pieces of his past he would rather forget. But the steady hum of comfort coming through the mind-link from his master helped him endure what otherwise would have been the unendurable shame of walking naked through a crowd of strangers.

Trying to keep his mind off his own nakedness, Wren noticed that he and Haven were one of the few same-sex master/slave pairs to be seen on the huge Tiberion warship. Most of the officials he saw were males and most of their slaves were female. The female Tiberions were considerably more attractive than the sand-lizard looking males, in Wren's opinion. They had the same muddy green skin tones but instead of a single strip of purple skin along the length of their skulls, they had a shawl-like fringe almost like hair which covered their head and shoulders in becoming waves.

Full breasts and wide hips seemed to be the feminine ideal and most of the slave girls Wren saw were scantily clad or else wearing nothing at all, aside from the ubiquitous slave collars in white, red, and black. White was the predominant color for both male and female slaves, he saw, followed by red like the one he was wearing. Only a few slaves wore the black collar, and most of the ones that did had a strange, empty look in their eyes that made Wren wonder if the black collar had some significance that wasn't immediately apparent.

The slaves that he saw, male and female, did have one other thing in common besides their collars, however -- all of them were branded. As the minister of the wardrobe had said, there was a two-inch-high initial burned into the skin of every slave he saw, either on the right upper bicep or on the tender skin of the pelvis, just a few scant inches from the genitals. Most of the brands looked old and a few had been blotted out with a larger brand. Wren supposed that was what happened when a slave got sold to a new master. His imagination worked overtime until he could almost feel the searing kiss of the branding iron and smell the odor of roasting flesh. What must it be like to be held down and burned over and over just so your owner could see his personal mark on the flesh of another sentient being?

Stop it, Wren, he told himself sharply. *That's never going to happen.* After all, it was one thing to play the part of a slave, but it was another to start really feeling like one -- to start believing the part he was playing. And it was ridiculous anyway. It wasn't like Haven was going to brand him. He would no more brand his novice than he would have sex with him -- no matter how much Wren might want it.

That thought sent his mind back to the incredibly hot feeling of submitting to his master's gentle touch in the dressing area, and for a moment Wren considered that it would be almost worth being branded if he could be fucked by his master as well. Yes, he very well might submit to the hot iron scorching his flesh as long as he could feel Haven's thick cock filling him up as part of the deal.

"*Wren, pay attention! We're almost to the audience chamber.*"

Haven's sharp order through their link brought Wren back to the here and now and he wondered if his master had caught any of his thoughts. Blushing, he looked up at the tall man from the corner of his eye but it was impossible to tell anything from Haven's broad, muscular back as he strode purposefully through the long multihued pearlescent corridors.

Up ahead, the hallway widened out into a massive passageway where the pearly pastels abruptly gave way to darker colors. Strips of black, crimson, and white silk descended from the ceiling in banners that looked to be over a hundred feet long. Armed guards in Tiberion armor, which seemed to consist of a chest plate made of buzzing touch-me-not and a less practical but more colorful pike, lined the long black and red carpet that led to an enormous archway.

"Hurry, hurry, Light Bringer!" Minister T'will hissed, all but pushing Haven and Wren onto the long stretch of carpet. "Audience hours are almost at an end. Go to the end of the carpet and wait until the guards signal you to go in. Hurry!"

Haven stepped onto the carpet deliberately and walked at what appeared to Wren to be a positively sedate pace, admiring the armored guards along the way. Wren followed his master at a trot, wondering why Haven was deliberately slowing their progress instead of rushing as Minister T'will was urging them to do. When at last they reached the edge of the archway where two especially large Tiberions stood, he saw why.

Sitting on a broad golden throne that floated three feet above the richly inlaid pseudo-wooden floor was a fat, bored looking Tiberion dressed in robes so encrusted with jewels and gold thread it was a wonder he could move at all. His tiny eyes were dull slits and the purple crest of skin at the top of his head drooped to one side as though it was about to go to sleep, like the rest of him. Standing beside him on the pure silver platform his throne floated over was a hugely muscular Tiberion with a hard look on his flat face. He was so tall he could lean over to whisper in the god-emperor's ear even though the throne was floating three feet off the ground. But the thing that made Wren look twice at him wasn't his height -- it was the fact that his eyes weren't the glowing red of most Tiberions. Instead, his irises were a deep, pulsing purple that was almost black.

Once you looked into those eyes, Wren found, it was difficult to look away. Then he realized that he had somehow locked stares with the strange Tiberion standing beside the throne and looked down quickly. What he saw on the floor in front of the throne was quite enough to distract him from both the god-emperor and his stranger advisor.

Kneeling on a pile of silk pillows, presumably placed there for exactly that purpose, was yet another Tiberion minister. On her hands and knees before him was a branded slave girl wearing a red collar much like Wren's own. None of that was unusual until it became obvious that the slave girl was kneeling on her hands and knees because she was getting fucked. With grunts and slaps of flesh on flesh, the Tiberion minister claimed his slave, thrusting a long, thick shaft into her open pussy again and again, apparently as an obeisance to his ruler, the god-emperor. Wren had no idea how having sex in public was supposed to honor the Tiberion monarch, but the minister and his slave were certainly going at it energetically -- or the minister was, anyway.

Because the pair was turned away from Wren at an angle, he couldn't see the look on the girl's face. But her body language spoke of complete submission, complete despair. As the minister continued to slam into her, she kneeled lower, burying her head in her arms and holding her ass even higher in the air. Clearly she was only waiting for the entire experience to be over so she could leave and let the next master and slave take her place.

The next master and slave…by the Light, that's us! Wren snapped out of the trance he'd fallen into watching the hapless slave girl getting rammed by the overenthusiastic Tiberion minister. Oh, gods, were he and Haven going to have to…? Wren couldn't even make himself think it. Even though a moment before he had been fantasizing about giving himself completely to his master, of being pinned beneath Haven's hard, muscular body and filled with his thick cock, the realization that his fantasy might soon become a reality still left him cold.

This wasn't how he wanted it to be, Wren realized suddenly. Fucking in front of an audience for the amusement of some fat foreign monarch wasn't the way he wanted to make love with his master for the first time. He wanted soft lighting, soothing music, and, after glimpsing Haven in the sonic shower and changing room from time to time and knowing the rather large dimensions of his shaft, Wren also wanted plenty of lubricant. But suddenly it looked like he wasn't going to get any of that.

"*Master,*" he sent through the link, trying hard to keep the panic out of his inner voice. "*Master, we're not going to have to...*"

"*Calm yourself, Wren. Of course not.*" Haven's deep inner voice sounded completely certain, but Wren saw the tense set of his master's broad shoulders and the grim look on his face. Haven was a Master of the Order of the Light, which meant he could call forth deadly weapons of havoc crafted from the living Light itself. But this wasn't a fight or flight situation -- it was a matter of protocol and if they offended the Tiberion god-emperor, *may he live forever,* Wren added automatically to himself, they might as well pull the trigger on the annihilators aimed at Gow gi Nef themselves.

Oh, gods, we're really going to have to do this, Wren thought, watching as the kneeling minister and his wretched slave girl finally finished their performance. *We're really going to have to...*

"Audience hours of his highness, the god-emperor Rudgez the Fourth, may he live forever, are now over!" a loud, imperious voice thundered from some overhead speaker. The pair of guards that stood as still as statues on either side of the archway came to life. The wicked looking spikes at the tops of their tall bronze and silver pikes suddenly clashed together, blocking the entrance to the archway and barring the way into the audience chambers with a finality that took Wren's breath away.

"*There, Novice,*" Haven sent with obvious satisfaction. "*Have some faith in your old master once in a while.*" He turned his head just enough to give Wren a sly wink and a half smile. Wren would have returned the gesture if Minister T'will hadn't come rushing up at that exact moment, breathless and angry.

"What? After all our preparation you missed the audience hours? I cannot believe this!"

"My deepest apologies, Minister T'will," Haven said, bowing deeply. "It is most unfortunate that I was unable to meet the god-emperor today. I suppose I will have to wait for the peace negotiations with the Gowans tomorrow to make his majesty's acquaintance."

"By no means!" T'will exclaimed, tapping his foot in irritation. "You cannot enter negotiations with the god-emperor, may he live forever, without first being formally announced and presented. It is unthinkable!"

"What?" Haven frowned. "Are you saying that we have to wait until the audience hours are over tomorrow to even begin these negotiations? Do I need to remind you that every man, woman, and child on the entire planet of Gow gi Nef is in fear for his or her life? We need to get this issue resolved."

"No, no." Minister T'will scowled. "There will be another opportunity for you to be announced and presented tonight at the Grande Promenade." He sighed in aggravation and threw up his hands. "Which of course means a new set of clothing for both you and your slave. Well, I will simply have to tell the minister of the wardrobe."

Wren's heart leapt into his throat at the thought of another "fitting." Who knew what he would be required to wear or do next time? Or how his master would be required to touch him. Apparently, Haven was thinking the same thing because his normally dark tan skin went decidedly pale and he asked, "Is it really necessary to go back to the dressing area at once? My slave and I have had a long journey to get here and we're very tired, Minister."

"No, no, the Grande Promenade doesn't start until this evening," T'will said. "Stay here and I'll get a servant to lead you to a room where you can get rest and refreshment before the evening's entertainments. The minister of the wardrobe has your measurements now so he can send you proper attire."

"Thank you." Haven bowed again. "That is most kind."

T'will made a short, cursory bow and left without answering.

Haven watched the Tiberion minister leave, a bemused look on his handsome face. "*Well, Wren, I guess we just wait for the servant to --*"

"*Master, behind you -- the Gowan ambassador,*" Wren interrupted.

Haven turned to intercept the fat, furry Gowan who was followed by his erotically shaved "slave girl." In the room full of Tiberions, Wren thought that the two Gowans looked like cats or rats in a room full of lizards.

"Master Haven." The Gowan ambassador did not look pleased. "What's this I hear about you and your slave missing the royal audience hours?"

"An unavoidable delay which is easily remedied, Ambassador," Haven said smoothly. "We're to be announced and presented tonight at the Grande Promenade so we'll be able to begin peace negotiations with the Tiberions as planned tomorrow."

"Well, I still don't care for the way this is being handled." The Gowan ambassador puffed himself up until his black fur made him seem twice as large and his round turquoise eyes glittered with indignation. "It is most irregular that you and your, nov -- ah, slave, could not manage to make the audience hours on time."

Haven frowned. "May I remind you, Ambassador, that it was you who asked for the intervention of the Order of the Light? If you do not wish our help --"

"No, no," the Gowan ambassador cut him off quickly. "No, it's simply that we're all so on edge and I was hoping to conclude these peace negotiations at the earliest possible time. My people, as I'm sure you can understand, are terribly frightened and upset. Fully a fourth of our population has already left the planet since the Tiberion threat has been declared. Unfortunately, the three-fourths that are left are unable or unwilling to leave. Such a state of chaos is unthinkable, and the offense we gave the Tiberions was truly unintentional, so I simply don't understand --" He broke off abruptly, his blue-green eyes growing wide as he stared at something over Haven's broad shoulder.

"Ambassador?" Haven stepped forward, a concerned frown on his face. "Is there something wrong?"

"*Master, he's staring at that massive advisor who was standing by the god-emperor's throne*," Wren sent through their link. "*He's coming this way*."

"*Thank you, Novice. I'm getting tired of being ambushed!*" Haven and Wren turned at the same time to see the huge Tiberion minister with the purple eyes approaching from the audience chamber where the god-emperor was now blatantly asleep and snoring in his floating throne. The minister was wearing a golden robe over a black shirt and pants but all his clothes had a severe military cut and he managed to make them look more like a uniform than formal court attire somehow.

"Be very careful what you say, Light Bringer," the Gowan ambassador hissed. "That is H'rak, the god-emperor's minister of war. He was the one who --"

But before they could find out exactly what H'rak had done, the massive Tiberion minister was upon them and the Gowan ambassador shut his mouth with a snap.

"Ah, Ambassador. Good afternoon." H'rak snapped out an efficient military bow that the Gowan ambassador and Haven both returned. "And I assume that this is the Light Bringer that you sent for to settle our little disagreement." He had a cold, colorless voice that managed to remain ironic despite its lack of expression.

"I am Master D'Lon Haven of the Order of the Light," Haven said, nodding. "And any argument which threatens to end an entire planet is more than a 'little disagreement,' Minister."

"Call me H'rak." The minister of war pronounced his name like someone choking on a bone. "And alas, Light

Bringer, if only the Gowans had not offered such mortal disrespect to our god-emperor, Rudgez the Fourth, we would not be in this position right now."

"I understand that the Gowans transgressed your protocols during routine trade negotiations by refusing food that was served to them and not having slaves as your customs demanded that they have," Haven said mildly. "But do you really think these are just causes to threaten to obliterate their entire world?"

The expression in Minister H'rak's flat purple eyes grew even colder. "You misunderstand, Light Bringer. They did not simply transgress our customs -- they committed blasphemy. They did not just refuse food -- they distained holy meat which was blessed by the god-emperor himself. And it wasn't their lack of slaves that offended so much as the fact that they were without the proper means to honor Rudgez the Fourth at the Feast of Clemency -- the most holy of days in the Tiberion calendar."

"Which we heartily regret," the Gowan ambassador gabbled hastily. He was so nervous that his long black whiskers trembled. "Please, esteemed Minister H'rak, the offense was unintentional. We Gowans are a peaceful people."

"Yes, so peaceful that you don't even have weapons strong enough to defend the outer limits of your planet," H'rak snapped, his cold voice heating a little. "So peaceful that you refuse to take responsibility for --" He stopped abruptly and shook his head. "But we will not speak of these matters now. Our councils are scheduled for tomorrow, as I understand it. That is soon enough to listen to your arguments on why we should not blast you out of the sky, Ambassador."

"But, Minister H'rak --" the Gowan ambassador began in a pleading tone.

H'rak made a peremptory gesture with one huge hand. "I will speak no more of it. You may go."

Dismissed, the Gowan ambassador bowed quickly and left, his slave girl courtesan following quietly behind.

Abruptly, Minister H'rak turned his attention to Wren, who had been standing quietly behind Haven, watching the entire exchange from the corner of his eye. "That is a very fine slave you have there, Light Bringer," he said to Haven, reaching out to stroke Wren's cheek with long, cold reptilian fingers. Wren stood absolutely still, keeping his eyes down. Somehow he managed to control the impulse to shiver at the repulsive, overly familiar touch.

"He is indeed. I have had him for many years," Haven said neutrally. Through their link, Wren felt a sudden surge of angry possessiveness, but his master kept his deep voice calm.

"High-spirited too. I could tell by the way he met my eyes earlier, though he will not do so now." H'rak cupped Wren's chin and forced his head up so that they were eye to eye -- or as close to it as they could be, considering that Wren was almost two feet shorter than the massive minister of war. Again, Wren had to force himself to control the shiver of disgust that wanted to run through him. "And you have him in a red collar, I see. A pity when black would suit so much better." The minister's glowing purple eyes traveled down Wren's body from the scarlet collar that circled his neck to the black leather harness and cock ring that kept his shaft at constant attention.

Oh, gods, if he touches me there... Wren bit his lower lip and fisted his hands at his sides. If the minister of war touched him, he would simply have to endure it to avoid giving further offense. But it would doubtless be one of the most loathsome experiences of his life.

"*Steady, Wren,*" he heard Haven whisper through their link, and the sound of his master's inner voice inside his head strengthened his resolve.

"Not many men possess the strength to master such a slave -- and a male slave at that," H'rak continued, giving Wren a cool, appraising smile.

"I don't find it to be a problem." Haven's tone had a slight edge to it now, and Wren could feel him calling the power of the Light to him, gathering strength for what might turn into a major confrontation. Maybe H'rak felt it too because he dropped Wren's chin abruptly and stepped back.

"I prefer a male slave myself. Much more challenging." He smiled coolly and turned his head. "Tallen, come!" he called sharply.

Suddenly, a male slave that looked to be a little younger than Wren appeared, though it was hard to judge his age since he was Gowan, not Tiberion. The slave's thick, luxurious brown fur had been shaved from the neck down, making his naked body look somehow even more bare and his large hazel eyes were dull with pain. Burned into the shaved flesh of his pelvis was a large capital H that looked old -- apparently the unlucky slave had belonged to H'rak for some time.

Looking lower, Wren winced when he saw that instead of a cock ring, the slave had on an elaborate series of leather straps that tied tightly around his erect shaft and only ended at the head of his cock, which was pierced. A large silver hoop had been passed through the tender nugget of flesh and the diamond trinket that dangled from it flashed whenever the slave moved. A thick black leather collar studded with similar diamonds circled his neck.

"This is your slave?" Haven asked, nodding at the young Gowan male.

"Indeed." Casually, H'rak reached down and began to stroke the leather bound cock of his slave, who tried to stifle a moan. "We do not esteem Gowans much, Light Bringer -- never have. But I find their assholes are as tight and pleasurable to fuck as any other slave's once all the disgusting fur has been shaved away."

"I see." Haven's voice was still cool and low, but Wren could feel his master's revulsion through their link.

"No, Light Bringer, I don't think that you do see. But you will." Reaching into his golden robe, H'rak abruptly produced a knife with a jeweled handle. It was a tiny weapon, no longer than Wren's hand from palm to fingertip, but the blade looked wickedly sharp.

"What do you intend to do with that?" Haven's voice was flat, but Wren knew his master couldn't stand by and watch the hapless slave murdered or mutilated and do nothing about it.

H'rak ignored the question. "Tallen," he snapped, still stroking the Gowan slave's cock with one hand and holding the knife in the other. “How long has it been since you’ve been allowed to come?”

The Gowan slave’s hazel eyes were wide now, following the glittering knife blade with desperate fear. “Six standard months, five days, and seven hours, Master,” he said, his voice low and trembling.

“Excellent, and would you like to honor this esteemed Servant of the Light who has come to mediate our dispute with your filthy people?” H’rak continued.

“N-nothing would give me greater pleasure, Master,” the Gowan slave stuttered, his eyes never leaving the blade in H’rak’s huge hand.

“Very well.” The knife moved with frightening speed. Before Haven or Wren could say anything, the black leather bindings that wrapped the slave’s erect cock were lying on the floor. H’rak gripped the newly freed shaft and fisted his slave exactly three times, a quick, jerking motion that looked more painful than pleasurable to Wren. He was wondering if H’rak had really kept his slave in such a state of sexual agony for more than six months when the minister of war barked, “Now!”

A sudden spasm wracked the Gowan slave’s slender, shaved body and jets of pearly white cum suddenly shot from the tip of his cock and landed on the black and red carpet at Haven’s booted feet.

H’rak dropped his slave’s cock at once and pointed at the droplets of cum that were already beginning to sink into the thick weave of the carpet. “Clean that up!” he demanded. Without a single protest, his slave, Tallen, dropped to his knees and began licking the evidence of his release from the rough nap of the carpet with a long, pink tongue.

Haven stepped back, giving the young Gowan male room to work, his face still carefully neutral.

"*Gods, Master, what was that supposed to be?*" Wren sent through the link. "*That poor slave!*"

"*I think it was the Tiberion idea of a gift of honor, Novice,*" Haven sent back dryly. To H'rak he said gravely, "You honor me, Minister."

"As you will honor the god-emperor tonight at the Grande Promenade." The Tiberion minister of war gave Haven a piercing look. "We Tiberions have a saying which I believe would translate into standard as 'a word to the wise is sufficient.' See to it that your obeisance is sufficiently respectful when you are presented to his majesty. Good day, Master Haven, I will see you and your fine young slave later." He bowed curtly.

"Good day, Minister H'rak." Haven returned his bow and they watched as the Minister of war and his miserable Gowan slave marched down the long red and black carpet, disappearing into the crowd of Tiberions lingering around the huge antechamber to the throne room.

Wren opened his mouth to mutter something to his master, but just then a short, round Tiberion servant came up and tugged on the sleeve of Haven's golden robe.

"Excuse me," he squeaked. "But are you Master Haven? Minister T'will sent me to lead you to your rooms."

"Thank you. That would be most agreeable." Haven nodded and they followed the servant across the carpet and through another long maze of pearlescent corridors. As they went, Wren wondered exactly what a "sufficiently respectful" obeisance consisted of. And though Haven was shielding his thoughts, he could feel his master's concern and dismay through their link as he probably wondered the same thing.

Chapter Five

Their rooms turned out to be a spacious arrangement, bigger than the entire space pod they'd spent the last week on, which caused Haven to breathe a sigh of relief. Unfortunately, there was only one bed, a huge gel mattress draped in pale blue and gold furs and stacked with multiple air-foam pillows. Wren went into the large bathroom at once, giving Haven only a quick glimpse of the broad pseudo-marble bathing pool before he shut the door.

Haven lay back on the bed, feeling the cool gel in the mattress beneath him conform to his shape. Taking a deep breath, he tried to meditate. Something was going on here besides just a breach of etiquette, he was certain. Something to do with Minister H'rak. Several times the massive Tiberion had seemed about to say something revealing and then had stopped himself. What was going on?

But no matter how hard he tried to concentrate on the matter at hand, his mind kept returning to the fact that in a couple of hours he and Wren were going to be presented to the god-emperor, Rudgez the Fourth. And they were going to be forced to perform some kind of sexual act if they wanted to avoid giving offense. But what would be "sufficiently respectful," as H'rak had put it? Would Haven be able to get away with something small like a kiss? Or would he be forced to publicly humiliate his novice by jerking him off at the god-emperor's feet, or worse?

Haven tried to consider the matter objectively, but he was torn, his mind gripped in a tug-of-war between lust and guilt. There was no way he ought to touch his novice in a sexual way -- it was expressly forbidden by the Council of Wisdom. And yet, if he wanted these negotiations to succeed, it looked like he was going to have to bend the rules. At the same time, though, even if he did have to touch Wren in inappropriate ways, he absolutely shouldn't enjoy it or continue to picture it in his head. He shouldn't imagine, for instance, the way it would feel to grip his novice's hard, slender shaft in one hand and stroke until Wren came, gasping his submission as he jetted cum all over Haven's palm. Or the way that cum would taste on his tongue if he sucked Wren and caught the thick, salty spurts in his mouth instead. Or the way it would feel to have Wren suck him, taking Haven's thick shaft down his throat and swallowing eagerly as Haven fucked between his novice's sweet, pink lips…

A muffled curse from inside the bathroom interrupted Haven's guilty fantasy session. He sat up abruptly on the gel mattress, aware that his cock was rampantly hard inside the confines of the tight black trousers he wore.

"Wren?" he called, wondering what his novice was up to and trying not to picture him in the black leather harness that doubled as a cock ring.

"Master?" Wren opened the bathroom door, a look of angry shame on his fine features. "Can you help me?" he asked, gesturing to the leather harness Haven had been trying so hard not to imagine. "The minister of the wardrobe wasn't joking about these inhibitor manacles -- the minute my hands get anywhere near my, uh, crotch, I get the most horrible shock."

"Come here and let me see what I can do about them." Haven beckoned to his novice, who came and stood between his knees. "All right now, let's see." Haven concentrated on the manacles, trying to ignore the fact that Wren's painfully erect shaft was inches from his face as he worked. But after ten minutes of intense concentration, he had to admit defeat.

"Master?" Wren looked at him hopefully, but Haven shook his head.

"I'm sorry, Novice, but the locking mechanism on these manacles appear to have a fail-safe. I could summon a Knife of Radiance to cut through them, but I'm afraid if we try to take them off without the key, the shock they deliver could kill you."

"You mean, I really have to wear them the entire time I'm here?" Wren groaned. "Gods, Master, that's going to be torture!"

Haven nodded grimly. "I know, Wren, I'm sorry. Maybe I can talk the minister of the wardrobe out of the key when he comes to bring us our new clothing for the Grande Promenade tonight."

"Oh, gods." Wren collapsed on the bed beside him, lying on his back so that his throbbing shaft stuck straight out in front of him. "I can't believe this. I'm already so hard I ache and now…" He shook his head, a look of shame coming into his large amber eyes. "Master, I hate to ask you this, but could you at least remove this damn harness thing? So I could, ah, go down?" He nodded down at his angry red cock, which did, in fact, look painfully hard.

"Certainly, Wren." Finding the angle difficult, Haven got on his knees at the edge of the bed so he could manipulate the black leather buckle that confined his novice's cock. It proved to be a difficult task since the leather was slippery with the oil he had used on Wren earlier. "And you don't have to be ashamed to ask me for help, either," he added, looking up to meet his novice's eyes. "I know we're in an uncomfortable situation here, Wren, but you can still rely on me to support you and help you in any way you need."

"Thank you, Master." Wren's clear tenor voice was soft with gratitude. "You're so good to me." He shifted his hips so that his hard, slender shaft slid lightly against Haven's fingers as he continued to work on the stubborn buckle.

Haven cleared his throat uncomfortably. Gods, there was no way he ought to take any kind of pleasure in the feel of his novice's cock in his hands, yet his own shaft was hard as a rock inside his trousers and there was nothing he could do about it.

"Master," Wren continued, apparently unaware of his discomfort. "What are we going to do at this strange Tiberion function tonight -- this Grande Promenade?" He lifted himself on his elbows and looked down at Haven, one golden brown eyebrow raised quizzically. "I mean, in order to avoid giving offense when you're presented to the god-emperor."

"I don't know exactly, Wren." Haven sighed and shook his head. "I've been trying to figure that out…trying to think about what would be the least, ah, invasive display we could get away with without offending the Tiberions."

"I suppose you could, um, touch me -- the way Minister H'rak did with his slave a while ago." Wren's face grew slightly red, but the throbbing shaft still confined by the leather cock ring harness plainly proved that he didn't find the idea at all off-putting.

"I was thinking more along the lines of a kiss, Novice," Haven said dryly, finally managing to get the stubborn, slippery buckle to budge.

"I suppose so." Wren sounded thoughtful. "I could get on my knees and kiss your cock, Master. That ought to be sufficiently respectful." He sent a quick mental image of himself kneeling on the floor before his master, with the tight black trousers opened and Haven's hard, naked cock jutting out of them. Wren's full, sensual mouth was open, performing a hot, sucking kiss on the broad head of his master's shaft while Haven threaded one large hand through his novice's spiky golden brown hair and urged him to take more, to suck deeper…

The image was so vivid that Haven could almost feel the moist heat of his novice's mouth enveloping the aching head of his cock. He had to bite back a groan and shield his emotions quickly.

"I really don't think that kind of thing is going to be necessary," he said, dryly, carefully keeping his tone light. "There, I think I've got it." Triumphantly, he pulled at the loosened harness, watching the black leather straps slither off his novice's naked body.

"I don't know, Master, we don't want to offend them." Wren looked at him with wide eyes and sat up on the bed. "And...and I just want you to know that if we have to do that, or anything else, I can... I mean, it won't bother me."

"Have you considered that it might bother me?" Haven got off the floor and sat beside his novice on the gel mattress, his hands on his knees. "Wren, don't you remember the promise I made you when I first took you away from Rigel Six? I told you that no one would ever use your body again without your will, and that includes me."

"I remember that, Master -- I remember it well." Wren's golden eyes were soft and bright. "But it wouldn't be -- against my will, I mean. Anything, Master, anything you need to do to me, or I have to do for you on this mission -- none of it could offend or hurt me as long as it's with you." He got off the bed and sank to his knees between Haven's legs, looking up seriously. "Master, don't you know that I would gladly take you in my mouth? That I would suck you deep in my throat and swallow every drop when you came?" He put his hands on Haven's knees lightly and leaned forward for emphasis. "And, Master, if you have to fuck me, I'll open myself for you. I'll submit to your cock in my mouth, in my ass, anywhere in my body. Anything you have to do, any way you need to take me, I'm yours -- yours completely."

"Gods, Wren." Haven could hear the ragged edge in his own voice, but he couldn't seem to control himself. He raked a hand through his blue-black hair and shook his head, trying to get rid of the erotic images his novice's words spun inside his head. "Don't...don't talk like that," he murmured, trying to sound stern and failing. "This mission…it's not going to come to that. We'll manage somehow."

"But, Master…" Wren stood up and leaned forward to brush his lips lightly against Haven's cheek, his breath warm against the side of Haven's throat. "We have to be realistic. We can't let the Tiberions obliterate the Gowans simply because we were too squeamish to follow their protocols and customs. So maybe…maybe we should practice."

Haven took a deep breath and kissed his novice lightly on the forehead before pushing Wren gently but firmly away. "What are you trying to say, Novice?"

"Only that…now would be a good time to…to practice what Minister H'rak showed us with his slave." Wren sighed and a look of shame crossed his face. "Please, Master, I didn't think I'd ever be asking you this but, well, I'm in serious pain here and I can't do anything for myself with these manacles on." He held up his hands helplessly, displaying the bulky black inhibitor manacles that encircled his slender wrists.

Haven looked down at the slim naked body and saw what his novice was talking about. Despite the fact that the cock ring harness had been removed, Wren's shaft was still achingly hard, pearly droplets of precum beading at its tender tip. Apparently, the conversation they had been having had done nothing to ease his novice's arousal. It had probably increased it, Haven thought dryly. Then he tried not to consider why it was that the talk of sexual submission -- Wren's submission to him -- should have such an effect on both of them. Because his own cock was still rock hard as well.

Aside from what he or his novice was thinking, should he do this? Guilt gnawed at him and then Haven remembered H'rak's miserable looking Gowan slave. The minister of war had taken great pride in the fact that he had kept his slave in a state of sexual agony for well over six standard months. Haven didn't want to do that to his novice, didn't want Wren to be in such physical pain that he couldn't concentrate on their mission. It would be cruel and wrong when, with just a few, impersonal strokes of his hand, he could ease the young man's ache. Wouldn't it? Abruptly, his mind was made up.

Apparently, Wren took his long silence for a rejection. "I'm sorry, Master, I shouldn't have asked. I…I just thought…" He trailed off, his voice full of misery.

"No, Wren." Haven cupped his cheek, tilting his novice's face until they were eye-to-eye. He sighed. "I just got finished telling you that you could ask me for help in any way. Of course, this isn't something we would ever do in the course of a regular mission, but I can't leave you in pain just because easing that pain isn't exactly what the council would consider proper."

"Thank you, Master." Wren's face filled with gratitude. "How exactly…?"

"I'm not sure of the exact mechanics, seeing that I don't exactly do this on a daily basis -- or ever for that matter," Haven said dryly. "But I think it would work best if I sat against the headboard and you leaned back against me. Here." He scooted back until the cool metal of the Tiberion bed's scrolled silver headboard pressed into his back and beckoned for Wren to sit between his legs and lean back against him.

"Yes, Master." Wren crawled on his hands and knees, the toned muscles sliding under his sleek, golden skin and Haven thought he had never seen anything more beautiful or erotic. Then he pushed the thought aside and tried to concentrate on the business at hand. *Bad choice of words*, he told himself. And yet, what else was he supposed to think about the fact that he was about to jerk his novice off? *Don't think about it -- just do it*, he advised himself. *Remember to keep it impersonal.* Impersonal -- right. Which was why he was currently encouraging his novice to lay back against him in a full body cuddle instead of simply taking him in hand and doing the deed quickly, as H'rak had done with his slave. But then Wren was settling himself so that his smooth, bare back was pressed against Haven's chest and all coherent thought seemed to leave his mind.

"Just relax and spread your legs for me," Haven heard his own voice saying. The young man in his arms obeyed at once, leaning his head back against Haven's shoulder and opening his legs wide to expose the slender, throbbing shaft.

"Please, Master," he murmured, his voice hoarse with need. "It hurts so much. I need you...need your hand on me. Please."

"Peace, Wren." Haven kissed his soft cheek lightly, tasting the slightly salty flavor of his novice's skin. "Close your eyes and let me touch you."

"Yes, Master," Wren murmured. But Haven noticed that the vivid amber eyes remained slitted, watching as he reached around his novice's body and took Wren's aching cock in his hand for the second time that day.

Carefully, Haven started at the root and stroked upward to the head, just as he had earlier when he oiled Wren before he put on the harness. Then his movements had been slow and tentative, uncertain of if he ought to be giving pleasure with his touch or not. But now Haven was deliberately working to make his novice come -- now he knew what Wren wanted, what he needed, and he was committed to giving it to him. He stroked again, holding the young man's cock firmly in his large hand and Wren gasped and bucked in his grasp.

"Oh, Master, oh..." he moaned, thrusting up to meet the hot rhythm Haven was setting. "Gods, that feels so good, your hand on me, stroking me..."

"That's right, Wren," Haven heard himself murmuring gently in his novice's ear. "I want you to relax and open yourself for me. Relax and let me make you come."

"Yes, Master...anything for you...anything you ask," Wren gasped, still pumping in time with Haven's hand. He pressed his head back hard against Haven's shoulder and his fingers gripped the material of Haven's black pants, squeezing convulsively as the pleasure built within him.

Through their link, which was wide open now, Haven could feel exactly what his novice was feeling. The hot, shameful pleasure of submission, of lying back against Haven's broad, muscular chest as his master stroked him. The need to thrust into the large, warm hand that held him so firmly, so knowledgeably. The rush of desire building inside his body, taut with imminent release as he prepared to let another man bring him to orgasm as he never had before...

And along with the feelings came Wren's thoughts -- the ones he usually kept shielded and buried, hidden away even from their mind-link.

Oh, Master, so good! How long have I wanted...needed...missed being close to you, love you so much! Missed pressing my head to your chest, hearing your heart, feeling your arm around me... Missed you. Love you. Love your hand on me...so hot! So hard now, going to...going to...

"Gods, Master, I can't help it!" Wren gasped in his arms. "Going to come now!"

"Come for me, my Wren." Haven kissed him again, lapping hungrily at the side of his novice's throat just above the scarlet collar, sucking, not caring if he left a mark. "Come now!" he growled demandingly in his novice's ear.

"Master!" With a final deep groan, Wren obeyed his master's order. Hot jets of pearly white cum jetted out over Haven's fingers as his novice cried and bucked against him, letting himself lose control, giving himself completely to the pleasure of his master's hand on his body.

"Good, that's good," Haven heard himself murmuring in encouragement. "Let it go, Wren. Let it all go."

At last the orgasm came to an end and Wren lay limp in his arms, breathing shallowly like a man who has narrowly escaped drowning. "Oh, Master," he gasped at last. "That was so sweet...so good. Thank you."

"You're welcome, Wren." For a moment, Haven lost himself in the sweet sensation of simply cradling the young man in his arms, of just being close to Wren as he used to when his novice was younger. Then he became aware that the erotic scene he had just participated in had affected him deeply. His cock was still hard and throbbing and his novice's warm, firm ass was pressed directly against his shaft. Haven shifted uncomfortably, knowing that Wren had to feel his hardness against his naked ass and yet the young man made no move to get away from it. Instead, he sighed contentedly and pressed closer, rubbing against Haven's cock in a way that made him grit his teeth with need.

Haven cleared his throat. "Ahem. Excuse me, Novice, but I think it would be better if you moved now."

"Why, Master? I'm so comfortable here. I love being close to you." Wren's soft voice had a dreamy quality to it that said he would be happy to lay naked in his master's embrace all day.

"I, um, enjoy being close to you too, Wren." *A lot more than I should*, he thought guiltily, being sure to shield the thought. "But I, uh, need to get a towel to wipe this up." He gestured with his still-sticky hand, the one that had so recently stroked his novice to orgasm.

"Is that all?" Without asking, Wren lifted Haven's hand with both of his own and began cleaning his master's digits with long, sensual swipes of his warm tongue.

"Wren…" Haven croaked and found he couldn't say anything else. His tongue was glued to the roof of his mouth and he couldn't take his eyes off the incredibly erotic sight of his novice lapping the sticky cum from his fingertips. The inside of Wren's mouth was so hot, so wet -- as he sucked each one of Haven's fingers into the moist, warm cavern, Haven couldn't help wondering what it would feel like to have his novice suck his cock instead. Gods, when had Wren become this incredibly sexual creature, when had he become so damn near irresistible?

Have to get control of myself, Haven told himself sternly. Sexually desirable or not, Wren was still his novice. It was one thing to ease his ache out of necessity. But it was something else entirely to hold his novice naked in his arms and dream of what it would feel like to have that soft pink tongue caressing his own cock, lapping at the head of his shaft before taking it all down his warm, willing throat...

Haven shifted uneasily. "Wren, you really have to move, now," he said, making his tone stern. "I...we can't lie like this anymore now that you're...satisfied. Besides..." He shifted again, trying to move the length of his aching cock away from the firm roundness of his novice's ass. "I, ah, have needs to attend to myself."

"Oh, Master." Wren turned suddenly in his arms so that his bare chest pressed against Haven instead of his back. "I'm so sorry," he said softly, rubbing his cheek against Haven's shoulder. "I didn't even think about how you must be feeling -- how hard you must be."

"Yes, well..." Haven tried to get up but Wren stopped him by putting a hand flat on his chest.

"Master," he murmured, looking into Haven's eyes. "Would you like me to...to help you? The way you helped me?"

"I…" Haven couldn't finish. His mouth went dry as his novice's hand slid slowly down from his chest to his crotch. Lightly, Wren cupped his throbbing shaft through the tight black trousers, his fingers gentle and knowing.

"I could touch you -- stroke you, the way you stroked me," Wren murmured. "Or if you wish it, I could suck you, Master. Would you like that? Would you like me to suck your cock? I would gladly pleasure you in any way you see fit." The soft hand between Haven's legs grew bolder, stroking firmly along the length of his pulsing shaft until a ragged groan was torn from his lips.

"Wren, no! We can't --" he began when suddenly a loud pounding sounded at the thick double doors at the front of the room. The sound acted like a catalyst on both of them. Wren jumped back as though he had been burned and Haven sat up quickly, scooting to the edge of the bed in one smooth motion.

"Yes?" he called as Wren looked in vain for something with which to cover himself.

"Dinner and your new clothing, Light Bringer," came a muffled reply from the other side of the door. Before Haven could reply, the door opened and B'orl, the minister of the wardrobe's assistant, came bustling in with a pile of new clothes over one arm and pushing a silver cart with the other. There were several plates with unrecognizable and unappetizing food stuffs piled on the cart, all of them under clear protective dome lids.

"Good evening, B'orl," Haven said, trying to appear calm, as though his naked novice hadn't just been crawling all over his lap and offering to suck his throbbing cock -- an offer

Haven was deeply ashamed to admit he had been desperately tempted by.

"Good evening, Master Haven." B'orl nodded at the cart. "The kitchens asked if I would bring your dinner along with the clothing you're to wear at the Grande Promenade tonight."

"I see. And what is this?" Haven lifted one of the clear dome lids and leaned down to sniff the delicate blue steam that rose from the plate underneath. A sour, rotten stench assaulted his nostrils and he jumped back and hurriedly replaced the lid.

"That's XXX," B'orl said, apparently speaking a word Haven's universal translator couldn't translate. "The meat of a d'nabure. It's a Tiberion delicacy," he said proudly. "You should try some -- it's delicious."

"Perhaps too delicious to eat all at once." Haven's stomach did a slow forward roll at the thought of putting the strange blue, sour-smelling meat in his mouth.

"Maybe we should save it for last -- to savor it, Master," Wren suggested from his position behind Haven's right shoulder. "*It smells vile, Master!*" he sent through their link. "*Maybe this is what the Gowans refused to eat -- if so, who could blame them?*"

"Maybe we should at that, Wren." Haven nodded. "*I'm inclined to agree with you on both counts, Novice.*"

"Well, you can eat later, Master Haven. Now, as to your outfits for the Grande Promenade..." B'orl bustled importantly around, spreading the pile of clothing he had brought over one arm carefully on the bed. Haven saw with dismay that he had a new deep blue shirt made of some silky material that appeared to only button a few inches past the navel, leaving the chest area bare as well as a pair of black leather trousers that, if possible, looked even tighter than the ones he currently had on. The crotch of the trousers had easy-open magno-tabs that looked likely to pop open suddenly and expose him in public. The long robe that went with the outfit was black silk with silver embroidery and B'orl had also brought him a new pair of high, shiny black boots, much more stylish than his old beat-up ones. They were the only part of the outfit Haven liked.

"*Master, what about me? What am I supposed to wear?*" Wren was looking at the clothes laid out on the bed with confusion. Through their link, Haven caught the thought that Wren hoped he would have at least a little more on for the Grande Promenade than he had worn for the audience with the god-emperor they had missed earlier.

"What about my slave?" he asked B'orl, nodding at Wren who was standing quietly at the side of the bed, still completely naked. "Will he, er, get a more formal outfit as well?"

"Oh, I'm glad you mentioned that -- I almost forgot!" B'orl snapped his thick fingers together and leaned down to reach the bottom rack of the tray that held the food. "Couldn't carry it all so I put your slave's accessories down here."

"Accessories?" Haven asked doubtfully, but his question was answered when B'orl stood up again, clutching an armful of supplies.

"Here we are," he said proudly, laying them out beside Haven's outfit. "I had to guess at some of the sizes, but I think these will do."

Haven looked in confusion at the strange assortment that was lying on the bed. There was a pair of black leather knee pads, a long red leash that would doubtless match the collar Wren still wore, and what looked like some kind of a long, silky black tassel attached to a thick black handle. There were also two small bottles of viscous liquid -- one red and one deep blue. Haven assumed they were more oil for lubrication. When he looked up, he saw that Wren was staring at the bed with a puzzled look on his face as well.

"*What's that weird tassel thing, Master?*" he sent. "*Are you supposed to whip me with it?*"

"*I certainly hope not.*" Haven frowned and turned to the minister of the wardrobe's assistant. "B'orl," he said. "Forgive my ignorance, but I'm not certain I understand how to put some of these, ah, clothes on my slave. Would you mind giving me a little instruction?"

"Not at all, Master Haven, although I would think most everything here would be self explanatory." B'orl picked up the leash. "To attach to his collar when you walk him. During the Grande Promenade, slaves are only permitted to walk by their master's sides on all fours -- that's what the knee pads are for. I've got some gloves here too, to protect his hands." He produced a pair of black leather fingerless gloves and placed them beside the pads.

"All right." Haven nodded. "So far I understand, but what is *this*?" He picked up the long silky tassel attached to the handle, noticing that it was strangely contoured with a bulge in the middle.

"His tail, of course," B'orl said, as though it was the most obvious thing in the world. "All the slaves must wear one for the Grande Promenade."

"Tail?" Haven arched one black eyebrow in question. "But how exactly does he wear it?" he asked, hoping against hope that his guess about the placement of the tail was wrong.

"Well, it fits in your slave's anus, of course." B'orl shook his head and picked up the black tasseled tail to demonstrate. "The handle, anyway," he said, motioning to the thick black leather handle attached to the tassels. "And then the harness has buckles in the back to hold it in place." He looked up at Wren and appeared to notice for the first time that he was no longer wearing the black leather harness. "Now that's a shame to be certain, Master Haven," he said, shaking his head. "Taking off your slave's harness and allowing him sexual release before the Grande Promenade tonight. I know you aren't familiar with our customs, but on Tiber unless a slave pleasures you exceptionally well, he or she isn't allowed sexual release. Did your slave pleasure you so well that you thought it wise to allow his erection to go down just before you needed him hard and ready for the Promenade tonight?"

"Well, I..." Haven shook his head, not certain what to say. His novice, however, didn't appear to have any problem answering B'orl's question.

"As a matter of fact I was just sucking my master's cock before you came into the room, B'orl," he said boldly, frowning regally at the small Tiberion. "He was about to come down my throat when your knock on the door interrupted us."

" *Wren*!" Haven shot his novice a warning look, trying to ignore the throbbing of his cock Wren's words inspired.

"*Just playing the part, Master.*" Wren gave him an innocent, big-eyed look that didn't fool Haven for a minute. His novice was deliberately trying to get a rise out of him -- in more than one way.

Unaware of their silent communication, B'orl nodded knowingly. "Just as well I interrupted you, then. Your master needs to save his seed to spend tonight before the god-emperor, may he live forever."

Haven cleared his throat uneasily. "Actually, I was wondering about that, B'orl. Wondering what a, uh, sufficiently respectful obeisance to make before the god-emperor would be. You see, I realize this may be hard to believe but my, uh, slave here is actually inexperienced in these manners and I would not choose to take him publicly without preparation if I could help it."

"Ah, as to that, you don't need to worry about it tonight. Penetration without preparation, I mean." B'orl gave them a sly wink. "You see, the finale of tonight's Grande Promenade is to be a public deflowering. The minister of finance has a new young slave, a girl from the inner planets that has never been had before. So your obeisance must be necessarily short in order to leave time for a proper show."

"I see." Haven felt his throat close up at the idea of taking someone's virginity in front of the entire Tiberion court. The thought of the humiliation and pain to be endured and not as an act of love but simply for the entertainment of the lazy monarch he'd seen earlier was repugnant. But there was nothing he could do about it. Through the link he could feel an echo of his own disgust from Wren. "Is...does this kind of thing happen often?" he asked, swallowing hard.

B'orl shrugged his shoulders. "It didn't used to but it's not uncommon now, especially since Minister H'rak has gained the god-emperor's ear -- may he live forever. He sets great store by following the old traditions, Minister H'rak does. Why, have you no such custom among your people?"

"I...we usually prefer to do such things in private." Haven frowned. "I can't help feeling for the slave girl who is to be deflowered by the minister of finance in such a public fashion."

B'orl chuckled. "Oh, don't worry about her. I know the minister of finance and he's not a bad sort. In fact, she'd better enjoy his attentions while she can. I hear he's selling her to Minister H'rak the moment the deflowering is over. He doesn't like used goods, does the minister of finance, not even when he used them himself."

"That seems a cruel fate," Haven said before he thought about it. He wasn't sure if he was talking about the slave girl being deflowered or being sold to the evil-eyed minister of war. Both, he supposed. But his speech didn't seem to have much effect on the short, round Tiberion.

"Well, be that as it may, Light Bringer, I need to get back to the minister of the wardrobe. He would be lost without me." B'orl smiled proudly. "But before I go, do you wish me to help you outfit your slave? I can show you how the tail is inserted -- you just use three parts of the blue calla-flower oil to one part of the red passion-seed oil. And mind you, don't mix up the ratios -- that's very important." B'orl took a step forward, reaching for the tasseled handle and the two new vials of oil, but Haven stepped smoothly between him and the bed where the supplies were laid out.

"I thank you but, no, B'orl. Now that I know what, er, goes where, I think I'll be able to manage with no problem."

"Very well." B'orl looked miffed but he shrugged again and turned to go. "See that you're both dressed and ready for the Grande Promenade within the hour. A servant will be sent to fetch you and show you to the Great Room." He bowed briefly and swept out of the room, leaving Haven and Wren to stare at each other over their new costumes.

Wren broke the silence between them by going over to the bed and picking up the "tail." "I suppose we ought to get this over with, Master," he said, nodding at the two vials of red and blue oil. "Both of us know we're not going to eat that glop they served us and anyway, I'm not hungry." He swallowed hard. "I'm too nervous to be hungry."

"I'm not hungry either," Haven admitted, sinking down on the bed. "But, Wren, don't you want to wait to the last minute to, uh, wear the…that thing? It might not be very comfortable and you don't want to have it in…I mean, *on*, for longer than you have to."

Wren sighed and sat on the bed beside him. "You're right, of course. I guess I just want to get the worst over with, Master. But I can wait until you get into your costume at least. Suppose you get dressed while I put this food down the waste chute in the bathroom?"

"Agreed, Novice. And try to do it quickly." Haven winced. "I don't think I've ever smelled anything more foul in all my travels."

Wren grinned irrepressibly. "Yes, it's a far cry from the dewberry bread you bought me with, isn't it, Master?"

Before Haven could answer, Wren was off the bed and wheeling the large silver cart into the bathroom. Haven stared after his novice for a moment, reflecting on the alarming fact that he was almost getting used to seeing Wren walk around naked and Wren seemed to be getting used to it himself. In fact, they were both getting entirely too comfortable in their roles -- a situation he would need to put an end to when his novice returned. Wren wasn't going to like it but Haven was going to have to put some distance between them before they lost all perspective.

He put on the shirt and boots and was just struggling to get the magno-tabs on the trousers fastened when he heard a long, low whistle. Turning he saw his novice leaning against the wall with his arms crossed over his chest, staring in appreciation.

"Very nice, Master." Wren nodded at the still open pants and Haven frowned and fastened them quickly.

"I'm glad you think so, Novice. It's a bit too provocative for my taste. If these pants were any tighter, I wouldn't be able to breathe and as for this shirt..." He frowned down at the dark blue silk shirt which parted in a wide vee to expose his broad chest.

"I like the shirt." Wren's gaze raked over Haven's bare chest, a hungry look in his amber eyes. "I like the way it shows you off, Master. Your body is amazing but no one would guess it beneath the shapeless tunics you usually wear." He came forward, both hands outstretched, but Haven caught them before his novice could place his warm palms against the broad planes of his chest.

"That's enough, Wren," he said quietly, looking the young man in the eyes. "I know you're just playing a part here -- we both are. But things are getting out of hand. We need to remember why we're here -- to save Gow gi Nef from destruction. And also *who* we are. I am your master and you are my novice and that's all. Understood?"

"Yes, Master." The hurt look that flitted across his novice's face squeezed Haven's heart but he knew he had done the only thing possible. They were getting too close, falling into their roles too easily -- especially Wren. It was one thing to perform in front of the Tiberions and play the part of a sexually submissive slave, but it was quite another to climb all over his master's lap as Wren had been doing and offer to suck his cock. Just the thought of it made Haven hard all over again and he took a deep breath, trying to release his improper urges to the Light.

"Well." Haven dropped Wren's hands and squared his shoulders. "I guess it's time to get you dressed."

"Yes, Master," Wren said again. "Do you think it would be easier to put back on the harness first or to put on the tail?"

"That's up to you, Wren." Haven was uncomfortably aware that he was going to have to re-oil his novice and also insert the tail since the inhibitor manacles would keep Wren from doing any of it himself. Well, he would have to simply remain businesslike -- cool and impersonal. As much as he cared for Wren, he would have to suppress his emotions during this difficult procedure and, if possible, for the rest of this mission.

Wren was silent for a moment and then he nodded at the long tassels of the tail. “Let’s get it over with,” he said simply. Without being asked, he climbed onto the bed on all fours and spread his legs. “Do it, Master,” he said, a grim look of determination coming over his face. “Don’t talk about it -- just do it.”

“Very well, Wren.” Reaching for the bottles of oil, Haven mixed them carefully in his hand. *Let’s see now, what did B’orl say? One part blue and three parts red? Yes, that’s it,* he thought, watching as the thick oil turned a deep shade of reddish-purple in his palm. He coated the thick handle of the tail thoroughly and stroked the rest of the mixture over Wren’s tight rosebud.

Once again he inserted two fingers, scissoring gently to open his novice for the coming invasion. He felt a surge of emotion from his novice as he penetrated Wren’s virgin opening, but it was quickly suppressed as Wren threw up his mental shields, cutting him off. Haven was momentarily hurt -- Wren had secrets and private thoughts as everyone did, but he had never made it so obvious before that he was trying to keep his master out of the mind-link between them.

Haven reminded himself that his novice was only doing what he had instructed him to -- setting limits and remembering who he was behind the role he was playing. Still, he knew how hard it had to be for Wren to submit to the humiliation of wearing a “tail” and of having his master insert it, so he stroked soothingly along his novice's soft lower back as he placed the blunt end of the black leather handle against the tight opening of Wren's body.

"Easy, Wren," he murmured as he pressed forward, watching as the black leather handle breached the tight ring of muscle guarding the young man's entrance.

"Yes, Master," Wren gasped and grabbed fistfuls of the blue and gold coverlet, his eyes squeezed tightly closed. Even through the barrier his novice had erected between them, Haven could feel his fear.

"Don't fight it, Wren. Relax and try to open up for me," he murmured, pressing the handle deeper into his novice's body. He only had an inch of the thick black handle inserted, and he was worried about what would happen when he got to the bulge in the middle.

"I…I'm trying, Master," Wren gritted, his eyes still squeezed tightly shut. "It's just…it's so big. I don't know if I can take it."

"You have to." Haven stroked his back, making his voice warm but stern. "Remember when you told me that you would submit to anything as long as it was by my hand?"

"I remember, Master." Wren looked up at last and the tears standing in his large golden eyes nearly did Haven in. But there was no help for it -- Wren *had* to wear the tail and he had to wear it soon. A servant would be coming in a matter of minutes to take them to the Grande Promenade, and they had to be ready to go or risk offending the god-emperor and breaking the Tiberion customs.

"I know you're a virgin here, Wren." Haven stroked his back and the rounded curve of his ass soothingly. "And I know this seems too big to fit inside you. But if you'll just trust me and open up for me, I promise it will be over before you know it."

Wren looked at him for a long time and then nodded once. "As you say, Master. I trust you and submit to you in this as in all things." Taking a deep breath, he let it out in a trembling sigh and buried his head in his arms. Then he spread his legs even wider, opening himself for Haven's assault in a gesture of trust so beautiful it almost hurt.

"My Wren," Haven heard himself murmuring. "You're so beautiful when you submit." Without waiting for an answer, he began working the thick black handle into his novice's body once more, pressing deeper and deeper to fill Wren with the tail.

Wren submitted quietly with only a muffled gasp when the bulge in the middle of the handle entered his body. Haven couldn't help thinking that it was a damn good thing that he wouldn't have to actually fuck his novice after all. Aside from the obvious reasons why it was a bad idea, the fact was that as thick as the black leather handle was, it wasn't nearly as big as his own cock.

"*Yes, Master, but if it was your cock in me instead of this cold handle, I might find it much easier to open for you,*" Wren sent through the link, and Haven realized that he had been thinking freely, assuming that since his novice had put a shield between them, he was no longer listening to Haven's casual thoughts. Obviously, that wasn't so. Hastily, he put up a shield of his own.

At last, the entire tail was in, the long black tassels hanging down to Wren's mid-thigh. Haven stoked the soft skin of Wren's trembling buttocks again and murmured soothingly, "It's all done, Wren. All the way in."

"Then put the harness on me too, please, Master." Wren's voice was muffled, his face still buried in his arms. "Let's get it all over with at once. That way I can try to get used to it before I have to wear it in public." *As if anyone could ever get used to wearing this kind of thing inside them*!

Haven caught the last thought through their link and was glad to hear that his novice had opened up to him again. Despite his own stern words to Wren, he didn't like being excluded from his novice's thoughts.

"Very well, Novice," he murmured, reaching across the bed where the black leather harness was heaped carelessly in a tangle of straps and buckles. "But I'm afraid you'll have to be, er, erect again for it to fit properly." He eyed his novice's slender shaft which was lying flaccid against one thigh with concern. Naturally, being forced to submit to having the invading tail placed in his body would have a dampening effect on his desire but it presented a daunting problem. Suddenly the ramifications of "helping" Wren find relief earlier became distressingly clear.

Wren looked up. "I'm sorry, Master, but you'll have to help me. I can't touch myself, remember?" He nodded at the bulky inhibitor manacles on his wrists and tried to smile. "If we stay here too long, I might forget how to touch myself altogether. Can't you just imagine me knocking on your door at three in the morning with a hard-on, begging for your help?" He sent what Haven was sure was meant to be a comical image of himself crawling naked into bed with his master, his slender shaft jutting out in front of him, painful with desire. The image continued with Haven holding open the covers to welcome his novice in beside him and stroking Wren as he had earlier to relieve his need.

Gods, this has to stop! He shielded the thought carefully, but was painfully aware that he was about to have to do exactly what Wren had sent him. Would this mission never end? And would they be able to look each other in the eye when it did?

"Let me get the oil again," he said aloud. Carefully, he mixed three parts red to one part blue oil in his palm, keeping his eyes on what he was doing instead of on his novice, who was still kneeling on hands and knees on the bed. "Kneel up, Wren," he murmured, putting one knee on the bed. "I need to be able to reach you."

Moving stiffly and carefully, obviously mindful of the tail buried deep in his body, Wren raised up so that he was kneeling in the same position he had been in earlier when Haven first oiled him and fitted him with the harness. "*I'm ready, Master*," he sent through the link, fixing his eyes on Haven trustingly. "*Do what you must.*"

It was the third time that day Haven had been forced by circumstances to handle his novice inappropriately, and he found to his mingled horror and relief that he was getting quite used to it. Gently, he grasped Wren's shaft in one hand and began to spread the reddish-purple oil over the young man's cock.

Wren drew in a breath and bit his lower lip.

"Am I hurting you, Novice?" Haven looked at him anxiously.

"No." Wren shook his head, obviously embarrassed. "It's just…your hands on me, Master. I know I should be used to the feeling by now but it still makes me feel…"

"Makes you feel what, Wren?" Haven asked, but his novice only shook his head.

"Never mind, Master. I'll be all right. All that matters is it's working. Look." Wren nodded down at his shaft which was coated in a thin, shiny layer of the reddish oil. It was as hard and pulsing as if Haven hadn't just jerked him off minutes before.

"It certainly is, Novice," Haven agreed dryly. Privately, he hoped that his intimate touch wasn't bringing back too much of Wren's painful past, but there wasn't much he could do about it at this point but be quick.

He finished buckling the harness on, securing the thick leather strap to the base of Wren's cock, which was already leaking precum again, and fastening the other straps around his thighs. They acted to hold the tail in place so there was no danger of it falling out. Then he helped Wren off the bed and buckled the black leather knee pads to his legs so that he could crawl in comfort.

"Barbaric of them to force you to crawl," he muttered finishing the job and stepping back to take in the entire effect.

"If that was the worst thing they'd done or were threatening to do, I'd gladly crawl behind you all day. But I'd probably better practice to be sure I get it right." Wren flowed off the bed suddenly, as sinuous as a cat, and began twining himself around Haven's long legs.

"That's enough, Novice." Haven put a restraining hand on Wren's spiky hair. "How…how does it feel?" he asked in a softer tone.

"Like someone is fucking me with every move I make." Wren's voice was flat and when he looked up at Haven, his large eyes were pleading. "It feels good and shameful at the same time, Master. I shouldn't want to be filled like this, should I? I shouldn't want to be fucked. Not after…" He shook his head, unable to finish the sentence, but Haven knew what he was trying to say. Not after what had happened to Wren as a child, not after the life he had led before Haven rescued him. He shouldn't want to be taken, used, fucked. And yet he did. To his intense shame, Haven felt his own cock surge at the thought. *It's not going to come to that*! he told himself fiercely, but somehow his own assurances to himself seemed a little less certain than they had before.

"Wren," he murmured, caressing his novice's soft cheek. "I know this is difficult for you. I know it's bringing back bad memories and associations and I'm sorry for that with all my heart. You know I would never ask these things of you if so much did not lie in the balance."

"Yes, Master." Trembling, Wren pressed against his side and let out a long, shaking sigh. "Yes, I know."

Haven knelt in front of him and pressed a kiss to the sweat-damp forehead. Looking into his novice's eyes, he murmured, "All I can tell you is to hold onto me -- stay close. I'm going to get you through this, Wren, I swear it by the Light."

"Yes, Master." Suddenly, Wren darted his head forward and pressed a light kiss to Haven's lips. Haven was taken aback, so surprised that he allowed the gesture to go on much longer than he should have. Long enough to notice that his novice's lips were every bit as soft as they looked. Finally, Wren drew back, a look of shame and worry stamped on his fine features.

"I'm sorry, Master. I don't...don't know why I did that. Don't know what came over me," he whispered.

"Don't worry." Haven tried to smile, making light of the situation. "We'll just consider it a dry run for the Grande Promenade tonight. I'm sure I'll have to kiss you there in front of the god-emperor."

"May he live forever," Wren finished dryly, and they both laughed.

Haven straightened up, relieved that the strange tension had been broken between them. But he couldn't help licking his lips, capturing the sweet taste of Wren's mouth on his even though he knew he shouldn't.

Chapter Six

Wren was glad when the Tiberion servant came to lead them to the Grande Promenade at last. The awkwardness between himself and his master seemed to be growing by the minute. He couldn't for the life of him understand why he had stolen that kiss. But when Haven's handsome face was so close to his own, it had suddenly seemed to him that he had to taste those red, sensual lips, had to explore that firm mouth, or die.

That was strange enough, but even stranger was the way he was feeling. The warm sensations that the oil had caused inside him where the tail was inserted and all along his painfully hard cock seemed to have spread to the rest of his body as well. His cheeks flushed with heat and his cock leaked steadily, just as though he hadn't come less than an hour before. Every step he took seemed to push the thick black tail deeper into his ass, and he couldn't help imagining it was Haven's cock instead, fucking him, filling him.

Wren shook his head. He wasn't usually this insatiable, even when he was daydreaming about his master. What was wrong with him?

He thought about letting his master know about his condition through their link but two things stopped him.

First, Haven had enough on his plate at the moment. They were in a precarious situation with everything hanging in the balance between the Tiberions and the Gowans and he didn't need to worry about Wren as well. And second, it would be too embarrassing. What was he supposed to say, "Master, I'm so horny I feel like I'm going to die"? No, Wren decided, he would just keep that piece of information to himself. He was sure when the Grande Promenade started he would be far too distracted to think of how he felt.

It certainly was a distracting spectacle. When they reached the large circular feasting hall where the event was being held, Wren was completely caught up in the sight of all the other masters and slaves around them. It was gratifying to see that he wasn't the only slave wearing a tail and, in fact, his was much less flamboyant than some of the others. He saw one unlucky female slave with what looked like a spread of peacock feathers sprouting from her backside. It made the black leather tassels adorning his own ass seem almost plain in comparison.

As each master and slave pair reached the entrance to the large, circular room, the slave would drop to his or her knees to be led by their master into the god-emperor's presence. The god-emperor, Wren saw by looking around the other pairs waiting to go before them, floated in a golden throne that hovered, as before, about three feet above the floor. From it, he could watch the obeisance made to him by the members of his court as they came to stand before him, each in turn. Beside him stood Minister H'rak as always, whispering into his ear.

The god-emperor had a bored look on his face despite the various sexual acts being performed in front of him. By now, Wren thought, he had probably seen it all many times over. How in the world had it become a tradition with these people to carry out what should have been intimate, private acts in public for the gratification of their ruler? Someone with a seriously twisted imagination had to be behind it. Someone like the Tiberion minister of war.

As if thinking of him had drawn his attention, Minister H'rak suddenly looked up. Catching Wren's eyes with his own cold purple ones, he deliberately ran his long, pointed tongue along his thin, slimy lips.

Wren shuddered and looked away, fighting not to betray the dismay and disgust he felt on his face. But Haven must have felt it through their link because he looked sharply at the towering minister before turning his attention to Wren.

"*All right?*" he sent through their link anxiously.

"*Fine, Master. He's just so...*" Words failed him but he shivered again, letting Haven know how he felt about H'rak.

"*I know, Novice. Unfortunately, we have to work with him in order to get to the god-emperor. Just don't look at him or meet his eyes. I don't want him getting any ideas about you.*"

The possessive note in his Master's mind-voice warmed Wren considerably. He thought guardedly that the best thing about this crazy assignment was the fact that he so obviously and completely belonged to Haven. He liked the idea of the older man mastering him in every sense of the word. It made him wonder if his desire to submit to Haven had to do with his childhood experiences or just the fact that he loved his master so much he wanted to give him everything. Before he could consider the question in depth, it was their turn to enter the circular feasting hall and he had to drop to his knees and follow Haven at a sedate pace around the perimeter of the room.

There were two master and slave pairs in front of them, which gave Wren the chance to look around. The red, black, and white theme had been duplicated here with a few minor exceptions. There were no runners of colored silk hanging down from the ceiling. Instead, the walls were painted in tricolored swirls with brief interludes of art depicting Tiberions in various sexual positions. The shiny black marble floor reflected everything like a mirror so that everyone in the room seemed to have a double somehow. It was a distracting effect until Wren learned to ignore it.

Three long feasting tables were set up across from where the god-emperor was holding court forming a U-shaped pattern. The two long tables on either side were occupied but the one in the middle was empty. From the gold and silver cutlery and plates, it was easy to see this was where the god-emperor would sit when the Grande Promenade ended. Platters of steaming meat and vegetables, none of them very palatable, could be seen at intervals all along the tables, making Wren hope that slaves were excluded from the feasting part of the evening.

He found it easy to forget about the decorations and the disgusting alien food as they got closer to the floating golden throne, mostly because he was wondering what his master had planned for them to do. Haven persisted in thinking that a kiss was good enough, but from observing the other pairs of masters and slaves in line before them, Wren wasn't sure that idea would fly. He watched with interest and trepidation as they got closer and closer to the throne and saw that Haven was doing the same.

As far as Wren could see, the theme that seemed to accompany every act was the "spending of seed" before the emperor at the climax of every exhibition. Just as Minister H'rak had "honored" them by forcing his slave to come on the carpet earlier, the masters who performed for the emperor made sure that the evidence of their release was on display at the end of each performance.

"*I guess I'm not supposed to swallow, Master*," he sent, watching the Tiberion master who was being fellated by his buxom slave. The master pulled his brownish-green cock out of her mouth just in time to shoot his seed all over her face and then they both bowed to the god-emperor and moved on.

"*I'm not going to tell you again that it isn't going to come to that, Wren*," Haven sent back sternly. "*I promised you long ago that you would never have to perform that particular service again, and I don't intend to break my word now.*"

"*But, Master --*"

"*No*!" Haven looked down at him, a warning expression in his dark blue eyes. "*Enough, Wren. This matter is not open for discussion.*" He turned back to watching the spectacle currently unfolding before the god-emperor, his broad shoulders tight with disapproval and tension under the elaborate tunic he wore. Sighing to himself, Wren did the same. He appreciated the fact that his master was determined to spare him any trauma that might bring back his past, but he hoped Haven's stubbornness didn't get them both in trouble.

The next master in line got creative. He had a small platform under one arm which he set down in front of the god-emperor's throne. When he clapped his hands, his slaved climbed nimbly upon it and knelt up, presenting a pair of truly enormous breasts. Stepping forward, the master produced his shaft and rubbed it between her pillowy mounds until with a low grunt he spurted his cum all over her chest. Then they bowed and moved on.

The next master…but there was no next master, Wren realized with a sudden flash of terror. He and Haven were up. He'd been so caught up in watching the performances of the other pairs in the processional that he hadn't noticed how close they were to being on display themselves. What was wrong with him? He usually wasn't this scatterbrained. It was as if his thoughts were clouded somehow. Shaking his head, he crawled sinuously at his master's heels as they took their places before the hovering golden throne.

"This is Master Haven, the Light Bringer the Gowans have summoned to speak on their behalf." Minister H'rak performed the introductions in a flat, cold voice, the sneer on his face making it obvious what he thought of Haven's presence aboard the Tiberion ship. "And this lovely young man," he continued, his oily voice warming a little. "Is Master Haven's slave boy, Wren. Haven has had him since he was a child. Isn't that right, Wren?" He leaned down to deliver the last sentence, his flat, greenish-brown face and glowing purple eyes entirely too close for comfort.

Wren swallowed, uncertain if he should answer or not, but Haven stepped between him and the Tiberion minister of war smoothly, blocking him from H'rak's view. "That is true, Your Eminence," he said, addressing the god-emperor directly and ignoring H'rak's glowering frown. "I have come all the way from Radiant where the Temple of Light is located, hoping to mitigate this delicate situation between your people and the Gowans. I am certain that with a little understanding on both sides, we can clear up this matter to everyone's satisfaction."

"Perhaps. It matters little." The god-emperor Rudgez the Fourth had a high, petulant voice, and when Wren dared to peek around his master's legs he saw that the royal Tiberion's enormous bulk was barely contained by the wide golden throne.

"It matters little?" Haven was clearly struggling to keep the incredulity out of his voice. "Your Eminence, the lives of an entire planet of sentient beings hang in the balance. Surely even your opulent lifestyle has not so jaded you as to believe that so many matter so little."

"I had not thought of it that way before. I suppose you have a point, Light Bringer." The god-emperor waved a pudgy hand glittering with rows of jeweled rings vaguely. "Still, as my good Minister H'rak points out, a slight against the Tiberion empire may not be ignored or others will follow." He nodded at the tall minister standing by his side. "Is that not right, H'rak?"

"Your Majesty is correct in this as in all things," H'rak growled, still glowering at Haven. "But I am afraid this Servant of the Light has mistaken his events. The mediations with the Gowans will not start until tomorrow. *This* is the Grande Promenade where you are to make obeisance to the god-emperor, may he live forever, Master Haven. So I suggest that you do so at once before you give serious offense."

"Very well." From the calm tone of Haven's voice no one would suspect the anger bubbling just beneath his surface. But Wren felt it through their link and he knew his master was hanging onto his temper with both hands. "Come, Wren," Haven said, interrupting his thoughts. He drew Wren upright, ignoring the fact that every other slave in the feasting hall was still on all fours, and cupped his face in both hands. Turning to the god-emperor he said, "I choose to honor Your Eminence with a heartfelt kiss between myself and this slave of my heart."

"A kiss, is that all you would offer the greatest ruler ever to take the Tiberion throne?" H'rak thundered, his purple eyes blazing.

"Master?" Wren looked at him anxiously but there was no uncertainty in Haven's dark blue eyes.

"To my people a kiss between two who care for each other is every bit as moving and intimate as more personal acts which are best reserved for the privacy of the bedchamber," he said firmly. Pulling Wren close, he wrapped his arms around the younger man and tilted his head down to fit his lips to Wren's.

To have his master kiss him on the mouth with love and tenderness was the stuff of Wren's wildest fantasies. He didn't care that it was just for show or that his master didn't really love him in that way; he gave himself up to the moment wholeheartedly, knowing there might never be another like it. Sighing, he melted against his master's body, opening his lips, inviting Haven's tongue to enter his mouth. His master seemed uncertain at first, but as Wren moved against him, he acted more purposefully. Cupping the back of Wren's head, Haven pulled him closer, deepening the kiss, exploring Wren's mouth as though he owned it.

And you do own it, master. You own all of me, body, heart, and soul. Wren wasn't sure if he was sending the heated thoughts through their private link or not, but as the kiss went on and on, he decided he didn't care. In fact, there was something about the way that Haven held him, something about the masterful way he was ravishing Wren's mouth that seemed to start a fire inside him. He felt the warmth from the oil that anointed his cock burst into heated flames that threatened to consume him from the waist up, and suddenly he was no longer content to stand submissively and allow his master to kiss him. Gripping the back of Haven's elaborate tunic, he kissed back, giving as good as he was getting. He pressed his naked body against Haven too, grinding his hard shaft against his master's thighs, rubbing as sensually and shamelessly as a cat in heat, making his needs known.

"*Wren? What are you doing?*" Dimly, he heard his master's dismayed tone through their link, but he was past caring. He only knew what he wanted -- what he needed -- was finally within reach. And what he wanted and needed was his master, in no uncertain terms. He wanted Haven. Wanted to love him, to touch him, to submit to him on every possible level. The urge was so driving that it forced Wren to his knees. The position brought his earliest memories flooding back and he knew exactly what to do.

"Wren?" Haven said aloud just as Minister H'rak was murmuring, "Finally. This is more like it." Then the magno-tabs that held Haven's tight black pants together parted and his master's cock was in Wren's hands.

"*Wren, no*!" But Haven's warning came too late. Wren was already stroking the long, thick shaft capped by a broad, plum-shaped head. His master's cock was beautiful. Hard and pulsing in his grip, it belied the warning and anger in Haven's tone. Here was the proof, Wren thought, almost delirious with lust and need. The proof that he affected Haven every bit as much as Haven affected him. Proof that his master had feelings for him that went beyond friendship and the proscribed relationship of master and novice.

"*Master, I love you*," he sent, rubbing his flushed cheek against the hard, thick shaft in his hands and breathing in Haven's warm musk. Without waiting for a reply from the still stunned Haven, he leaned forward and took his master's cock into his mouth.

It had been over ten years since his days as a slave boy on the streets of Rigel Six, but Wren hadn't forgotten the proper way to suck cock or the elusive skill of deep throating a shaft once it was in his mouth. He swirled his talented tongue around the broad head to start with, lapping at the droplets of precum like a cat drinking cream, and then took Haven deeper. He heard his master's hoarse cry as the thick shaft slid between his soft lips and went down his willing throat and thrilled at the deep desire he heard in it.

Wren swallowed, milking Haven's cock, trying to increase the flow of salty, delicious precum from a trickle to a river. He was rewarded with his master's hands in his hair, to pull him off or push him forward, Wren didn't know. Nor did he care. He only knew that he was where he belonged at last, on his knees before his master, giving his complete and total submission to the man who owned his heart.

"*Wren, no. We must not do this -- you have to stop. Stop before I --*"

"*Before you come? But I want you to, Master. I want to suck your cock and swallow your cum, every last drop.*" Wren looked up, meeting the troubled dark blue eyes of the man he loved most in the universe.

"*It's wrong,*" Haven protested, his big hands twining restlessly in Wren's spiky golden brown hair. "*Wrong to let you do this on so many levels. I am your master, not your lover, my Wren. And I promised you that you'd never have to perform this act again.*"

"*But I want to.*" Wren pressed against Haven, taking his cock even deeper, rubbing his nose against the soft, fragrant nest of curls at the base of his master's shaft. "*I love you, Master. I need you. I was born to do this -- born to get on my knees and submit to you. To suck your cock.*"

"*Wren, will you listen to yourself?*" The look in Haven's eyes was half anxious worry and half overwhelming pleasure but the pleasure was winning, thanks to Wren's excellent technique. "*This isn't what you were born for -- this is what I rescued you from. You were born to be a Servant of the Light, not some sexual toy, not even for me.*"

"*You may have rescued me from that life but I have never forgotten it. Tell me, Master, were you never tempted to try my mouth even once? Never tempted to take me the way so many men did before you*?" Wren held his master's gaze as he drew back and lapped at the head of Haven's cock sensually.

Haven's blue eyes were tortured but he didn't answer Wren's taunting question. Instead, he shook his head firmly and sent, "*No more talk. This has to stop now*!"

Pulling back from Wren's hungry mouth in what was obviously a superhuman effort of will, Haven stood, holding his pulsing cock in his hand and breathing hard. Wren knew that his master probably wanted to just stuff the hard shaft back into his trousers and forget about this embarrassing scenario, but he couldn't -- Wren had taken him too far and he was too close to the edge. So instead he gripped his shaft in one hand and stroked, obviously intent on spilling his seed before the god-emperor as the other masters had done. But Wren couldn't let him do that. Couldn't let his master's cum, which he had worked so hard for and so longed to taste, go to waste on the black mirrored floor before the golden floating throne.

As Haven's thick cock began to spurt, Wren lunged forward again and captured the plum-shaped head his mouth. Before his master could protest, he was swallowing eagerly, drinking the thick jets of hot cum as they spurted from the tip of Haven's shaft, savoring every salty drop.

As he swallowed, Wren looked up to see that his master's blue eyes were wide with disbelief and anxiety. He stood still, no longer trying to stop Wren in his single-minded pursuit. Instead he buried one hand in his novice's hair and pulled him close, allowing Wren to suck him dry, spilling not a single drop before the golden throne. It was a gesture of defeat, and through their link Wren could feel both Haven's immense pleasure in his hot, wet mouth, and a terrible sadness.

At last there was nothing left to drink, and Haven's shaft began to lose its rock hard solidity. But the fire still burned in Wren. He was still savoring his master's salty flavor and was reluctant to release the thick cock from his mouth. He nursed gently at the tip, coaxing the last few droplets out until Haven carefully drew him away.

"*Wren*," he sent, his mind-voice tinged with sadness. "*What have we done? What have I allowed you to do?*"

"*You've only allowed me to love you, Master, the way I've always wanted to. The way I want to every night for the rest of our lives.*" Wren knew he shouldn't be revealing his inner thoughts, his secret desires guarded so carefully for years, but he couldn't help it. The flames licking inside him seemed to have burned down all his barriers and he couldn't keep his feelings quiet anymore.

"*I have broken my promise to you in the worst way possible.*" Haven's dark blue eyes were filled with regret.

"*No, I --*"

"Well, that was certainly a heartfelt display all right. But I think your slave has the wrong idea. You're supposed to spill your seed before the god-emperor, may he live forever. Not swallow every last drop."

Chapter Seven

Minister H'rak's grating voice broke into their private mind-speech, and Haven realized that while he and his novice had been having a moment they had almost completely forgotten the existence of everyone else in the room, even Rudgez the Fourth and his dour minister of war. *Of all the dangerous, foolish, unforgivably stupid things to do…* Haven berated himself. A true Servant of the Light always kept his eyes open and his wits about him. Letting anything, even the bewildering and emotional event that had just taken place between himself and Wren, steal his focus was beyond careless.

"You must forgive my slave's eagerness," he said, tucking his now flaccid cock back into his tight, black pants. "Though I have had him since he was a child, I have been reluctant to, er, break him in as it were. This sort of display is new to him."

"So we gathered, Light Bringer." The god-emperor was sitting up straight in his throne and his beady red eyes showed a hint of genuine interest for the first time all night. "He is very beautiful, your slave boy." His high voice had taken on a note of husky desire as he devoured Wren with his greedy gaze. "Is he, by chance, for sale?"

If nothing else had been enough to dampen the fire that seemed to burn inside Wren, this question did it. He dropped back down to his hands and knees and buried his face in Haven's leg, trembling. Haven felt his terror and despite his anger and worry about what had just happened between them, a surge of protectiveness rolled over him.

"I am afraid not, Your Eminence," he said, working hard to keep his face blank and his voice emotionless. "He has been bonded to me in an irrevocable manner. He would be no good to any other master."

"Very well then." Rudgez the Fourth looked distinctly sulky, but to Haven's relief, he appeared to be willing to let the matter drop. Haven bowed deeply and prepared to move on.

"But bonds may perhaps be broken?" Minister H'rak's question stopped Haven in his tracks. "Broken and reformed to a new master?" His tiny purple eyes narrowed in concentration as he stared at Wren.

"*Master, please, I'm sorry I displeased you but you won't...you wouldn't...*"

"*Of course not, Wren. I would die rather than give you up -- you know that!*" Haven couldn't think what in the world had gotten into his novice. Wren wasn't acting at all himself this evening. First insisting on sucking his cock, even though it was expressly forbidden both by the rulings of the Council of Light and by Haven himself. And then thinking that Haven could ever, under any circumstances, be induced to sell him to the fat, disgusting ruler of the Tiberions. Or to anyone else for that matter.

"I am afraid, Minister H'rak, that the mind bond which binds Wren to me is quite different from a Tiberion symbol of ownership. You cannot simply make one mark over another the way you lay one brand over another on your own slaves," he said aloud, making sure that his novice was hidden behind his legs as he spoke. He knew how appealing Wren looked, naked except for the tail and harness, and he didn't need the god-emperor dwelling on his novice's beautiful golden body.

Rudgez the Fourth opened his mouth to ask something else, but the minister of war held up a hand to silence him, an act Haven was sure no other Tiberion would have dared to commit.

"How very interesting, Master Haven," he said, twisting his thin lips into a sneering smile. "Thank you for that insight into the bond between you and your slave, but I am afraid your time is up. There are several more members of the court who yet need to make their obeisance to the god-emperor, may he live forever, before the deflowering can commence. So if you wouldn't mind moving along…?"

Haven bowed briefly and led his still trembling novice away from the hovering golden throne to a seat at one end of the long feasting table to their right. He sat down on the low bench which appeared to be carved out of some expensive and fragrant wood and got Wren settled between his feet. At once his novice pressed close to him, nestling between his legs and rubbing his cheek against Haven's inner thigh. Despite the fact that he had come so recently, Haven felt his cock beginning to rise again at Wren's nearness and seductive actions.

"*That is enough, Novice!*" he snapped through their link, reaching down to push the young man away. "*I refuse to have another display like the one we just put on in front of the god-emperor. What is wrong with you tonight?*"

"*Master, please don't push me away! Please touch me! I need you -- want to show you how much I love you. Let me suck you again -- please?*" Wren's mind-voice was filled with unrequited lust, and Haven looked down with concern to see the bright pair of amber eyes staring up into his own from under the table. Their pale golden hue was eaten almost entirely by the drowning black of Wren's pupils and Haven realized his novice's eyes were dilated with lust. He was filled with guilt for the improper activity they had just engaged in but now, even more, he was worried.

"*No, you can't suck me, Wren,*" he sent, feeling surreal. "*But if you sit still and be good, I'll touch you.*" Reluctantly, he ran a hand through the spiky golden hair even though he felt that they needed some serious time apart after what had just happened. What was going on with Wren, he wondered for what felt like the hundredth time that night. His novice was seemingly insatiable, not to mention disoriented, a strange combination for a young man who had always had a level head on his shoulders. Wren's common sense was one of his defining attributes, almost as much a part of him as his beautiful amber eyes. What had happened to it now? Could it be restored? More to the point, could Wren be restored to his former self? And even if he was, how could Haven explain all that had passed between them to the council?

Haven's worried thoughts were cut short by a loud squealing blast that seemed to come from a twisted metal horn being played by one of the attendants at the end of the table. Obviously this was the Tiberion idea of music. Wincing, Haven forced himself not to put his fingers in his ears. Being an emissary of goodwill, he usually tried not to judge other cultures, even ones that were strange to him. But by their customs, manners, food, and even their music, the Tiberions were proving to be the most barbaric and disgusting race he had run across in a long time -- perhaps ever. Did these people have any sense of class or taste in anything they did?

"And now, for the pleasure of his eminence, the god-emperor, may he live forever, the minister of finance would like to present a public deflowering with his new slave from the fourth moon of the Tyndall system," the attendant announced.

Suddenly, two guards in full Tiberion regalia entered the circular feasting room. Chained between them wearing inhibitor manacles and nothing else was a young, humanoid woman. She was little more than a girl, Haven estimated, surely no older than Wren. She had pale pink skin, a waterfall of pale lavender hair, and large, sky blue eyes which were wide with fright. She trembled as the guards dragged her forward, shaking her head and saying something over and over in a language Haven's universal translator didn't know. But he didn't need any kind of translation to see that she was not a willing participant in the upcoming ceremony -- he could feel her misery and pain radiating through the room and knew Wren probably could too. Two large wooden posts were present in front of the end table where Rudgez and Minister H'rak now sat, and the guards chained the naked girl between them and stepped back.

Haven tensed as the minister of finance, a tall, thin Tiberion with slanting, deep-set crimson eyes walked forward. His lizard-like body was covered in a single long coat of copper-colored cloth with deep pockets and wide cuffs trimmed in black. He bowed low to the god-emperor, who had lowered his throne enough to stuff his face with the same sour blue meat that Haven remembered B'orl had told them was considered a delicacy. The minister then made another, slightly less formal bow to Minister H'rak, who was staring at the slave with a hungry light in his purple eyes and ignoring the food. There was a plate of the blue meat not far from Haven that he wished he could ignore. But the rotten odor drifting up to him made that impossible. The stench would have spoiled his appetite if it hadn't already been ruined by the spectacle that was about to take place.

"*Master, what are you doing?*" Wren's mind-voice broke his concentration, and Haven realized he was halfway to calling a Sword of Brilliance into being through the power of the Light as he contemplated the scene in front of them.

"*I cannot let this happen,*" he told Wren, wondering what he could do to stop it that wouldn't mortally offend the Tiberions and cause them to immediately blow Gow gi Nef out of the sky.

"*There's nothing you can do. You can't save her.*" Wren's voice was soft and sad but there was truth in his words.

"*I can't just sit here and see her raped!*" Haven looked down to meet his novice's eyes again. Wren's pupils were still dilated to their widest point, erasing his hope that his novice might be coming back to himself. But at least he was talking sense, as little as Haven wanted to hear it.

"*Do you know how many men took me before you bought me?*" Wren asked, rubbing his cheek against Haven's inner thigh, dangerously close to his cock. "*Do you know how many used me? Fucked my mouth? Left me bloody and crying in the dirt before you came along?*"

Haven's mouth went dry. Wren had never talked so much about his past before. It was always something he had wished to put behind him, and Haven had never pressed the young man for what were obviously painful details. But tonight for some reason all of Wren's emotions were out and on display. "*How many?*" he asked, not wanting to know the answer.

"*I cannot even count their numbers, Master, but you couldn't save me from that fate and you can't save her from this one. Maybe later when the negotiations are concluded and we are about to leave you can rescue her as you rescued me. But if you do anything now…*"

"*I'll doom the negotiations before they start. You're right, Novice. It's just so hard to watch.*"

"*Would you like me to take your mind off it, Master? You're half hard already and no one would see if I sucked you under the table.*" Soft fingers found the rigid lump of his cock and stroked in a distracting manner before Haven could catch his novice's hand and push it firmly away.

"*No, Wren,*" he sent as sternly as he could. "*We're not going to be doing anything else tonight. Something is going on with you and I intend to find out what. But for now, be still!*"

"May it please Your Majesty, I am proud to deflower this slave before you," the minister of finance was saying when Haven raised his head. He stepped forward, reaching into his deep pockets and produced two vials of oil -- one red and one blue. Carefully, he uncapped them both and poured a small amount of the red oil and a much larger amount of the blue oil into his palm before replacing the vials dexterously. He mixed the oils by rubbing his hands together and then began to spread the bluish-purple mixture over the slave girl's naked breasts.

The slave moaned and tried to pull away as the minister's scaly hands cupped her tender mounds. Haven bit the inside of his cheek and frowned, willing himself not to go to her rescue. He had to remind himself that billions of souls on Gow gi Nef were hanging in the balance in order to keep from drawing a Sword of Brilliance or at least a Knife of Radiance from the air above him and charging the scene.

"Hold still, slave!" The minister of finance made a motion to the guards who had chained her to the posts in the first place. "Widen her stance and chain her legs," he demanded. "I won't have her dancing about like this while I am attempting to honor the god-emperor, may he live forever."

The two guards did as he commanded and soon the hapless slave girl was forced into a spread-eagle stance between the two posts. Her naked body quivered as the tall Tiberion minister approached her again.

"Shame me in front of the god-emperor, would you?" he hissed in a voice so low Haven never would have caught it without his specially trained senses. "Well, we'll see how reticent you are with a triple dose of passion-seed oil in your pussy, my dear." He pulled the vials of oil out of his pocket where he had put them for safekeeping. This time he mixed a very little bit of the blue oil and a great deal of the red oil in his palm. Then, with an ominous smile, he approached the chained slave and reached between her open legs.

She moaned and begged in her strange language but there was no stopping the tall Tiberion. He parted her naked pussy lips with rough fingers and began rubbing the reddish-purple oil mixture into her vulnerable inner cunt. Haven's big hands clenched into fists under the table and he could feel Wren's distress at the sight as well. But then something strange began to happen to the slave girl -- she actually began to react to the minister's scaly touch.

Instead of moving her pelvis to try and avoid the long, reptilian fingers that entered her, she suddenly began thrusting toward them, attempting to get more of them into her cunt. The words of negation she gasped became moans of pleasure, and suddenly she spread her thighs for the Tiberion minister, her pale blue eyes dilated to drowning black with lust.

Haven felt like an electric current had just passed through him. Her eyes -- the slave girl's eyes were exactly the same as Wren's! And she had gone from fear and revulsion to obvious enjoyment of the situation with the application of the oils. Suddenly B'orl's voice rang in his head: *You just use three parts of the blue calla-flower oil to one part of the red passion-seed oil. And mind you, don't mix up the ratios -- that's very important.*

Of course, he had been so preoccupied with getting Wren into his costume that he had mixed up the ratios! No wonder his novice was acting so strangely. And he would continue to act that way until the oils were washed off. Haven only hoped he hadn't caused any permanent damage with his stupidity.

He wanted to get up and leave at once, but he was fairly certain that would be a huge insult to the god-emperor. So he forced himself to sit still, watching as the Tiberion minister of finance bared his greenish cock and prepared to take the slave girl from behind. Far from trying to avoid his invasion, she tilted her pelvis back, welcoming him in with drugged cries of lust. Even when he rammed his shaft into her bare pussy to the hilt and began to thrust violently inside her, she only moaned and backed to meet him, apparently oblivious to any pain his rough treatment was causing her.

"*Gods, Master, look at the way she submits.*" There was definite longing in Wren's voice and through their link Haven could catch glimpses of his novice's fantasies. He saw himself taking Wren from behind as the minister was taking the slave girl, saw Wren begging and moaning for more of his thick shaft as he penetrated the beautiful golden body to the hilt with his cock…

Enough! Haven slammed down a mind-barrier between them, uncomfortably aware that his cock was hard and ready all over again. *Have to get that oil off him as soon as possible*, he thought to himself guiltily. *I'll scrub him off myself if I have to.* Of course he *would* have to, he realized, because of the damn inhibitor manacles Wren was wearing. But that particular thought only caused a fantasy of his own, he and

Wren waist deep in the bathing pool in their room, their limbs entwined as he slowly, sensually fisted his novice's slender cock to wash away the offending oil.

Haven shook his head to clear the image. What was wrong with him lately? Was it this place? Something about the air inside the Tiberion ship? Or were his long suppressed improper desires simply coming to the surface in the decadent and debauched Tiberion lifestyle they were being subjected to? Whatever the reason, he knew he was going to have a terrible time trying to explain why he had touched his novice so improperly and even worse, allowed Wren to fellate him. *I could have stopped him*, he thought guiltily. *At least when he was swallowing my cum, I could have pulled him off me.* But what had he done instead? He'd tangled his fingers in Wren's soft, spiky hair and pulled his novice closer, allowing, even encouraging the intimate kiss as Wren swallowed every drop. Why had he done that? If he couldn't think of an adequate reason for himself, Haven was sure he couldn't think of one the Council of Wisdom would accept.

"*Master? Master, it's over now. People are leaving.*" Wren's soft mind-voice brought him back to himself. Haven looked up from his untouched plate and saw that it was true; the Tiberions who had been sitting on either side of him and Wren had left silently, taking their slaves with them. The head table where the god-emperor and Minister H'rak had been sitting was deserted, much to Haven's relief. The last thing he needed was another confrontation with that fat floating idiot or his sadistic minister of war.

In fact, the circular feasting hall was almost completely empty except for the slave girl who had been deflowered.

She was still chained to the wooden posts, her head hanging low in either sorrow or shame -- Haven couldn't tell which. On the inside of one pale, pink thigh there was a trickle of cum and a smear of blood, proving that she had indeed been a virgin before the ordeal began.

Haven's heart went out to her, and without thinking, he walked around the table and went to stand in front of her. Reaching out, he attempted to lift her chin with one hand, but she jerked away, her eyes wide with fear. They were blue again, Haven saw, her pupils a normal size, and the emotions on her face were the exact opposite of the flagrant lust she'd displayed earlier. He frowned, wondering why she had returned to normal when the slick passion seed oil mixture still coated her inner thighs and pussy. But there was no time to wonder long -- the guards were returning for her, their booted feet ringing against the cold black marble as they marched.

"I'm sorry," Haven told her quietly, even though he knew she couldn't understand. "I wish I could help you. I will do what I can to see you freed before my novice and I leave this ship."

She only shook her head, tears welling up in her large blue eyes as she looked at him. Then the Tiberion guards unchained her roughly and led her away, her pattering footsteps almost lost in their tramping pace.

"*You must let it go, Master.*" Wren's soft mind-voice made sense, but it still hurt Haven's heart to let the violated slave girl be led away to who knew what other atrocities in the huge ship. He looked down to see his novice curling around his legs again like a cat, his slender shaft still hard and dripping precum on the black marble floor.

"Come, Wren," he said aloud, pulling the young man to his feet. "It's time we scrubbed that oil off."

* * *

One hour and thirty standard minutes later, Haven was beginning to wonder if getting the oil off his novice was going to be possible. He had started by sending Wren into the huge, sunken bathing pool that dominated their bathroom and ordering him to soak in the bathing pool until the oil came off. Wren had soaked for a while and then come out of the bathroom wrapped in a towel. He had then dropped to his knees, offering to take Haven down his throat again because he so longed to taste his master's cum.

Red in the face, Haven had led his novice back into the bathroom and put him back in the bathing pool. This time he watched as Wren soaked in the tub and spread his legs which allowed the warm bath waters to penetrate his virgin rosebud anus until even Haven had to admit the young man was squeaky clean. Once again Wren climbed out of the tub, but this time he leaned up on tiptoes and kissed his startled master, rubbing his still hard cock against the tight black pants Haven wore.

Controlling his anger and lust as well as he was able, Haven had then drained the tub and refilled it with clean, soapy water. Undressing himself even though he knew it was a dangerous move, he got into the water with Wren and touched him inappropriately for the fourth time that day. Or was it the fifth? Haven had lost count. He only knew he had to bite the inside of his cheek until he bled to keep himself from kissing Wren as he touched him. He sat his young novice on the edge of the bathing pool and stroked his slender shaft with a soapy hand, making sure to leave not a single inch unwashed.

Wren moaned and came almost at once, his cock pulsing in Haven's big hand, pumping jets of pearly white cum into the air with his release. Trying to ignore the way his own cock was throbbing by this time, Haven had turned him around, leaned him over at the waist and instructed him to prop his elbows on the side of the pool. As soon as Wren did as he was told, Haven pulled his legs apart and inserted two long fingers into his novice's tight rosebud. Wren cried out and gasped, his cock instantly hard again as Haven fucked his fingers gently into him, allowing the warm water from the tub to wash his novice clean inside and out. He was more than aware of the impropriety he was committing, but he didn't know what else to do -- how else to get rid of the oil and with it, Wren's lustful urges. At last, he considered that his novice was clean enough.

But he proved to be wrong yet again. The moment Haven withdrew his fingers and instructed Wren to get out of the tub and get dressed, the young man ducked under the water and tried instead to capture Haven's cock in his mouth. He succeeded for a moment and Haven was treated to the exquisite torture of having his novice's hot, wet mouth engulfing his shaft once more before he pulled Wren dripping and gasping up from the depths and made him get out and dry off.

Firmly, Haven sat his novice down on the side of the huge bed platform and examined his handiwork. Despite all the soap and elbow grease that had gone into getting Wren clean, there was still a thin, reddish film of oil on his cock and presumably coating the inside of his anus as well.

With orders to Wren to stay where he was, Haven went to the communiqué device imbedded on one wall of their bedchamber. Angrily, he punched in the series of coordinates that B'orl had left under one of the plates of food they had flushed down the waste chute earlier that evening.

"Yes, Master Haven?" B'orl's flat face on the communiqué monitor was puffy with sleep, proving that at least one Tiberion had the decency to be in bed instead of debasing slaves and deflowering virgins.

"This oil -- the passion-seed oil -- how do I get it off?" Haven demanded. He knew he wasn't being very polite but he was beginning to panic. Wren was acting like someone drunk on lust wine from the Nebulon system, and if he didn't stop his incessant advances soon, Haven was very much afraid he was going to do something he would regret forever. He had lost count of how many times Wren had offered to suck him again or begged Haven to fuck him. They had to get the damn oil off, and yet despite repeated scrubbings, it and its effects were still there.

"Passion-seed oil?" B'orl blinked owlishly and then appeared to remember what Haven was talking about. "Oh, the oil! Yes, Master, is there a problem with it?"

"Yes, there's a problem -- I mixed up the ratios." Haven was too desperate to dissemble. "And now my novice, er slave, is showing the effects most disturbingly. He, uh, won't be satisfied and I must get my sleep for the mediations tomorrow. How do I get it off?"

"Oh, well that's easy enough." B'orl yawned, treating him to the sight of several rotten back teeth. "Semen is the only known solvent for passion-seed oil. Specifically, the semen of the one who put the oil on in the first place. You oiled your slave yourself, did you not?"

Haven felt himself go pale. "Are you saying I have to…?"

"Simply come in him, Master Haven." B'orl shrugged again as though it was no big deal. "Precum will probably be sufficient to dissolve the coating of oil on his cock but if you also inserted the oil into his anus…"

"I did," Haven snapped, feeling like his world was spinning out of control.

"Then fuck him." B'orl yawned again. "Fuck him and come in him and the problem will be taken care of."

"I…I don't choose to do that," Haven said stiffly. "Wren is a virgin and I don't choose to use him that way. Not now."

"But you put the tail in him," B'orl protested as if that refuted Haven's entire argument.

"The tail, yes," Haven said testily. "But he's never had a…a cock inside him. And I don't mean for him to start tonight."

B'orl shook his head and clicked his tongue. "Well, if I'd known that, I never would have offered you the oil in the first place, Light Bringer. Why didn't you put him in a white collar if he's a virgin?"

"What difference does the color of his collar make now?" Haven was beyond exasperation.

"A great deal of difference in our culture, Master Haven. A slave wearing a white collar is a virgin or exclusive to his master's use. A red collar means anyone who wishes can use the slave -- most masters who enjoy watching their slaves get fucked more than fucking them themselves choose that color. And a black collar means a pain slave -- the slave can be fucked *or* punished by anyone who wants to." He shook his head. "I thought you knew all that. I was quite surprised that you picked the red for your slave when it was so clear you wanted to keep him to yourself."

"Forget about the damned collars for a moment! The question is, how am I supposed to get this oil off of him?"

"Very carefully, I'd say, Master Haven," B'orl said with a completely straight face. "I wish I could be of more help but there is no other solvent. See, the passion-seed plant --"

"Never mind about the plant or its properties," Haven snapped. "I don't have time; I have to go tend to my slave."

"Very well, Light Bringer." B'orl bowed respectfully, the top of his pointed skull disappearing from the monitor for an instant as he performed the obeisance. "I'll send along a white collar for your slave to wear tomorrow. If, that is, you'll still be requiring one?"

"What? Yes...yes, of course I will. Send one." Haven wasn't sure exactly how he was going to manage this, but he did know one thing -- he hadn't saved Wren from degradation and rape all those years ago in order to degrade and rape the young man himself. Somehow he had to get the oil off and out of his novice without taking Wren's virginity and he was determined to do it.

Slapping off the communiqué, he walked over to the bed where Wren lounged against the blue and gold furs. The slender shaft jutting from between his golden thighs was every bit as hard as it had been before he'd come all over Haven's hand, and it leaked precum freely. Haven reflected morosely that it was too bad not just any cum would do because it would have made things so much simpler -- Wren had plenty to spare and he seemed able to go all night.

"I heard what B'orl said, Master." Wren twisted sinuously and suddenly he was up on his hands and knees, spreading his legs to present himself in a posture of submission.

"Wren, what…stop that at once," Haven demanded, trying not to look at the erotic pose his novice was striking.

"But, Master." Wren looked over his shoulder, his large eyes still dilated with need. "If there's no other way, then we'll have to do it. I told you that I would gladly submit to anything you wanted to do to me. So if you have to fuck me for my own good --"

"I am *not* going to do that." Haven ran a hand through his blue-black hair, trying to think how to proceed. "Get off your hands and knees and lay on your back with your legs spread," he directed. He had an idea now of how he was going to proceed -- he just hoped he could keep control of himself while he put his plan into action. Light help him, but after being teased and touched and sucked all evening by his novice he had never wanted anyone as badly as he did Wren right now.

His novice complied with his orders at once, flipping over onto his back and spreading his thighs wide in submission. "Do what you need to, Master," he said softly. "I don't mind."

Yes, but you will once the effects of this damn oil wear off, Haven thought, careful to keep a barrier between them so his novice couldn't hear him or feel his desire. He had to go about this carefully and clinically, had to treat it like any other situation where he'd been called upon to heal the young man who was under his care.

He got on the bed with Wren and moved into position between the young man's thighs. Taking his erect cock in one hand, he tried to coax a droplet of precum to the slit at its tip so that he could rub it over Wren's straining shaft. He wasn't getting very far and was just thinking that it was going to take all night when his novice surprised him by wrapping his legs around Haven's waist and pulling him down.

"Wren…" he said warningly, but the young man shook his head.

"Just listen to me for a minute and don't move, Master. This way is easier -- see?" He shifted under Haven until both their shafts were nestled together, rubbing against each other with a delicious friction that made the older man bite back a groan.

"Wren, I don't know," he said uncertainly, but his novice only smiled.

"But you're already producing much more precum. This way you'll have the oil off me in no time -- thrust against me and see."

Drawing back, Haven made a long, slow, gliding thrust against his novice's straining shaft. This time there was no way he could hold back the groan that rose in his throat.

"*Feels good, doesn't it, Master? Feels right.*" The intimacy of having Wren speak inside his mind as their throbbing cocks rubbed together was almost too much for Haven. With great difficulty, he reminded himself of the task at hand.

"Wren," he said, speaking aloud deliberately to avoid the intimacy of their link. "This isn't about pleasure -- it's about necessity. I'm just going to rub against you until I've, uh, eradicated the oil on your shaft."

"Yes, Master," Wren practically purred. "But what are you going to do about the oil inside me?"

"I'll let you know when the time is right," Haven assured him. "In the meantime, help me get this oil off of you." *Before you drive me insane*, he thought privately.

"Yes, Master. But please, would you…could you kiss me just a little while we do this? It seems so…so clinical otherwise." Wren looked so sad, the wide amber eyes pleading softly that Haven found himself agreeing. After all, he did love his novice -- not as a lover, he told himself, despite what they were doing at present. But he didn't want Wren to feel that he disliked him or hated what they were doing. He just needed to keep the situation in check. But surely a small kiss couldn't hurt, especially if it would make Wren feel better.

"Well, I suppose it couldn't hurt," he said gruffly. "Come here, my Wren."

Wren leaned up to meet his lips eagerly, and before Haven knew what was happening, what had started as a brief, closed mouth peck quickly became a hot, open mouthed kiss as they rubbed together, trying with their mutual efforts to spread his precum over Wren's slender shaft.

He was having no trouble producing the sticky liquid now, Haven found, as he explored Wren's mouth with his tongue, tasting his novice thoroughly. His cock was weeping from the delicious friction and the feel of Wren moving under him. He tried to control his possessive, dominant emotions, but it was very difficult when he was touching his novice so intimately, stroking over and over against Wren's cock, and Wren was so obviously eager to submit.

"*Take me, Master,*" he sent through their link fervently. "*Take me, stroke me, fuck me, use me any way you want. I'm yours to do with as you wish. Just don't stop touching me.*" His taut young body undulated under Haven's, opening to him as Wren gave himself up completely to this forbidden act of love.

Haven thought he was going to lose his mind. The clinical act to rid his novice of the oil and the quick kiss had turned into something he'd only ever dreamed of before. And even then he didn't allow himself to dwell on such images but forced himself to release them into the Light. But now, not only was he dreaming of touching Wren, he was acting on those dreams. He had his novice pinned spread-eagle to the bed, rubbing his naked cock against Wren's while he ravished his mouth and prepared to fuck him…

No, not that. Never that! The thought jarred Haven back to reality, and he forced himself to pull away from Wren's clinging arms and legs. Sitting back on the bed, he panted harshly, trying to regain his breath after the intensely sexual experience. At least, he reflected rather grimly, the first part of his plan had been a success. Wren's cock, though still hard, was shiny with their mingled juices and Haven was willing to bet that not a single centimeter of its surface remained dry.

"Master, why did you stop? I was so…so close." Wren's large amber eyes were wide with desire and his mouth was red and swollen with Haven's passionate kisses. With his beautiful naked body spread out on the bed and that expression on his face, he looked to Haven like a debauched angel. A beautiful boy fallen from the heavens into the hands of one who had used him hard and well. *Except I am that one,* Haven reminded himself severely. *And it has to stop now.* Yes, because if he lost control during the next part of his plan, the relationship between him and his novice, the most important relationship in his entire life, would be ruined completely.

"I stopped because I didn't want to come," Haven said matter-of-factly, answering his novice's question as forthrightly as he could. "We need…*I* need to get my cum inside you, Wren. But no, before you ask, I am *not* going to fuck you. I don't want to take your virginity completely -- I just need…need to get the head of my cock into you before I come." He could feel himself getting red as he explained, but he went doggedly on. "Just the head. No more than that, I swear. And I wouldn't even do that if there was any other way."

"So you're not going to fuck me?" Wren was positively pouting now and Haven reflected that he would be more than glad when this was all over. He wanted this tempting little angel gone so that the levelheaded young man who was his friend and partner as well as his novice could return. That thought more than anything else gave him the strength to continue.

"No, I'm not going to fuck you. I just told you I won't," Haven said sternly. "I need you to roll on your side for me, Wren, and try to open up."

"Yes, Master." Wren rolled obediently onto his side. He seemed to know what Haven had in mind because he lifted his top leg invitingly, exposing his tight virgin rosebud to view.

"Gods, Wren," Haven nearly groaned at the erotic sight. If only Wren wasn't so beautiful, he thought. If only that slender, golden body didn't draw him so. If only he didn't have to do something that was so terribly wrong. He wished himself a thousand miles away, anywhere else, so that he wouldn't have to do this. But there was no other way.

His own cock was rock hard and ready both from the events they had just been through and the sight of Wren spread so invitingly before him. Sliding onto his side, he pressed close to the young man he loved so much and lined the head of his cock up to Wren's tender opening.

Slowly, carefully, he began to push, intent on breaching the ring of muscle that guarded Wren's rosebud. He heard his novice gasp and saw Wren wince and bite his lower lip as the broad head of Haven's cock began to slip inside. The agonized expression and the stretching pain he could feel

Wren experiencing through their link almost made him stop. But if he didn't do this now, he knew he would never have the nerve again. It had to be done.

Reaching around his novice, Haven grasped Wren's now semierect shaft and stroked it firmly from root to tip. "Just the head, Wren," he murmured in the young man's ear. "Try and relax. Let me in just far enough to come in you, and then it will all be over."

"Yes, Master," Wren moaned softly. He shifted a little, thrusting into Haven's palm and at the same time opening himself wider, submitting despite the stretching pain. His submission was so beautiful it touched Haven to the core. His heart ached with the perfect trust Wren had in him, and bled with the thought that he was betraying that trust with this act. Because no matter how necessary it was, the fact was he was still putting the head of his cock into his novice's virgin ass, still preparing to fill Wren full of his cum at any moment as the young man lay quietly, letting it happen.

"Just a little more, my Wren," he murmured softly. And with a last shallow thrust, he felt the head of his cock pop through the ring of muscle and enter the heat of Wren's body. Haven was in.

"Gods, Master, I feel you in me," Wren moaned softly. "You're so big, so thick."

"Does it hurt, my Wren?" Haven whispered, his voice hoarse with need and love.

"Some…but it feels good, too." Wren pressed back experimentally, causing another thick inch of his master's cock to enter his tight ass.

"Stop." Haven put a hand on his hip warningly. Although there was nothing that he wanted to do more than to ram his cock home to the root in Wren's soft, wet heat, he refused to do it. "I promised I wasn't going to fuck you, Wren," he whispered roughly in his novice's ear. "I'm just going to fill you with cum and then I'm going to pull out."

"But, Master, how can you come if you don't fuck me at least just a little?" Wren asked softly. He pulled forward so that the forbidden inch of cock left his body and then pushed backward again, taking two inches inside him this time.

"Wren, don't." Haven tightened his grip on his novice's shaft, effectively stopping the young man's movements. "Hold still," he ordered, withdrawing until only the head of his cock was inside Wren again. "Hold still and let me come in you, Wren. I don't want this to go too far."

"Please, Master, just a little. Just as far as you've gone before," Wren begged softly. "I want to feel you deep in me. Wouldn't it be better for you to put your cock all the way inside me just once so that when you come it will really fill me up?"

"No," Haven said firmly, although it was taking every ounce of strength he had to keep from following Wren's twisted logic. "I'm sure it will work just as well with only the head of my cock inside you. But if you promise to hold still and not take more than I'm willing to give, I'll thrust just a little, all right?"

"I'll be still, Master," Wren whispered. "Just fuck me. Just fill me up with your cum."

"I told you, Wren, I'm not fucking you," Haven grated. But as he plunged forward, making the shallowest thrusts he could, it certainly felt like it. He was only going an inch or so past the head of his cock into Wren's tightly stretched rosebud, but somewhere deep inside him he longed to go deeper. Longed to bury his cock to the hilt in the beautiful, unresisting body and fuck until Wren moaned and begged and writhed under him.

The forbidden thoughts coupled with the intense sensation of Wren's body squeezing the head of his cock was finally too much. With a low groan, Haven felt himself beginning to come, spurting his seed into Wren's tight ass. At the same time, he felt the slender shaft in his hand begin to pulse as Wren allowed his master's orgasm to trigger his own.

Love you, Wren, he thought, too far gone to know if he was shielding the forbidden emotion or not. *Love you so much. You are so beautiful when you give yourself to me. So beautiful when you come...*

When he was finished, he felt so worn out with emotion and the physical exhaustion of holding back even as he came that he didn't even have the strength to withdraw from Wren's body. They lay panting together for a while, the head of Haven's cock still pressing inside his novice until he felt Wren stir.

"Master?" His novice's voice sounded soft and uncertain, but the purring note of seduction was gone.

"Wren? Are you back?" Haven rose up on an elbow and looked down at the young man still spread out on the bed beside him and half under him in a wanton pose of submission.

Wren looked up at him, his amber eyes back to normal but filled with hurt and confusion. "Master, I don't understand. I thought I was having a very vivid dream but this… Why are we naked? And…why are you inside me?"

Chapter Eight

"Gods, Wren, I'm so sorry." Haven drew away and Wren could feel his shame through their link. Haven was wondering how he could possibly explain the reason behind his actions. He was terribly afraid that Wren would feel he had been betrayed, abused, molested when that was the last thing Haven wanted to do.

"It's all right, Master," he murmured, turning to face the older man. It felt so strange to actually be naked in bed with his master, to feel Haven's cum dripping out of him and know they had been intimate, even if not as much as he remembered wanting.

"No, Wren, it's not all right. None of what I've done to you since we got on this Gods damned ship is all right." Haven rolled away from him and reached for his clothes which lay in a discarded heap at the foot of the bed.

Wren's heart ached for his master's pain. Quickly, he slid off the bed and went around to kneel at Haven's feet. "*Please, Master, talk to me*," he begged through their link. "*I'm not angry or upset, just a little disoriented*."

"Which is exactly why I should have found another way to do what I did." Haven's deep voice was savagely unhappy and the barrier he had built between himself and Wren felt as deep and wide as the vast black reaches of space. "It was the oil," he continued as he finished dressing. "It was my fault -- I mixed up the ratios. And it made you…not yourself."

When he had first awakened from the strange dream state he seemed to have fallen into, Wren hadn't been able to remember exactly what he had said and done. But details were coming back to him now, memories that made him blush from the tips of his toes to the roots of his hair.

"Master," he said softly, still kneeling on the floor. "Did I…did I really suck you tonight?"

"Yes, Wren, I'm sorry. I tried to stop you but not hard enough." Haven ran a hand through his thick, blue-black hair in obvious distress. "I should have tried harder not to break my word to you. I promised you that you'd never have to do that again and then I did it to you myself."

"No, Master." Wren looked up the tall length of the man he loved. "If I remember correctly, *I* did it to *you*. You tried to stop me -- there was no blame in your actions."

"Yes, there was -- there is!" Haven began pacing angrily, his hands knotted into fists behind his back.

"But the passion-seed oil -- there were extenuating circumstances," Wren protested. It hurt him to see his master so upset.

"No excuse is good enough for what I did to you," Haven said roughly, rounding on him. "Please, Novice, I need to be alone. I need to meditate on my actions and think of how I will explain them and myself to the council once we get back to Radiant."

"The council?" Wren felt himself go cold all over. "But…but, Master, do they really have to know?"

"Listen to yourself, Wren. Of course they have to know. Thinking to hide the things we have done is wrong. Do you see?"

"I see, Master." Wren nodded and swallowed hard. "But, well, will the council let us stay together after…after they know?" If he lost his master because of his actions that night, he knew he would never forgive himself. Because despite the fact that he had been under the influence of the passion-seed oil, there was nothing he had done that he would take back. In fact, he would go further if he could, would give himself to his master completely. Wren knew it was wrong and improper to feel so, but he loved Haven with all his heart and the thought of being parted from him was an agony he couldn't bear. "Please, Master," he whispered when Haven didn't answer his question. "Please say that you won't let yourself be parted from me. I…I couldn't bear it."

"My Wren." Haven cupped Wren's flushed cheek in one hand, his blue eyes softening. "I would never let anyone take you from me if I could help it, little one," he rumbled, stroking Wren's face gently. "Though I can scarcely believe you can still care to be my novice after all that I have done to you here."

"Oh, Master, I care. I care so much!" Wren flowed into the warm, strong arms that had comforted him so many times in the past, pressing himself against Haven's hard, muscular body and burying his face against his master's neck. He longed to tell Haven that he wanted to be more than his novice, that he wanted to be his lover, his partner forever.

But he knew that he couldn't say as much to his master. He had already revealed too much tonight. Doubtless Haven thought it had been the passion-seed oil talking, but if he suspected otherwise, that Wren was in love with him, then his strict sense of honor would surely demand that he give Wren up as his novice and Wren couldn't bear that. So he shielded his true feelings carefully and contented himself with nuzzling against Haven's broad chest.

"Wren..." Haven pushed him away gently but firmly. "The ruling of the Council of Wisdom is final. Which is why we must not let any more improper actions pass between us."

"What is improper about me hugging you?" Wren demanded. Already he missed the comfort and shelter of his master's arms.

"Nothing if you had any clothes on," Haven said dryly. "Wren, as long as we're here and you are forced to go around dressed...or rather undressed like a Tiberion slave, I think it would be better if we kept from touching each other. I'll still help you in and out of your harness -- that can't be helped. But I'm afraid you must try to endure your sexual urges and wait for self-gratification until these negotiations are complete and we get back to the pod." He shifted on the bed and looked at Wren thoughtfully. "I can see now that all our problems started with that first touch -- with me allowing myself to help you when you were in need." His eyes flickered down to Wren's cock and then back up to his eyes. "I wanted to touch you no matter what I told myself about easing your pain -- I wanted to stroke and caress you and make you come for me. I see that now, although I couldn't admit it earlier. Had I not given into that improper urge, none of the rest of what we have done may have followed."

"I am sorry, Master." Wren looked down, feeling like he was going to cry. "I…I never should have asked you to do that in the first place. But…but can we really not touch, not even to hug?"

"Not while you're unclothed. It's not proper." Haven's deep voice was stern, but then, seeing the hurt in Wren's eyes, he sighed and went on. "You tempt me, little one. I am shamed to admit it even to myself, but it's true. You're not the ragged little slave boy I bought so many years ago -- you've grown into a beautiful young man and I can't ignore that anymore, not with you parading around nude or next to nude in that damn harness." He shrugged sadly. "If I can't look at you without having improper thoughts, then it's not right for me to touch you either. Do you see?"

"I see, but, Master, it's so hard." Wren felt tears wetting his eyes and had to look away. He knew that in a way his master's words ought to make him glad -- Haven was actually admitting he had feelings for him that went beyond the master/novice relationship they had shared for so many years. How many times had he fantasized about something exactly like this? Fantasized about Haven admitting that he wanted Wren as a lover and not just as a novice and then taking him, dominating him completely as Wren surrendered body and soul to his master's demanding touch? But now that the time had actually come, he felt sad instead of elated.

He should have known that once his master realized his improper urges toward his novice he would put some distance between them. But so *much* distance -- never to hug Haven again, never to be held in those strong arms and comforted, never to hear his master whisper, *my Wren* in that deep voice that seemed to pierce right through him. It was almost more than Wren could bear, and yet he knew he had to. As much as he loved Haven and he knew that Haven loved him, his master's sense of propriety would never allow them to have more than a close friendship. It was forbidden by the council and their word was law, a law Haven was not about to transgress again.

"Wren…I can feel your hurt and I am sorry, truly sorry for your pain," Haven murmured, breaking into his thoughts. "But we are on a slippery slope. We have to stop now -- right now -- if we want to remain together when we return to Radiant. You say that you don't want to be parted from me, but if we tell the council what we have done, no matter how good our excuses, they will surely separate us. Unless we can show that we took steps to stop ourselves from committing any more wrong. Which is what I am trying to do now."

"Very well, Master." Wren blinked the tears from his eyes and stood up. "I would rather have you in my life as my master and never touch you again than lose you by giving in to my impure urges. I will be strong."

"We'll both be strong." Haven gave him a small smile.

"Yes, Master." Without thinking about it, Wren started to go to him for a comforting hug. Then he realized what he was doing and turned aside. "Sorry, Master," he murmured, looking down at his feet. "Force of habit."

"Indeed. A habit I shall be sorry to break." Haven sighed. "Well, let's try to get some sleep, Novice. Tomorrow will doubtless be a long day, even if the mediation between the Gowans and the Tiberions goes well."

"True," Wren agreed, beginning to arrange some of the sleeping furs down at the foot of the bed. He dimly remembered being eager to share this bed with his master when he first saw it. He had anticipated being wrapped in Haven's strong arms as they slept, but that was out of the question now. Or ever again.

"What are you doing?" Haven asked as Wren curled up in the small nest he had made for himself. "That can't be comfortable, Novice."

"I thought it would look better for me to sleep at your feet as befits a true slave," Wren murmured, meeting his master's eyes. "And, well… it keeps us out of temptation's way."

Haven nodded. "Very good thinking." He settled in his own part of the bed and yawned, obviously getting ready for sleep. As he turned on his side, there was a deep rumbling gurgle from the direction of his stomach.

"Master? Are you hungry?" Wren looked at him anxiously but Haven only shook his head.

"Don't worry about it, Wren. I can wait until morning -- we'll just have to hope that Tiberion breakfast cuisine is better than what they serve for dinner."

Wren laughed. "Indeed, Master. It could hardly be much worse. But we have some meal bars back in the pod. It would only take me a few minutes to fetch them." In truth, he knew he ought to be hungry himself. He hadn't eaten any more than Haven had since they'd boarded the Tiberion ship. But the events of the day had left him without an appetite.

"No, Wren." Haven turned over again and shook his head. "I can wait until breakfast. Until then I will simply release my hunger to the Light." *All of my hungers*, he thought privately, but Wren caught the words anyway and knew what they meant. His master was going to be meditating for strength -- the strength to stay away from him and not think impure thoughts.

The idea made him feel sad and he wished that he and Haven had never come on this mission in the first place. Before this the love and lust he felt for his master had been a private thing, but at least he'd still had Haven's comforting touch, however casual, to sustain him. Now he had nothing but his master's presence to feed the fire of his love. And he might lose that if he wasn't careful.

I'll be careful, he promised himself. *I won't do or say anything else that might jeopardize our relationship*. Life without his master was unthinkable -- a black hole that Wren didn't even want to look into let alone live. So from now on, no matter how much he burned for the tall, dark-haired man that he loved with his whole heart, he would keep himself in check.

Feeling sad but resolved, Wren turned over in the small nest of sleeping furs and sighed. He was still sticky and thought about going to the bathroom and cleaning Haven's cum from between his thighs but remembering the painful shock of the inhibitor manacles, he decided it probably wasn't such a good idea. Besides, if this was the last physical reminder he would ever have of his master's touch, he wanted to keep it on and in him for as long as he could. He only wished that Haven had gone all the way and truly taken his virginity, that he had thrust his thick shaft to the hilt in Wren's body before coming inside him. It probably would have been painful; the stretching sensation when his master put only the head of his cock inside him was evidence of that. But Wren would have welcomed the pain -- at least it would have given him something more tangible to remember his master's intimate touch by. As it was, he had only sticky inner thighs and a sore heart.

* * *

He woke up a few hours later with his own stomach rumbling. Apparently, the worry and sorrow he had been feeling earlier weren't enough to keep hunger at bay indefinitely.

Wren knew he should release his hunger into the Light as his master had, but Haven had ten years' more experience in the ways of the Light than he did, not to mention considerably more willpower. He tossed and turned for almost half an hour before deciding that it wouldn't hurt to go get the meal bars out of the pod. After all, who knew what the Tiberion idea of breakfast was? What if it was as bad as or worse than the sour blue meat they liked so much for dinner? There might not be time to fetch the bars if he waited until tomorrow, and he didn't like the idea of Haven having to conduct the mediation on an empty stomach. For a moment he wondered if it was safe for him to go out alone without Haven to act as his master and shield him from unwanted advances. But surely, even as perverted as the

Tiberions were, they had to sleep sometime? And if most of them were tucked safely into bed, he could go out without worrying about running into any of the more predatory members of the court. Minister H'rak came to mind and Wren shivered. But then his stomach rumbled again.

I'll just run out to the docking bay and come straight back, he promised himself. *It won't take five minutes.*

Slipping out of the furs, he searched around until he found the loose green tunic and fitted brown trousers he had worn when they first boarded the ship. There was no way he was going to run around in that embarrassing slave harness unless he had to. For a quick trip to the pod, he wanted his own clothing. He pulled on his novice's uniform quickly, not bothering with the boots. He didn't want to attract attention on his midnight wanderings and knew he could move more quietly barefoot.

Feeling immeasurably better once he was decently dressed, Wren slipped out of the bedroom and into the reaches of the huge Tiberion warship. The glows in the corridors had all been dimmed, rendering their vulgar splendor in a gloomy half-light. Wren didn't mind the lack of illumination, however. It allowed him to walk more freely and he moved like a cat, passing from shadow to shadow.

He found the docking bay easily and quickly and located the small, homey pod he was already beginning to miss in moments. Popping the lock, he rummaged around until he found the flat, palm-sized bars made up of concentrated nutrients and dried fruits and nuts. Packaged in slick silver wrapping, they were hard as a rock but quite tasty, and one of them could keep a man Haven's size going for a whole day. *Or a greedy novice going for an hour*, Wren thought with a smile, remembering the way his master always teased him about his fondness for the meal bars.

When he was younger, just after Haven had bought him from Dungbar the slaver and taken him back to the temple, his master used to hide one or two bars in his tunic whenever he came to see him. To their mutual delight, Wren would climb the tall man like a tree, going on his own private treasure hunt to find the bars that he knew his master had brought just for him. It had been Haven's gentle way of teaching him that not all touch was painful or sexual, his way of helping Wren get over his early childhood trauma of being a slave. Gods, how he'd loved climbing all over his master, searching for the meal bars! But even better were the warm, wonderful bear hugs Haven would give him when he found one, praising him for being clever and brave and letting Wren know how much he was loved.

Wren's smile faded when he remembered that such casual touching was now prohibited between them. How had it happened? Was it his fault for teasing his master too much, for pushing Haven past all boundaries of propriety? Wren was very much afraid that it was. *I should have released my lust and need into the Light as Master does*, he thought ruefully. *Should have fought my impure urges instead of giving in to them, dwelling on them.* Yes, it was definitely all his fault. Wren had wanted too much, had pushed his master into recognizing and acknowledging the sexual tension and desire that lay between them. And now he would never feel those warm, comforting arms around him again, even in a platonic hug of friendship.

Stop thinking about it, he ordered himself, closing the pod and making his way back to the maze of corridors. *You ought to be concentrating on the mission. Billions of Gowan lives hang in the balance, and all you can think about is your forbidden love for the one man in the universe you can never have. You've been acting less like a Servant of the Light lately than a cat in heat and it serves you right that --*

His thoughts were interrupted by low voices drifting out into the corridor from a room up ahead to his right. The hall he was walking through had no carpeting, only some kind of exotic stone floor that was cold on his bare feet, and the echoing tones were too distinct to miss.

"....fully expect the mediation tomorrow to fail utterly," someone said in a familiar grating tone.

"But what about the Light Bringer? The Gowans seem to set great store by Master Haven's counsel," a higher pitched, more nervous voice answered the first.

"Don't tell me you're worried about the Servant of the Light that fat fool of a Gowan ambassador called in, T'will," the first voice answered. "Their order is nothing more than a few delusional monks with the ridiculous belief that they can manipulate the universe to their own ends through their ancient religion."

"That's not all they can manipulate," Twill's voice protested. "It's said they can call weapons right out of the air -- terrible fiery swords that can cut through anything and reduce a man to ash in seconds."

"And you believe that?" The first speaker snorted in derision. "Next you'll tell me you think the boy traveling with Haven is really his pleasure slave."

Wren froze outside the doorway, listening intently to the exchange taking place in the room ahead. He had a bad feeling he knew who the grating voice of the first speaker belonged to -- it was Minister H'rak. To be caught listening in on his private conversation would probably be extremely hazardous to Wren's health. But now he had to know exactly what the minister of war knew about himself and Haven and how he was planning to derail the peace negotiations tomorrow. Quietly, he crept a little closer to the doorway and crouched low, listening intently.

"The boy is not really a slave?" Twill's high twittering voice rose in disbelief.

H'rak made an incredulous noise. "Do you know nothing of the Order of the Light? I can't be certain, but I suspect the boy is actually Haven's novice."

"Novice?" T'will echoed, sounding uncertain.

"A Light Bringer in training, mind-linked to an older, more experienced master in order to learn their ways," H'rak said impatiently. "A novice obeys his master in all things. Including, in this case, playing a role that would be considered an abomination among their kind. As far as I know, Servants of the Light keep no slaves, especially not sexual ones. They prefer to drown their natural urges in self-righteousness rather than act on them."

"But he acts the part so well! I saw the way he took Master Haven into his mouth and sucked him tonight at the Grande Promenade," T'will protested. "He sucked his master to completion and swallowed every last drop of Haven's cum. If they abhor sexual misconduct as you say, how is this possible? He *must* be a slave."

"I don't know how it's possible." H'rak's voice was musing. "I asked myself the same thing. My guess is that they are willing to do anything, even transgress their own principles, to save that planet full of puling cowards we presently have our annihilator aimed at." He laughed, a low rasping sound that sent a shiver through Wren's entire body. Clutching the stack of meal bars in one sweating palm, he crept closer to the open door.

"It will be extremely interesting to see exactly how far they can be pushed without revealing their true relationship," H'rak continued. "If Haven admits that the boy is his novice and not actually his lover and slave, we can accuse them of transgressing our customs and giving offense, exactly as we did the Gowans. And if he doesn't, he faces the repugnant task of molesting the innocent young man he is supposed to be training and caring for."

"A conundrum indeed -- *if* the boy isn't really a slave," T'will remarked. "Still, your theory would explain why Haven became so flustered when the god-emperor, may he live forever, asked if the boy was for sale -- why, he practically jumped out of his skin to protect him. Most real masters aren't that protective of a common pleasure slave."

"No indeed," H'rak agreed, chuckling coldly. "And the way he spoke of the bond between them -- it was clear he would rather cut off his right arm than lose his novice to the clammy clutches of Rudgez the Fourth."

"But they have passed as master and slave up until now and the god-emperor, may he live forever, was quite taken with them, or at least with the boy," T'will protested. "And you can prove nothing against them. The god-emperor's word is law, H'rak -- not even you can change it once he's made up his mind. How can you be sure Haven's presence won't sway him during the mediation?"

"I can be sure because the god-emperor is an easily led, weak-minded fool that I have under my thumb completely," H'rak growled. "He will do as I tell him and I will have my revenge on the Gowans, Light Bringer or no Light Bringer."

"Minister H'rak, you go too far. You forget yourself." T'will sounded shocked.

"Not at all, T'will. I'll simply dangle a new virgin before his eyes until he does as I say. You know how he loves a good deflowering. In fact, don't you have a new slave girl yourself that has never been used?"

"I do but I don't care to take her in front of the entire court, H'rak." T'will sounded peevish. "I don't know why you had to bring back that ancient practice of taking pleasure in a slave before the god-emperor, may he live forever -- it's most embarrassing to be forced to perform every time we have a court function."

"Maybe." H'rak chuckled coldly. "But it keeps the god-emperor's tiny mind too busy with the pleasures of the flesh to worry about affairs of state. And while you might dislike performing, don't pretend you don't enjoy watching while others do. Remember the pain slave I worked over the other day for his majesty's enjoyment?"

"Worked over, is that what you call it? You whipped his back to bloody ribbons." T'will sounded distinctly queasy. "Such a display is very hard to watch while one eats, H'rak. So off-putting. I found myself quite --"

He was interrupted by the clattering sound of the entire stack of meal bars slipping from Wren's sweaty palm to the hard stone floor.

Gods, what have I done? Wren didn't stay to be found out. Turning, he ran as quickly and as silently as he could back toward the docking bay, hoping to hide in the pod until the coast was clear.

But before he could get more than three steps down the echoing stone corridor, a large cold hand caught him in a merciless grip and turned him around.

"Spying are we, *slave boy*?" H'rak's grating voice demanded. "Well?" He shook Wren, his long fingers digging into the tender flesh at the nape of his neck.

"No, Minister." Wren widened his eyes, attempting to look innocent. He knew now that the Tiberion minister of war suspected the real nature of his relationship to his master, but his life might well depend on convincing H'rak otherwise. He had to continue to play the hapless, helpless pleasure slave to the hilt and hope that H'rak bought his act as genuine rather than forced. "I was only fetching my master some food from our space pod. He found himself still hungry even after the delicious feast at the Grande Promenade tonight." He nodded at the pile of meal bars lying in a heap on the stone floor.

"I'm certain he did since he didn't eat a bite," H'rak snarled. "And what about you, little slave, is your belly full too? Perhaps full of your master's cum?"

Wren blushed and dropped his eyes modestly. "It is my pleasure to service my master with my mouth, Minister," he murmured. "Although I am not used to doing so in such a public place."

"Or at all, I'll wager," H'rak growled. "How much of my conversation with Minister T'will here did you hear?"

Wren bit his lip. If he denied hearing anything, H'rak would assume he had heard everything. But he certainly couldn't let the huge minister of war know that he had heard his plans to annihilate the Gowans in order to fulfill some personal vendetta, or that Wren knew that H'rak suspected the true nature of his relationship with Haven.

"Speak!" H'rak shook him so hard the room spun. Wren wished briefly that he had passed his trials and was a master in his own right, able to call forth weapons of Light. A Knife of Radiance in his guts would doubtless do the Tiberion minister of war worlds of good. But even if he had been able to form a knife, Wren knew what Haven would say -- this situation called for subtlety, not force.

"I heard you ask Minister T'will if he had a new virgin slave because the god-emperor, may he live forever, enjoys watching a deflowering," he gasped, trying to look frightened. "And he said that he did but that he didn't wish to take her in front of the entire court. And that's all I heard before I dropped the meal bars on the floor by mistake, I swear, Minister H'rak."

"A likely story." H'rak grated. "About as likely as that blowjob you gave your master tonight at the Grande Promenade. I wager that was the first cock you ever had in your mouth -- am I right, *slave boy*?"

"I promise you, Minister H'rak," Wren said with complete truthfulness, "My performance tonight with Master

Haven was not my first such experience by far. My master bought me from a slaver by the name of Dungbar on Rigel Six -- he was selling my mouth to any who would buy at five credits a suck. I've had more cocks in my mouth than I care to count."

H'rak's purple eyes narrowed to slits and then he gave Wren a cold, humorless smile. "Well, then you won't mind sucking mine. On your knees, boy, and shed those ridiculous clothes." With one horribly strong hand, he pushed Wren down to the cold stone floor and with the other began to unbuckle the military style belt around his waist.

Gods, what am I going to do? Wren took a deep breath, willing himself not to panic as he slowly removed his green tunic. *I have to preserve my cover. I've done this before*, he reminded himself. *With men more repulsive than H'rak. Well, almost as repulsive.* He closed his eyes and remembered kneeling in the hot, dusty back alleys of Rigel Six while cruel men fucked his mouth and shot bitter, salty cum that tasted like tears down his throat. Being mouth fucked by the tall, scaly Tiberion was going to be no pleasure cruise, but he could live with it if it kept H'rak from suspecting that he was right about Wren's true relationship to Haven.

"H'rak, you're an animal." Minister T'will, who had been standing by watching disapprovingly, finally spoke up. "Surely you're not going to make the boy suck you here and now?"

"No, as a matter of fact, I don't think I will." H'rak stepped back and examined Wren, his purple eyes still narrowed in thought. "It's not nearly a good enough punishment -- especially if the boy has had as many cocks in his mouth as he claims. Swallowing my cum would hardly faze him, now would it?"

"As to that, I couldn't say." Minister T'will frowned.

"No, I think I'll fuck him, instead." H'rak laughed, a deep, ugly sound that made Wren feel sick to his stomach. Having the minister's thick, scaly cock in his mouth was bearable but to have it in his ass...no, he couldn't. He just couldn't.

"I beg your pardon, Master H'rak." Wren tried to keep his voice level and respectful. "I'm afraid that my master would not look kindly on you using me that way. I'm his exclusive property and while I've had many cocks in my mouth, my ass is virgin -- he's saving it for himself."

"Is that so?" H'rak snarled. "Then why do you wear a red collar, slave?"

"My master didn't understand the color coding system of your slave collars when we came here." Wren talked fast, trying to keep the panic out of his voice. "In fact, B'orl, the assistant to the minister of the wardrobe only explained it to him tonight. He said he was going to have a white collar sent over for me to wear in the morning so that everyone could see I was a virgin and my master's exclusive property."

He hoped that H'rak would buy his story or at least go check it with B'orl instead of insisting that he take off his pants as well as his tunic. Just one glance between his legs and the jig would be up. There was no way he would get the dour minister of war to believe that his master had only put the head of his cock inside his virgin rosebud. No way he could convince H'rak that Haven hadn't actually fucked him tonight.

"I don't believe you," H'rak said bluntly, shattering his hopes. "You're a filthy, lying little slave and you've got the right color collar to fuck." He gave Wren a cruel smile and lifted his chin with cold fingers to stare into his eyes. "I've been wanting to fuck your tight ass from the moment I first saw you, little Wren, little *slave*. I only wish you were wearing a black collar so I could flog you before I fuck you."

"H'rak, stop -- think what you're doing." Minister T'will put a nervous hand on the minister of war's bulging bicep. "What if the boy is telling the truth and he really is a virgin?"

"What if he is?" H'rak brushed off T'will's hand, his attention still focused on Wren.

"Well, think about it!" T'will sidled closer and hissed in H'rak's ear. "What if you're right and he's Haven's novice instead of his slave?" he asked. "Do you really want to be responsible for deflowering a Servant of the Light? The repercussions would very likely be deadly. Haven is a serious man -- I wouldn't take his anger lightly if I were you. Or the anger of any other Light Bringers he might bring with him to avenge his novice's rape."

"I don't fear those delusional idiots," H'rak growled. "My cock's been hard for this little one since the moment I laid eyes on him."

"But what if the head of their order complains to the god-emperor, may he live forever? Are you really so sure of his regard that you will willingly abuse the hospitality he has offered to the Servants of the Light? The penalty for such a crime is demotion or death, as you know," T'will persisted.

"Very well." H'rak gave Wren a shove and he fell in a heap on the hard stone floor, skinning the palms of his hands painfully. "But at the very least we're going to have an inquest into this." He gave Wren an evil grin filled with sharp, yellow teeth. "I'm going to find out who you really are and why you were creeping around without your master, little Wren. And then we'll see who gets first use of that sweet virgin ass of yours."

Chapter Nine

"For the last time, Minister H'rak, my slave was doing no wrong. I sent him to get the meal bars from our pod because I was still hungry after the feast. If allowing him to go unaccompanied to our ship was an offense, I should have been warned about it when I came aboard." Haven glared across the table at the tall minister of war, challenging H'rak to refute him. The inquest he'd been called to first thing in the morning was not a good way to begin his day but he'd actually been awake for hours before the summons came…

* * *

"*Master, don't be angry, but I think I'm in trouble.*" Wren's soft mind-touch had wakened him from a troubled sleep, causing Haven to sit up on the side of the huge bed, instantly alert.

"*Novice, where are you?*" he sent, realizing that the young man wasn't in the room with him.

"*In some kind of holding cell, I think. I can't see much, but it's dark and cold and somewhere near the center of the ship.*"

"*Be calm, I'm coming for you.*" Haven was already feeling around for his clothes, but Wren's next words stopped him.

"*No, Master, you can't rescue me or they'll know that we're mind-linked and H'rak's suspicions will be confirmed.*"

"*H'rak's suspicions? What are you talking about?*"

"*He knows I'm not really your slave -- strongly suspects it, anyway.*" In a few short sentences, Wren told him everything he'd overheard in the conversation between T'will and H'rak. It confirmed Haven's suspicion that the dour minister of war was behind the Tiberion's aggression against the Gowans and that he was the puppet master pulling the god-emperor's strings. Unfortunately, it also let him know that Haven and Wren's master and slave act, while more than enough to damn them before the Council of Wisdom, was not convincing enough to completely fool Minister H'rak.

"*We'll have to be careful, Master,*" Wren sent him from wherever he was being held. "*H'rak will try to ferret out our deception and use it to discredit you as a mediator. With no one to fight for them, the Gowans will be extinct before another standard day passes.*"

"*Did he not give any reason for this vendetta, this hatred he has for them?*" Haven asked. "*Think, Novice, there must be something he said.*"

"*He only said that he would have vengeance. I'm sorry, Master, but who knows what goes on in such a twisted mind?*"

"*He could hardly have picked a less likely target,*" Haven mused. "*The Gowans are a peaceful people -- to my knowledge they've never perpetrated an act of aggression against any other sentient species and have remained stubbornly neutral during any and all outside conflicts.*"

"*I know, Master. But the search I did before we came aboard indicated that the Gowans' neutral stance has made them a favorite layover for space pirates. They refuse to extradite anyone no matter how heinous their crimes. All sins are considered to be wiped clean the moment a person sets foot on the soil of Gow gi Nef, and unless they commit an offense on the actual planet itself, they are safe from any outside justice. The Gowans' policy ensures that while a good portion of their population are wanted criminals, they have almost no crime to deal with themselves.*"

"*Hmm.*" Haven rubbed his chin, staring into the blackness. "*As predatory and corrupt as the Tiberions are, you'd think they would appreciate the Gowan attitude of 'innocent despite being proven guilty elsewhere.' Are they perhaps giving asylum to someone H'rak has a personal hatred for?*"

"*I hardly think he'd blow up the entire planet for that,*" Wren sent dryly. "*He'd probably just go down to Gow gi Nef and kill whoever it was personally. Or demand that the Gowans give him up -- I'm sure they'd break their non-extradition rule in this case.*"

"*True, Novice. But what if H'rak already killed whoever it was that he was after and his lust for revenge still isn't sated?*"

"*It does seem likely that nothing less than the extermination of an entire planet would satiate H'rak's bloodlust,*" Wren admitted. "*Considering what his other appetites run to.*"

Haven was instantly alert to the quiver of fear in his novice's mind-voice. "*Did he hurt you, Wren? What did he do?*" he demanded.

"*Don't worry, Master, I'm still a virgin -- but only by the skin of my teeth.*" Haven listened with growing anger as his novice explained what H'rak had planned to do to him. "*It's my fault,*" he concluded at the end of his explanation. "*I knew I ought to stay in the room with you, but I was hungry and restless. I gave in to my appetites and look where it landed me.*"

Haven knew his novice was talking about more than physical hunger -- although the words remained unspoken between them the subtext was clear. "*No, Wren,*" he sent. "*It was my fault for not asking the significance of the collars in the first place. I should have known a culture as warped as this one would attach sexual meanings to everything -- even the color of a slave's collar.*"

"*But if I hadn't gone out, H'rak couldn't have caught me in the red collar. Now he can say that I was out without my master and refused to service him sexually even though I was marked as available.*" Wren's mind-voice sounded distressed, and Haven wished he was close enough to pull his novice into his arms and give him a comforting hug. Then he remembered that he himself had outlawed any kind of physical contact between them. Even if Wren had been sitting right beside him on the bed, there was no way Haven could have touched him. But that didn't mean that the despair in the young man's voice didn't affect him.

"*You're not available to anyone but me*," he sent back fiercely, balling his big hands into fists. "*I hope you told him that, Wren.*"

"*I did, Master. I knew what I ought to do for the sake of our mission and I...I thought I could stand to suck him if I had to. After all, I'd done it enough with men I hated and loathed before you rescued me as a child. But when he threatened to...to fuck me...*" Wren's voice dissolved into inarticulate misery and Haven ached to hold him again.

"*My Wren*," he murmured soothingly through their link. "*He will not touch you. I swear it by the Light. Despite everything that has happened between us recently, you are still my novice to train and protect. I will shield you with my life if necessary.*"

"*Oh, Master. I wish I was there. I wish... I wish you could hold me.*"

The broken, yearning tone of Wren's mind-voice made a lump rise to Haven's throat. It reminded him of the battered and abused boy he had rescued from poverty and sexual degradation so many years ago. Of the nights that Wren had cuddled in his arms, seeking comfort and refuge from the nightmares of his old life. All he wanted to do at that moment was to gather Wren close and hold him until the fear left his wide amber eyes. But he couldn't, he reminded himself. Never again. The thought caused a lump to rise in his throat and he had to get up and pace the length of the huge bedroom.

"*I wish I was there too*," he sent when he was able to control the emotions that threatened to drown him. "*I wish I could hold you. I am so sorry...sorry for everything that's happened between us since we got to this ship.*"

"*I am too, Master, but in a way I'm not.*" Wren's mind-voice sounded pensive and quiet. "*I mean, I know what happened between us was wrong but...but I wouldn't take it back. The only thing I wish is that I could remember it more fully.*"

Haven felt shame descend on him as heavily as a lead blanket. "*I'm glad you can't remember, Novice,*" he sent grimly. "*The way I broke my promise to you --*"

"*I never asked you to promise what you did,*" Wren interrupted. "*I don't feel betrayed or hurt by what you did to me, Master -- by what we did together. I just...Master, can I ask you a question about tonight?*"

"*Certainly, Novice.*" But Haven felt a heaviness around his heart. He wished Wren would just try to forget what had happened -- it would be less emotionally damaging than dwelling on the details. Yet he felt he couldn't refuse to speak about it if Wren wanted to.

"*Was...was I pleasing to you?*" Wren's mind-voice was so soft Haven could barely hear him. "*Did you enjoy the feel of my mouth on you when I sucked you? The feel of my body wrapped around yours when you...when you entered me?*"

"*Gods, Wren...*" Haven closed his eyes tightly in the blackness of the bedchamber, trying to control the surge of lustful emotion that threatened to swamp him. Was Wren trying to kill him? But he felt compelled to answer.

"*Master?*" Wren asked uncertainly.

"*Yes, Novice,*" Haven sent back at last. "*Yes, I enjoyed the feel of your body joined to mine. I have never had greater pleasure than when you took me between your hot, soft lips. And I have never had to control myself so rigidly as when I was trying to enter you without taking things too far.*"

"*I wish you had gone farther, Master. I wish you had taken me while we had the chance,*" Wren sent passionately. "*I wanted to feel you in me, fucking me, taking me completely. I wanted to feel you use me as hard and as deep as you could before you filled me with your cum.*"

Haven shut his eyes briefly, trying to release the burning need his novice's words raised inside him to the Light. "*You must not talk that way, Wren,*" he sent back. "*You must not wish such things. The council would separate us for certain if we did such a thing.*"

"*I know it's wrong, but I can't help it.*" Wren's voice was little more than a whisper. "*I can't help the way I feel about you, Master.*"

"*You can and you must, Wren,*" Haven sent firmly. "*Release your improper urges into the Light and I will do the same.*"

"*I'll try, Master. I don't want to lose you, to lose the most important relationship in my life. But at least...at least now I know that the feelings I've been hiding for so long...that I'm not the only one to feel them.*" He sent a brief image of himself and Haven entwined in a kiss, his master's large body covering his, holding him close with loving dominance as he devoured Wren's sweet mouth hungrily.

The sweet, forbidden vision made Haven's entire body ache with longing. "*You must not dwell on such thoughts, Novice,*" he sent gently. "*They are wrong. The feelings we have allowed to grow between us are wrong, too, and must be discouraged and ignored. We must not speak of them again. You know it is true.*"

"*I know, Master.*" There was a wistfulness in Wren's mind-voice that nearly brought tears to Haven's eyes. "*It's just... I've loved you so long it's hard to stop now.*"

"*You don't have to stop, Wren,*" Haven told him. "*You can always love me as a mentor. The way I love you as a student, one I am so very proud of.*" Haven knew it wasn't enough, but it was all he could offer the young man now -- all he could offer either one of them.

Even when Wren became a master in his own right, the council would frown upon any kind of romantic relationship between them. The master and novice roles they had played for so long were sacred to the Order of Light and to taint them with any kind of sexual desire was forbidden. So he had to discourage anything but the correct feelings between himself and Wren -- even though he ached to feel his novice's slender, firm body pressed against his, to taste those sweet lips again. Haven shook his head. Gods, he wished he had never allowed himself to go down this road in the first place because it was terribly hard to go back.

"*It's late, Master. Or early, rather,*" Wren sent with a mental sigh. "*You should try to get some rest. In the morning you can come looking for me.*"

"*I'll say I fell asleep waiting for you to come back and was disturbed when you weren't in the room when I woke up. I'll come for you first thing in the morning,*" Haven promised. "*Will you be all right until then?*"

"*I'll be fine.*" Wren's mental tone was less certain than his words, but it was clear he didn't want Haven to worry. "*Good night, Master.*"

"*Good night, my Wren.*" Haven sent a warm, gentle wave of comfort through their link -- a mind-hug, Wren used to call it when he was young. It was the only kind of hug he could give his novice now, and Haven put as much care and love into it as he could, though it seemed terribly inadequate.

* * *

"He should not have been out on his own creeping around." Minister H'rak's grating voice interrupted Haven's reflections on the night before and brought him back to the present. He sat at a gold inlaid table across from the minister of war and the god-emperor in a small but opulent conference room used to conduct official business. It was where he had been summoned by the royal Tiberion guards when he stepped out of his bedchamber that morning, and he had gone with them without hesitation, eager to see his novice again and make sure he was all right.

He hadn't heard from Wren since the night before, and his attempts to contact his novice had been met with a wall of silence. He could tell Wren was there but for some reason he wasn't answering Haven's mind-touch. Haven couldn't think of why his novice would be blocking him -- maybe he was thinking about what had passed between them earlier and wanted to shield his forbidden thoughts, but it wasn't like him not to answer his master's call at all. It worried Haven and he had gone with the royal guards eagerly, hoping to see his novice safe and sound. But he had been there arguing with H'rak for the better part of an hour now while the god-emperor looked on with a bored expression on his fat face and they had yet to bring Wren in. Haven was beginning to run out of patience.

"Where is Wren?" he asked, refusing to be drawn back into H'rak's argument. "He belongs to me and I demand to see him at once."

"Very well, Master Haven," H'rak sneered. He nodded at the guards flanking the ornately carved doors. "Bring in the little spy."

"Wren is no spy." Haven frowned at the minister of war.

"But neither is he truly a slave," H'rak countered. "He is your apprentice -- a Servant of the Light in training that you brought here under false pretenses in order to gather information about affairs of state that do not concern you."

Haven opened his mouth to refute the allegations, but at that moment the doors of the small room burst open and Wren was pushed inside. He stumbled once and went to his knees, his head hanging low.

"Wren!" Haven ran to his novice at once and knelt on the thick carpet beside him. "Wren, are you all right?" "*Why didn't you answer my mind-call?*" he sent.

"Fine, Master." Wren's light tenor voice was hoarse as though his throat was sore. When he looked up, Haven saw the trickle of blood running from the corner of his full mouth and a dark bruise beginning on one high cheekbone. "*H'rak came to me this morning, very early. He wanted to make me admit I wasn't really your slave. I didn't tell him anything even though...even though he hurt me.*"

"*Why didn't you tell me?*" Haven demanded, cupping Wren's hurt cheek in his hand tenderly.

"*I knew if you found out what he was doing you'd want to come rescue me, and it would prove to him once and for all that we were mind-linked and that I was your novice, not your slave. I couldn't risk it, Master -- that was why I blocked you. I'm sorry.*"

"*No, I'm sorry, Wren. I should have come for you earlier no matter what H'rak thinks.*" Without thinking, Haven started to send a pulse of healing power to the bruised cheek he was touching, but Wren pulled back abruptly.

"*No Master, if you heal me, it will only strengthen their suspicions about us.*"

Haven knew Wren was probably right, but it only made him angrier than he already was. Rising, he turned to H'rak, who was staring at him intently, his purple eyes narrowed in concentration. Clearly, he was waiting for Haven's reaction.

"What have you done to my slave?" Haven struggled to release his anger and keep his voice calm and cool, but it was difficult when all he wanted to do was call a Light weapon into existence and chop off the Tiberion minister's ugly head.

"Only asked your novice a few questions, Master Haven. He was most uncooperative, I'm afraid." H'rak gave him a lizard-like smile, the corners of his thin lips curling up coldly. "Don't worry, though, he is still a virgin -- as long as one of the guards didn't become overly enthusiastic after I left him this morning."

"Wren is my slave --" Haven began, but he was interrupted by the god-emperor.

"The slave boy is a virgin?" He sat up eagerly, his immense bulk wobbling in the golden throne that hovered only a few inches off the floor. "Then why does he wear a red collar?"

"Your pardon, Your Eminence," Haven said smoothly, turning from H'rak to the suddenly interested god-emperor. "I was ignorant of the color-coding system of your slave collars when I came aboard, which led me to pick incorrectly. But, yes, by rights, Wren should be wearing a white collar."

"I know you've owned him since he was a child, but his charms are considerable. How have you resisted taking him?" There was a greedy light in the god-emperor's small red eyes that Haven didn't like.

"Well, Your Majesty --"

"He hasn't fucked the boy because Wren isn't really his slave," H'rak snarled, cutting Haven off. "The boy is in training in the Order of the Light and Haven is his mentor."

"Is this true? You don't really own the boy?" Rudgez the Fourth asked, still eyeing Wren hungrily.

"I bought Wren over ten standard years ago on Rigel Six," Haven said steadily. "He is mine in every sense of the word, Your Eminence, and I am deeply offended that Minister H'rak would suggest otherwise." He took a deep breath. "Since I have been aboard your ship, I have been insulted and my slave has been damaged -- under other circumstances, I would demand satisfaction of Minister H'rak. However, I didn't come here to fight duels or answer false accusations. I am here as a mediator to settle the conflict between your people and the Gowans, and that is what we ought to concentrate on right now."

"Oh, the Gowans." The god-emperor made a shooing motion with his hand, as if the subject bored him.

"Yes, Your Eminence, the Gowans. The people whose planet you have threatened to annihilate," Haven said, struggling to keep his voice calm.

"The Gowans who offered a mortal insult to Your Majesty and offended the dignity of the Tiberion throne," H'rak growled, turning to the god-emperor. "Much as Master Haven has offered a mortal insult in coming aboard our ship without a true and proper pleasure slave to service him for Your Majesty's honor."

"For the last time, Wren is mine! He belongs to me." Haven struggled to keep his voice cold and quiet, allowing just a hint of threat to creep into his tone as he stared H'rak down.

"Prove it!" The minister of war stood suddenly, slapping his palm on the ornate table for emphasis.

"I didn't come here to prove anything to you, Minister H'rak," Haven said coldly. "I came on behalf of the Gowans -- a people you plan to destroy utterly in an act of cold-blooded genocide. Not because they truly offered your god-emperor any insult, but because of some personal vendetta you have against them yourself."

"That is my business -- I knew your little novice was a spy." H'rak's muddy complexion turned dull red with anger. "We Tiberions have a custom called Pain or Pleasure, Master Haven -- a little game that proves the truth or treachery of the one who is subjected to it. I suggest that you and your 'slave boy' should be put to this test. If you agree to it, we will know once and for all that Wren is your slave. If you don't, well, the penalty for offering offense to his majesty, Rudgez the Fourth, may he live forever, is death, as the Gowans are about to find out."

"You dare threaten a Servant of the Light?" Haven rose, calling on the power around him, the power of the living Light, the energy of all pure goodness contained in the universe. Between the fingers of his clenched right fist, a pulsing burst of radiance began to grow. He could feel it solidifying in his hand, a beam of energy so pure it would burn away any wickedness or evil it touched. Slowly, almost gently, he drew the brilliant tip along the inlaid table before him. Gold melted and wood hissed, releasing a thick black smoke as the Knife of Radiance passed over its rich surface.

Across from him, H'rak stood perfectly still, his purple eyes narrowed to slits. "I heard that such things were possible but I didn't believe." His grating voice was flat -- not fearful but cautious. Beside him, the god-emperor shrank back in his chair, his own eyes wide. He stared at the brilliance in Haven's fingers with a dull fascination, as if hypnotized.

"Believe," Haven told them softly. He had called only a knife into being, though he could have raised a much more deadly weapon. His purpose was to let H'rak know they were serious, not to actually fight. "Wren and I may be alone in this place, but we are not helpless," he told the minister of war. "It is a mortal insult to threaten a Servant of the Light, especially one who comes to you on an errand of peace."

"And it is a mortal insult to draw a weapon in anger in the presence of the god-emperor," H'rak snarled in return.

"Well then, we're even." Haven allowed the Knife of Radiance to die slowly in his hand, fading away to nothing. Then he turned to the god-emperor, deliberately ignoring H'rak. "I suggest that we stop talking about myself and Wren and settle the question of your threat against the Gowans, Your Eminence."

"The Gowans, the Gowans, I am sick to death of hearing about the Gowans." Now that the knife was gone, the animation had returned to Rudgez the Fourth's pudgy face.

"Then Your Majesty should give me leave to blow their third-rate planet to bits," H'rak said smoothly, sitting down beside the god-emperor himself. "It's the only way never to be bothered by them again."

"But I thought we were to have a game of Pain or Pleasure." The hungry gleam was back in the god-emperor's eyes, his attention turned once again toward Wren. "Master Haven and his slave are such a pretty pair, and with little Wren there still a virgin, it would be a shame to miss it."

"The Light Bringer and his novice choose not to oblige Your Majesty," H'rak said, casting a contemptuous smirk at Haven and Wren, who was still kneeling on the floor beside him. "They prefer to talk endlessly of the Gowans, who ought to be exterminated."

"Your Eminence, the Gowans are a peaceful people who --" Haven began, but H'rak interrupted him.

"Who have offered mortal offense to the Tiberion Empire, as have Master Haven and his slave, Wren, who isn't a slave at all."

"H'rak, for the Gods' sakes, I don't care what he is." The god-emperor shot his minister of war an impatient glance. "Only that I get to see him play. I tell you what," he said, leaning forward in his golden throne and addressing Haven. "If you'll agree to undergo our custom of Pain or Pleasure, I'll sign an unbreakable peace treaty with the Gowans right now. We'll leave their space and never bother them again -- there's nothing of interest to do in this quadrant of the galaxy anyway."

"What?" H'rak nearly shouted, turning to face the god-emperor with fury in his glowing eyes. "Your Majesty, think what you are saying -- you cannot allow the Gowans' insult to go unpunished. You must make an example of them or --"

"Or what? The rest of the universe will know that we waste our time on boring little backwater planets who don't even have the weapons to give us a good fight?" Rudgez the Fourth frowned petulantly. "No, H'rak, my mind is made up. I want to see Master Haven and his slave play Pain or Pleasure, and then I want to leave this miserable piece of space and go back to Tiber at once." He turned to Haven eagerly. "So, will you play?"

"What exactly is involved?" Haven could feel Wren's anxiety through their link but he also felt his novice's excitement. After all that they had been through, Rudgez was offering to just hand them an unbreakable peace treaty and fly away, never to bother the peace-loving Gowans again. And all in exchange for playing some sort of game. Of course, knowing the Tiberions, it might be something completely bizarre and disgusting, but Haven thought he could stand a lot in order to save the lives of the billions of innocents below on Gow gi Nef. He could tell Wren felt the same.

"Different actions are inscribed on the sides of a pair of dice. The dominant player -- that would be you, Master Haven -- rolls and must choose either the pain or pleasure aspect that has come up to subject the submissive player to -- that would be your slave boy, Wren."

"What sort of pleasure or pain are we talking about? I won't do anything that will put my slave in mortal danger or cause him lasting harm," Haven said sternly.

Rudgez the Fourth waved his hand dismissively. "It's only a game, Light Bringer. Of course no lasting harm will be done. Now, will you play or not? I can have Minister T'will draw up a peace treaty in a moment if you choose to cooperate."

"*I say let's do it, Master*," Wren sent through their link before Haven could ask. "*Think of the lives we can save -- this opportunity has been presented to us by the Light. We must take it while we can*."

"*You're sure*?" Haven couldn't risk looking behind him to where Wren still knelt on the floor, but he sent the question with as much warning as he could. The decision ultimately had to be Wren's, since he was the one that would be acted upon.

"*I'm sure*," Wren sent firmly.

"*Very well, Novice, I hope we're not getting in over our heads*." Aloud, he said to the waiting god-emperor, "Very well, Wren and I will participate in your game in exchange for an ironclad peace treaty that states you will never bother the Gowans or come near Gow gi Nef again."

"Done! Let us move to the Pain and Pleasure room at once." The god-emperor manipulated some controls on the arm of his golden throne and it rose to its normal height of three feet and maneuvered easily around the table. The guards hastily threw open the doors, and H'rak followed the floating throne, a scowl pasted on his flat face.

"You think you've won, Light Bringer," he snarled at Haven as he passed. "But we'll see how well you do when the dice are cast and your precious novice is at risk by your own hand."

"*What does he mean, Master?*" Wren was getting carefully to his feet and Haven turned to offer him a hand up.

"*I don't know, Novice, but I don't like the sound of it.*" He frowned grimly as they followed the god-emperor and Minister H'rak out of the small room. "*Nor the fact that they have an entire room devoted to this custom or game -- whichever it is. I'm beginning to be sorry we agreed to play.*"

"*But think of all the innocent lives we're going to save -- surely that is worth some discomfort, Master,*" Wren protested, following along behind Haven as they left the room.

"*Discomfort, yes. But knowing the Tiberions, there may be quite a bit more than that involved,*" Haven sent. "*And to hear H'rak tell it, the danger is mostly yours, Wren. A danger or pain by my own hand.*" He frowned, not liking the thought.

"*They hurt me this morning and I didn't break -- why should I fear anything that might come to me by your hand? No, I am not afraid, Master.*" Wren was walking beside him now, his chin lifted defiantly as he looked Haven in the eye. Haven felt a surge of respect and affection for the young man. Wren had been through so much since they had come aboard the Tiberion warship, and yet his spirit was unbroken and the Light still shone through him. Even now, dressed as he was in only the tattered remains of his brown trousers and with a bruised cheek and a cut lip, he still held himself straight and tall. There was no shame or fear about him, only a determination to do the right thing no matter what the cost. Truly, any Master would be proud to have him as a novice.

"*Wren,*" he sent, resting his hand briefly on the young man's shoulder and looking into his clear amber eyes. "*We have been through much together on this mission, but you have handled yourself beautifully. I chose well when I took you as my novice. I'm proud of you.*"

"*Thank you, Master.*" A warm blush appeared across Wren's delicate cheekbones. "*I'm glad you feel that way.*"

Haven could feel him wanting to say something else and holding himself back, but no words were necessary. Wren's beautiful eyes spoke eloquently if silently about his love for his master. A love that was no less pure and sincere because it was forbidden.

"*Oh, Wren,*" he thought regretfully, taking his hand off Wren's shoulder and putting some distance between them. "*If only things were different. But it can never be between us, little one. The council forbids it, and if we transgress their laws again, we will be separated for certain.*"

"*Then we must not transgress,*" Wren sent back simply. "*Because I can't live without you, Master.*"

"*I love you too, Wren,*" Haven sent gently. Then a small golden door appeared before them and their trip through the opulent halls of the Tiberion ship was over.

Chapter Ten

The Pain or Pleasure room wasn't much bigger than the small meeting room they'd just left, Wren saw, looking around. It was circular and carpeted in some rich blue material that felt soft under his bare feet. On one side there was a tiny silver table with a golden cup placed just in the center of it. Beside it was a small, plush couch covered in the same dark blue material as the carpet. Directly in the center of the room there was a pair of golden posts with chains hanging from them. They reminded Wren ominously of the wooden posts the hapless slave girl had been chained to the night before for the deflowering at the Grande Promenade.

"Here we are." The god-emperor seemed almost gleeful with anticipation. "Guards, come and bind the boy to the posts -- strip him first, of course." He clapped his bejeweled hands together and nodded imperiously at Wren. Haven was frowning like a thundercloud when the two Tiberion guards came to take him, but Wren submitted meekly and went with them quietly to the golden posts.

"*Cheer up, Master,*" he sent, trying to project calm and hide the jittery fear that had been eating him ever since they'd walked into the room. "*It will all be over soon.*"

"*That's what I'm afraid of, Novice.*" Haven shook his head as he watched Wren being bound by his wrists between the two posts.

"Now, Master Haven," Rudgez the Fourth chirped, interrupting their private conversation. "You must go to the table and shake the cup. When you roll the dice you may pick one option -- either that which is displayed on the pain die or the one displayed on the pleasure die. But you must pick one and perform it completely -- no halfway actions, please, or our deal is off."

"I understand, Your Eminence," Haven said quietly. "And when is the game concluded?"

"After four rolls of the dice, you and your slave or novice or whatever he is may go. You may leave this room with a copy of the peace treaty to give to the hapless Gowans and fly away freely from our ship. But" -- he held up one fat finger -- "you must agree to never have any kind of contact with the Tiberion Empire again."

If the god-emperor thought they would have a hard time with that last condition, he was completely wrong. As far as Wren was concerned, never having contact with the Tiberion Empire or anyone in it was the sweetest part of the deal, after saving the lives of the Gowans, of course.

"Very well," Haven said and walked up to the small silver table.

Wren watched him pick up the golden cup and couldn't help shivering. It felt strange to be naked again in public, even though the only other people in the room besides himself and his master were the god-emperor, the still glowering Minister H'rak, and the pair of guards that flanked the door.

H'rak sat on the small blue couch, his entire large body clenched in rage. Clearly, the dour minister of war was still simmering over the fact that he didn't have the god-emperor under his thumb quite as much as he had thought. And just as clearly, Rudgez the Fourth didn't care. He had settled his golden throne beside the small blue couch, his fat face alight with anticipation. All that mattered to him was being entertained, Wren decided. Anything that was boring or difficult was of no value or interest to the spoiled Tiberion ruler. *I just hope we can put on a good enough show to save the Gowans*, he thought to himself.

Apparently, his master was thinking the same thing because he lifted the golden cup and shook two ivory dice inscribed with silver script out onto the tabletop with great ceremony.

"Well? Well, what do the dice say?" The god-emperor clapped his fat, bejeweled hands together, as excited as a child.

Haven's lips were white but he showed no other emotion as he read the two directives from the pair of dice. "Kiss," he said. "Or strike."

"Excellent. And which do you choose?" the god-emperor wanted to know.

"I don't know yet, Your Excellency. I must consider." Haven's deep voice was tight with tension. "I would perhaps be better able to make a decision in silence."

"Very well." Rudgez the Fourth nodded. "If it makes you uneasy to be asked questions, then H'rak and I will be silent.

You won't even know we're here." He nodded to one of the guards. "Dim the outer lights and make no noise," he commanded imperiously. The guard moved hastily to obey and soon the perimeter of the room was plunged into darkness. The only light left was a small but brilliant glow directly over Wren's head. It made him feel like he was on a stage with a spotlight trained on him, which in turn made him feel more naked and vulnerable than ever. But at least he could no longer see the greedy, avid face of the god-emperor or the enraged Minister H'rak. The darkness hid them from view, giving the illusion that he and his master were the only ones in the room.

"*Well, Wren?*" Haven turned to face Wren completely. Clearly he wanted the choice of the dice to be up to Wren.

He's treating me like a partner, giving me this choice like an equal, not just his novice, Wren thought, uncertain if he was flattered or worried by this new deference Haven was showing him.

"*You have proved yourself worthy of my respect over and over again*," Haven sent, clearly having heard Wren's thoughts. "*And so I give you the choice, Wren. Should I kiss you or strike you?*"

Wren didn't hesitate. He knew the consequences if he and his master crossed the line again, no matter what the reason. The Council of Wisdom was notoriously stiff-necked and unbending when it came to such cases. They wouldn't care if Wren and Haven saved an entire solar system by committing an impropriety; they would still see them separated. And that was something Wren couldn't bear.

"*Strike me, Master,*" he sent, lifting his chin. "*Do it hard and give the god-emperor no reason to back out of his deal.*"

"*Very well, Wren.*" The emotions coming from Haven were a mixture of desperate unhappiness that he had to do this and powerful pride that Wren was strong enough to choose the harder option. This would be almost as hard for him as it was for Wren -- harder even, Wren thought, because his master had never once struck him in anger in all the years they had been together. But Haven knew the penalty for transgressing the council's rules as well as Wren, and he was just as eager not to be separated from his novice as Wren was to stay with his master.

With no more hesitation, Haven walked forward and struck him, a hard, open handed blow that landed on his unbruised cheekbone with a stinging slap and made Wren's ears ring. The pain was nothing compared to what he had withstood from H'rak and his bullying guards that morning as they interrogated him, but the look on his master's face still brought tears to Wren's eyes. Haven looked so grim and drawn, so terribly unhappy that it hurt Wren's heart to see it.

"*My Wren, I am sorry,*" Haven sent, reaching up to wipe at the tears that trickled down Wren's tingling cheek.

"*Not at all, Master. You are only doing what you must. Go on and roll the dice again. We have only three more rolls and then we're free of this place forever.*"

Haven nodded shortly and went back to the small silver table with stiff, awkward steps. Reaching for the cup, he placed the ivory dice back inside it and shook it until they chattered around inside like small, angry animals. Finally, he poured them out onto the silver surface of the table and bent low to read the words inscribed on them. There was a breathless moment of silence and he turned to Wren.

"Bite or stroke," he intoned aloud for the benefit of their silent, invisible audience. Then he looked at Wren, silently asking his choice.

"*I don't suppose that means you could stroke my hair,*" Wren sent nervously, trying to joke. But Haven only shook his head.

"*You know that isn't what the dice call for, Novice.*" He sent a brief mental picture of his own large hand encircling Wren's shaft and pumping it slowly until his novice came, fountaining cum over his master's fist.

Despite his vulnerable and uncomfortable position with his arms chained over his head to the posts and his public nudity, Wren still felt a surge of excitement and desire at the image of his master touching him. The feel of that large, warm palm was forever etched on his memory, and he longed to have Haven stroking him again, taking him to the edge and beyond. But he knew that it couldn't be -- he had to think about the future and what would become of them after this mission was over. He had to take the path of pain instead of pleasure in order to stay with the man he loved.

"*Bite me, Master,*" he sent, turning his head to one side to expose the long line of his throat. "*Mark me hard, I don't mind.*"

"*Very well.*" Haven walked forward and pulled Wren into his arms -- as much as the chains that held Wren to the posts would allow, anyway. Pressing the length of his big body against Wren's slender, naked one, he lowered his head to the offered throat.

Wren shivered and forced himself to relax in his master's arms. Even as Haven's white, even teeth sank into the tender flesh at the place where his neck met his shoulder, he made no protest. He refused to struggle or fight against the pain, as sharp as it was -- it was being inflicted on him by his master and as such he received the bite as gladly as he would have taken a kiss. He could feel the big body moving over him, feel the warmth of Haven's skin through his clothes as the bite went on and on. And despite the piercing pain in his neck, he felt his cock growing hard against his master's thigh. He couldn't help it. It wasn't the pain that aroused him, but rather his own total submission to his master. There was a pleasure that transcended pain in opening himself and allowing Haven to do anything to him. A pleasure so deep he could scarcely bear it.

At last Haven released his hold and straightened up. There was a small smear of blood at the corner of his mouth and Wren could tell from the warm trickling sensation he felt at his injured shoulder that it was his own. He could also tell that Haven was desperately unhappy but he didn't speak of it to Wren, even through their link. He simply turned and went back to the small silver table like a man in a trance. Wren understood. *He wants to get it over with*, he thought, watching as Haven loaded the hateful dice back into the golden cup and shook them once more. *Only two more rolls of the dice and we're free.*

Haven poured the dice on the table and bent to consider them a moment. Then he turned to the dark area where the god-emperor and H'rak sat quietly and shook his head.

"Well, Master Haven?" Rudgez the Fourth's high voice floated out of the darkness. "What do they say?"

"The dice say…they say suck or cut." Haven's voice was steady, but Wren could feel the turmoil bubbling just below his calm surface. By now his master was heartily wishing they had never agreed to play the twisted Tiberion game but it was too late -- they were in the middle of it and there was no backing out.

"And which do you choose, Light Bringer?" the god-emperor wanted to know.

"You said no lasting harm would come to my slave through this game." Haven's deep voice was accusing. "And yet now one of my choices is to cut him -- how is that not lasting harm?"

"Oh, pish." The god-emperor suddenly hovered into view, his golden throne floating a few feet above the floor. "Don't be so squeamish, Master Haven. A few light scratches with a knife will hardly disfigure the boy for life."

"That depends on how much and where I am expected to cut him." Haven frowned at the chubby figure in the gold throne. "I am not in the habit of mutilating my slaves, Your Eminence."

"Mutilating indeed." The god-emperor made a shooing gesture. "It's not like we're asking you to cut off one of his fingers, Master Haven. Simply carve your initial into his flesh somewhere -- traditionally on the skin of the upper arm or the pelvis. Here -- you may use my own personal knife to do it." He hovered closer and held out a tiny knife with a jeweled handle and a sharp, thin blade as though conferring a great favor. "That is," he said, "If you are determined to choose the option on the pain die again."

"*Well, Wren? I would rather cut off my arm than harm you like this, but the choice must be yours.*" Haven flicked his eyes back in Wren's direction. He was shielding his own emotions closely, obviously not wanting to affect Wren's decision.

Wren thought briefly and longingly of how it might feel to have his master's hot mouth envelop his cock. He could picture Haven on his knees before him, laving him with his tongue, taking Wren deep until he came so hard…And the worst thing was he knew his master desired it too. Try as he might to shield his emotions, some of the deep hunger that Wren felt himself came slipping through the chinks in Haven's mental barrier. Truly, Wren thought ruefully, the feelings they had allowed themselves to acknowledge in their time aboard the Tiberion ship were hard to contain. And yet they must contain them -- or be separated forever.

"*I choose the knife, Master,*" he sent at last. "*I'm yours completely, heart, body, and soul -- you might as well make it obvious by signing your name.*"

"*Wren, if you are choosing this option because you think I would hesitate in any way --*"

"*No, Master," Wren cut him off gently. "I know you would gladly love me with your mouth as I have loved you with mine. But that road leads to our separation in the end -- I can't bear that.*"

"*I can't either, Novice. But neither can I stand to carve my initial into your flesh in cold blood.*" Haven's mind-voice was tight with misery.

"*I can stand a little pain to stay with you,*" Wren told him. "*I'd rather be cut by you than kissed by anyone else, Master.*"

"*My Wren. Only you would say such a thing. Very well then, I'll try to be quick.*" Haven turned and took the knife carefully as though it were a poisonous creature that might turn on him at any moment. Then he turned back to Wren. "*Where?*" he asked simply.

"*My pelvis -- just inside the hipbone,*" Wren sent at once.

"*Of course,*" Haven sent dryly. "*It would be difficult to explain why I had signed your arm the next hot day on Radiant when you want to wear short sleeves.*"

"*Not at all, Master,*" Wren protested. "*I am proud to wear your mark on my skin. It's just that, well...having you cut me there instead of on the upper arm seems so much more intimate. I want this to be just between the two of us, something I can remember and cherish forever.*"

"*You want something permanent to remember me by if they separate us anyway, don't you?*" Haven asked, kneeling before him so that his face was on the level of Wren's waist. "*Well, this is permanent, all right. I doubt even a healing with the power of the Light will be able to erase the scar I leave.*"

"*I don't want it erased, Master. I want to remember forever that I belong to you, no matter what the council says,*" Wren sent. "*So do it, Master. Cut me.*"

"*Close your eyes, Wren. Don't look,*" Haven cautioned. The knife looked tiny in his large hand and its tip was poised just over the smooth golden skin between Wren's right hipbone and the shaft of his semierect cock. Why he should still be partially hard despite what was about to happen, he couldn't say. Maybe it was as he had told his master, a very intimate act. It was as though Haven was claiming him in a way he never had before, and Wren could think of no one in the universe he would rather belong to.

Wren closed his eyes obediently, hissing only slightly when the miniature blade bit into his flesh. As he had promised, Haven was quick. A few short, clean strokes and it was done. When he opened his eyes and looked down, Wren saw a capital H outlined in red carved into his pelvis.

"*That wasn't so bad, Master,*" he sent, relieved that it was over.

"*No?*" Haven looked up at him briefly. "*And yet it was the worst thing I've ever had to do in my life.*" He threw the knife aside and blotted the wound carefully with the edge of the cape he was wearing as part of his outfit today, careless of the crimson stains left on the pale blue material. When he was sure the bleeding had stopped, he pressed a soft kiss to Wren's hip. "*I'm so sorry, Wren,*" he sent, and the pain in his mind-voice nearly brought tears to Wren's eyes again. He wished his hands were free so that he could throw his arms around his master and hug him tight. He was sure Haven would allow it, despite their earlier resolve not to touch anymore. These were definitely extenuating circumstances.

Finally, Haven stood and went back to the table.

"*Cheer up, Master,*" Wren sent him. "*One more roll and we're done. The worst is over.*" But he wondered uneasily as Haven loaded the ivory dice into the golden cup if he was right.

A quick shake of the dice and then Haven was dumping them out on the table once more. He leaned over to look and then the broad shoulders under his pale blue cape went stiff and tense. "*No,*" Wren heard him think through their link. "*No, I will not do it. Not for anything or anyone. I can't!*"

"*Master?*" he sent, concerned, but Haven was already turning to stare at the god-emperor who was once again hidden in the darkness.

"The dice say brand or share, Your Eminence." His deep voice was cold. "Would you care to explain?"

"Well, you can choose to leave a more permanent mark on your slave, Master Haven," Rudgez the Fourth said, hovering into view. "Or you can choose to share him with someone else in the room." He smiled at Wren hungrily and Wren fought to keep his face blank. There was no question about which option he would choose. Between the pain of having his master's initial burned into his flesh or submitting sexually to either the fat god-emperor or the tall, angular Minister H'rak, he would take the branding iron without hesitation. However, Haven didn't appear to be willing to take either option.

"You said no lasting damage would be done," he told the god-emperor. "Either one of the suggestions on the dice would lead to irreparable harm to Wren. I absolutely refuse to make this choice."

"Well then, maybe someone should make it for you." H'rak, who had been quiet all this time, suddenly loomed into view. He smiled grimly at Haven, his long fingered hands clenched into fists. "I have always fancied the boy, myself, Haven. I'll be more than happy to rid him of that pesky virginity for you."

"Stay back." Haven put himself between H'rak and Wren and began calling the power of the Light.

H'rak's hand went to the hilt of his sword -- it was ornate and obviously ceremonial in nature, but it was just as obviously extremely sharp. The single overhead light glittered on its silver blade just as a brilliant radiance began growing between Haven's hands.

"Now, now, no need for that." The god-emperor hastily maneuvered his throne between them. "This is really most unnecessary."

"I refuse to brand Wren or to share him. He belongs to me and no other," Haven said sharply.

"Well, this always is an unpopular roll," the god-emperor chattered conversationally. "What with there being so many possessive masters and all the trouble of getting a branding iron ready…"

"Still, it is a choice which must be made," H'rak grated, pulling his sword completely free of its sheath.

"H'rak, you're ruining the game. Go sit down at once," the god-emperor said sharply. For a moment it seemed that the huge minister of war would disobey him, but then H'rak slid the ceremonial sword back into its sheath with a low growl and stalked back to the couch. For his part, Haven allowed the weapon he had been calling to die but didn't completely dissipate the energy he had gathered. Wren could still feel it crackling in the air between them and he was sure the god-emperor could feel it too.

"Well, Your Eminence?" Haven raised an eyebrow at the hovering Rudgez the Fourth.

"The rules state that you can refuse exactly one roll of the dice." The god-emperor held up one chubby finger. "But only one, Master Haven. So I hope you like what you get on your next try better. If you refuse to perform one of the options again, I will allow H'rak more freedom with his sword." He floated his throne back to the darkened area beside the couch and called out, "Proceed."

"*That was a close one, Master,*" Wren sent, letting out a breath he hadn't known he was holding. "*Just so you know, I would have chosen branding over being touched by either one of those two.*"

"*And I would have chosen death over either burning my initial into your flesh or watching either Rudgez or H'rak paw you, Novice,*" Haven sent, leaning over the table and picking up the dice.

"*You would have chosen death not only for us but for the Gowans, Master,*" Wren reminded him gently. "*We must think of the mission. You must not refuse to choose again.*"

"*My Wren. When did you grow so wise?*" Haven's mind-voice held a hint of grim humor as he dropped the dice into the cup.

"*I think it was sometime after I met you, Master,*" Wren sent, trying for some humor himself. But he was as tense as Haven was as his master shook the golden cup and poured out the dice for the fifth and final time.

Haven bent over the silver table for a long time, staring at the dice before he finally straightened up. Turning, he faced Wren, ignoring the god-emperor and Minister H'rak completely this time.

"The dice say flog or fuck." His deep voice was as dry as a desert and his face was impossible to read. But Wren could see the pain dancing somewhere deep in his master's dark blue eyes and knew what Haven was feeling. It was pretty much what he was feeling himself. Faced with a choice between having what he wanted most in the world -- complete intimacy with the man he loved -- and reliving the childhood nightmare of Dungbar's belt across his back, he hardly knew what to do. And yet Haven was watching him, clearly waiting for an answer. An answer that Wren didn't know how to give.

"*Master,*" he sent hesitantly. "*You know how much I want you, want to feel you in me, filling me, taking me completely. But if we do...*"

"*The council will separate us for certain,*" Haven finished for him. "*I never should have agreed to play this twisted game, Wren. Either choice is completely unbearable.*"

"*But one of them must be borne, Master,*" Wren sent. "*We must choose, not for our sakes, but for the Gowans. The entire planet of Gow gi Nef hangs on our choice.*"

"*Then choose, my Wren. For I cannot.*" Haven's deep blue eyes were troubled, his lips compressed into a thin, tight line. Wren knew what he had to do.

"*I'll take the flogging, Master,*" he sent, trying to keep the fear out of his mental voice. "*Just do it as you did the cutting -- quickly and without hesitation -- and I'll be fine.*"

"*Neither one of us is ever going to be fine again,*" Haven sent darkly. "*Are you certain this is your choice, Novice?*"

"*Yes, Master. I'm sorry, I know it won't be easy for you.*"

Haven frowned unhappily. "*It's liable to be considerably harder on you, Wren.*" He turned to the god-emperor and H'rak and said, "We choose the flogging."

"Oh?" Rudgez the Fourth came into view again, a disappointed look on his face. "The flogging is most brutal, Master Haven -- usually reserved for only the most troublesome slaves. I was certain you would choose to deflower young Wren here instead."

"I'm afraid not, Your Eminence," Haven said shortly. "And if you don't mind, I would rather get this over with."

"But of course." The god-emperor clapped his hands together. "Guards, bring this Servant of the Light a flail."

One of the royal guards left and was back in half a minute with a long, thin flexible cane. He shook it once, and the three leather thongs that had been wound around its handle came loose and dangled about three feet below the tip. Something shiny was tied to each thong but from where he was standing, Wren couldn't see what.

Haven took the cane in one hand and examined it, paying special attention to the tips of the thongs. After a moment, he looked up at the god-emperor.

"The die specified that I must flog my slave, not skin him alive. There are pieces of sharp metal here -- they'll cut him wide open."

"The better to teach a disobedient slave a lesson, Light Bringer," Rudgez said gravely. "That is actually one of the less damaging whips we use. There is another, called a flayer, which has metal and broken glass affixed all up and down the length of each thong. I can have the guards fetch it for you if you like."

"Your Eminence is too kind," Haven said icily. "But no thank you." He swept the flail through the air several times as if trying to get the hang of it, although Wren suspected he was trying to buy time.

"There is a trick to it," the god-emperor said helpfully. "A way of twisting your wrist so the tips catch in the flesh as the lash falls across the slave's back to do maximum damage. H'rak is quite skillful at it if you'd like a demonstration."

"Again, no thank you," Haven grated.

"Very well, then. You must give ten lashes of the flail in order to meet the requirements of the game. As soon as the last blow falls, you and your slave boy are free to go with the treaty in your hand. Understood?"

"Understood." Haven stared at the flail in his hand for a long moment and then he turned to face Wren. "*Wren*," he sent softly. "*Are you sure*?"

Wren swallowed convulsively, his eyes fixed on the wickedly sharp metal tips attached to the three leather thongs. It was going to hurt like fire, he knew. If Haven wielded the flail correctly -- and he had no choice since holding back in any way would cause the god-emperor to renege on their deal -- then it was going to feel every bit as bad or worse than the heavy silver buckle of Dungbar's belt had when he was a child. The instrument Haven held was going to lay his back open to the bone, and knowing that his master could heal him of the wounds and pain, if not of the scars, later on when they were alone was little consolation. Even being branded would likely not hurt as badly and yet...Wren imagined a life without his master, without the tall man with the deep blue eyes and gentle hands who had rescued him so many years ago. A life without Haven was no life at all, he decided.

"*Master, I'm sure*," he sent. "*Just do it quickly. Get it over with.*" He braced himself against the golden posts, digging his toes into the thick blue carpet and gritting his teeth, getting ready to bear the pain. There was a low whistling in the air behind him as Haven drew back the flail and Wren braced himself for the first blow...but it never came.

"I cannot do this," Haven growled in a low, desperate voice. Then his master was behind him, winding strong, muscular arms around Wren's waist and pressing his face to the side of Wren's neck. "Forgive me, Wren," he whispered hoarsely. "But I love you too much to hurt you so -- it would be easier to tear out my own heart. I fear I must overrule your choice and pick the other option."

"Master," Wren whispered, tears of relief pricking at his eyelids. "I submit to your will. Do as you wish with me -- I'm yours."

"*I shouldn't want to do this*," Haven murmured through their link, even as he spread Wren's thighs with his large hands. He withdrew for a moment and then returned, this time with something slippery and warm on his fingers, which he pressed gently into Wren's tight rosebud. It felt like the same oil that had been used on him the first time he'd been put in the Tiberion slave harness. "*I shouldn't want to take your virginity*," Haven continued as he stretched Wren gently. "*The same virginity I bought so many years ago to preserve -- not to take myself. Light help me, what have I become?*"

"*You've become the man I love*," Wren sent. "*And, as you say, you bought my virginity. So why should you not be the one to take it?*" He looked over his shoulder at Haven, pleading with his eyes. "*I love you, Master. I always have, from the moment I looked up and saw you standing over me in that dark alley on Rigel Six.*"

"*My Wren, you've changed so much since then. And this isn't how I would have chosen to take you.*" Haven's mind-voice was regretful. "*I wish we were someplace quiet and private.*"

"*Someplace where I wasn't chained up, perhaps?*" Wren asked lightly. "*It doesn't matter, Master. None of it matters. As long as you're the one to take me, I don't care how or where it happens. It's enough to know that I will finally be yours -- yours completely. You've owned my heart forever and now you'll own my body as well.*"

Haven gave no answer, but the two long fingers stretching Wren's tight entrance began to move deeper, scissoring gently inside him to stretch him wide. Wren moaned softly, spreading his legs to try and be open enough for his master. He knew this was nothing to what was coming, and he anticipated both the pain and pleasure he knew awaited him when Haven entered him with his cock.

He didn't have long to wait. With a soft but audible pop, Haven opened the magno-tabs on his trousers and released his cock. Wren couldn't see it, but he could feel its thick, heated length sliding gently between his open legs. He moaned again as his master's shaft slid against the tender sac that cradled his balls, setting every nerve in his body alight with fire. Gods, how long had he wanted this? Forever it seemed, and now he was finally going to get it, finally going to feel his master take him all the way.

"*Please, Master,*" he sent, his breath hitching in his chest. "*Please, I want to feel you inside me. All the way inside me.*"

"*And I want to be there. But I don't want to hurt you.*"

"*I'll welcome the pain along with the pleasure, Master. Just, please take me.*"

"*Very well, Novice. Spread your legs a little wider and tilt your pelvis back toward me,*" Haven instructed.

Wren did as he was told, arching his back eagerly to give his master easier access to his body. Then he felt the blunt, moist probe that must be the head of Haven's cock pressing lightly against his rosebud. Gripping Wren's hips lightly in his large hands, Haven began to press forward, slowly breaching the tight ring of muscle that guarded the entrance to Wren's body.

Taking rapid, shallow breaths, Wren concentrated on opening himself to his master. He knew Haven was taking care to go slow, but it still felt as though he was being skewered by the thick cock that was entering him so carefully. He knew at least the head of his master's shaft had been inside him the night before, but at the moment it didn't seem possible. He wished he could remember more of what had happened between them while he was under the influence of the red passion-seed oil, but everything was an erotic blur.

"*Is the pain too much, Wren?*" Haven's mind-voice was thick with passion and full of concern at the same time. He had stopped his advance, the head of his cock only halfway inside Wren, and seemed prepared to pull out at any moment.

Wren took a deep breath. "*No, Master. Never too much. Take me all the way.*"

Haven seemed to know what he needed because with one last, forceful push, the head of his cock slipped into Wren's body.

Wren moaned and tried not to stiffen up. Haven's cock was so large -- much larger than the black leather tail he'd been forced to wear during the Grande Promenade the night before. It pulsed inside him, stretching him even when his master wasn't moving and only the broad head of it was inside his body. Despite the stretching pain, Wren wanted more.

"*Master, I'm all right,*" he sent, pressing back to take another inch of Haven's thick cock into his body. "*But I need more, more of you inside me.*"

"*Very well, Wren.*" Haven gripped his hips more tightly and began to press inward and upward. With one long, slow, erotic thrust, he opened Wren's rosebud completely and sank his shaft to the hilt in his novice's unresisting body.

"*Gods, Master,*" Wren whispered. "*So deep...I can feel you in me so deep.*"

"*That's right, Wren.*" Haven's deep voice echoed in his mind as he lapped and kissed at the spot on Wren's neck he had bitten earlier. "*I'm inside you now, taking you, owning you. At this moment, you belong completely to me. Now I need you to loosen up enough for me to fuck you.*"

"*Yes, Master,*" Wren sent. He was glad they had a mind-link to communicate with because at that moment he was breathless with both pleasure and pain. His vocal chords were locked by the intense sensations going on deep inside him, and he couldn't have done anything but moan if his life depended on it. Deliberately relaxing his muscles, he let himself fall back against his master, leaning his head on Haven's broad shoulder as he opened himself completely to the thick cock that was already leaking precum deep inside his body.

"*So beautiful,*" Haven mind-whispered as Wren leaned back against him. "*So beautiful when you give yourself to me, my Wren. When you submit.*" Slowly, carefully, he pulled back and plunged in again, filling Wren completely with his shaft. He held Wren in place for his slow assault, and his hands began to roam over Wren's naked body, stopping to caress and pinch his nipples before finding their way further down to Wren's hard cock.

Wren moaned softly as the head of his master's cock rubbed hard over a spot in his body that made pleasure spike through him. "*Master, I was born to submit to you. Born to take your cock deep inside me, born to feel you fuck me.*"

"*Maybe you were at that,*" Haven returned. He stroked slowly but steadily in and out of Wren's body now, his thick shaft spreading the tender flesh of Wren's ass while his large hand encircled Wren's long, slender shaft.

"*Yes, Master.*" Wren gasped softly as his master fucked into him, filling him completely in the way he had dreamed of for what seemed like forever. The pain was mostly gone now, replaced by the deep, throbbing pleasure of finally having his master inside him, claiming him completely.

"*This is what I wanted to do last night.*" Haven sent an erotic picture of the two of them entwined naked on the bed while he entered Wren carefully, trying hard not to go too far. "*I didn't want to hurt you but Gods, Wren, I wanted to be inside you so badly. You opened yourself for me so sweetly, just as you are now, and you pressed back against me, taking more of my cock inside you even when I told you to stop.*"

"*Like this?*" Wren pressed back, meeting his master's thrust, joining the rhythm Haven had begun when he started to fuck in earnest. The large hand that fisted his shaft tightened momentarily, and Haven drew a deep breath against the side of Wren's throat.

"*Yes, Novice, exactly like that,*" he sent, thrusting harder. "*It was as though you were trying to milk the cum out of me, as though you were determined to feel me in you no matter what the consequences.*"

"*And so I am, Master,*" Wren sent teasingly. He pressed back harder, opening himself wider for his master's thick cock. "*I'm determined to make you come deep inside me and this time I'm going to remember every moment of pleasure.*"

"*I'm not the only one who's going to come, my Wren,*" Haven mind-whispered to him. The large hand on Wren's cock tightened again, fisting in the same deliberate rhythm Haven was using to fuck him. Wren gasped at the increased sensation and moaned as the pleasure that was building inside him spiked higher and higher. His master was actually doing it -- he was fucking Wren, taking him completely. And at the same time he was stroking him, making him feel completely surrounded and opened by the thick cock skewering his ass and the large, warm palm encircling his shaft.

"*Master,*" he sent. "*I can't hold out much longer. It feels too good, too right...*"

"*Then don't hold out, Wren. I wish I could make this moment last forever, but more than that I want to feel you coming around me, want to feel your pleasure as we are joined completely,*" Haven sent. Wren could feel the sorrow under his master's pleasure and he knew the cause -- this would be the one and only time they could do this before being separated by the Council of Wisdom. He would never feel his master inside him again and might never see him again after they got back to Radiant. But he knew he would carry this memory inside his heart forever, no matter what happened.

"Master!" he moaned aloud as the pleasure reached its peak and hot cum spurted from his shaft. "Master, take me, come in me -- I'm yours!"

"My Wren," Haven rasped against the side of his neck. He pressed forward hard, thrusting his thick cock to the hilt in Wren's tight rosebud, filling him completely. Then he too began to come, pulsing inside Wren's body as he allowed Wren's orgasm to trigger his own.

They stayed locked together for an endless moment as Haven finished the most forbidden act he could possibly have committed with his novice. The Council of Wisdom would look upon it as a violation, an unpardonable act of sexual aggression against the young man he had been entrusted to train and care for. But Wren knew better. It was an act of submission, a physical manifestation of a love so deep and wide there was no other way to express it than to open himself and take Haven in. He had given his master everything and regretted nothing.

But he knew that the consequences of their actions would be terrible.

Chapter Eleven

Haven pulled out of his novice in a long, slow slide. Wren's legs trembled with the effort of holding himself upright and Haven supported him gently. He saw the thick trickle of cum -- his cum -- on the inside of Wren's thigh and felt a stab of shame. What had he done? Had he actually fucked his novice? Fucked him and come inside him even though he knew how wrong it was? But then, why had it felt so right? There had been no disturbance in the living Light around them as he took his novice. To the contrary, Haven had almost felt it bathing them with peace as he consummated his relationship with Wren in a way that was never meant to be. But that must be his imagination working, trying to justify what he had done. For Haven had committed the ultimate sin and once they returned to the Temple of Light on Radiant, both he and Wren would have to pay for it.

"A beautiful deflowering, Light Bringer. So much more gratifying to watch than a simple flogging." Rudgez the Fourth's high, annoying voice snapped Haven back to the here and now and he suddenly felt dirty and exposed. Stuffing himself back into his pants hastily, he turned to face the god-emperor.

"You left me little choice, Your Eminence. I didn't wish to see my slave's back in shreds if I could prevent it."

"But you see, that is the truth and the beauty of the game," Rudgez said gravely. "It reveals the true emotions of all who play it. It is plain to see that you love young Wren with a rare and abiding passion."

"I am glad you were amused, Your Majesty, but Wren and I should really get going now. We need to tell the Gowan ambassador that his planet is no longer in danger."

"Indeed." Rudgez swung his throne around and called into the darkness, "Guards, come release the young slave. And H'rak, bring me a copy of that peace treaty we had T'will draw up."

As the Tiberion royal guards rushed forward to unlock the chains from around Wren's wrists, H'rak stalked forward, his flat face dark with anger. In his large fist was a rolled piece of parchment but he didn't hand it to the god-emperor at once. "Your Majesty, may I ask you once more to rethink this action," he said, staring Rudgez in the eye. "I feel you may regret allowing the Gowans to get away with their insults in the near future if you don't."

"Pish." Rudgez waved his hand dismissively. "Come, H'rak, the deal is done. I got to see a lovely show in return for proving what a kind and generous ruler I am -- there is no way I can go back on the deal. Especially since Haven cannot go back on his end -- young Wren will never be a virgin again, you know."

"Yes, Your Majesty, I know," H'rak grated, "But --"

"But nothing," Rudgez snapped, snatching the rolled piece of parchment from his fist. "You cannot go on forever moping about your niece. Yes, don't look so surprised, I know all about it," he continued as H'rak's purple eyes grew wide. "I also know you think you're the power behind the throne. And it was useful to let you think so for a while, but now it bores me. So stop sulking, H'rak. That is an order."

"Yes, Your Majesty." H'rak's muddy complexion was nearly purple with anger, but he bowed low and withdrew silently, presumably to fulfill whatever function it was that a minister of war who had suddenly been deprived of his target was charged with doing.

Now that he was released from the chains holding him up, Wren sagged in weariness. Haven reached down and lifted the young man into his arms, holding him protectively close. Eyes closed, Wren put his arms around his master's neck and gave a sigh that was a mixture of contentment and pure weariness. Haven thought that his novice had probably been up all night between the uncomfortable holding cell and H'rak's brutal inquisition. He would need to sleep for at least the first day of their trip home.

"It looks like you've got an armful, Master Haven," the god-emperor said, holding out the rolled piece of parchment. "I know you're eager to go, but I have to ask one more time: are you certain young Wren there isn't for sale?"

Haven gave the Tiberion ruler a level look. "Your Majesty, I could more easily rip out my own heart and sell it to you than I could part with Wren."

"That would be a no then, I take it." Rudgez the Fourth was pouting again, but Haven was in no mood to flatter his vanity any further.

"You're correct," he said shortly and managed to take the peace treaty from the god-emperor's fat hand despite the fact that he was holding Wren. "Now, if Your Majesty will excuse me, my business here is finished."

"Certainly, go, by all means, Light Bringer." Rudgez the Fourth waved airily. Haven didn't wait for a second invitation; he turned and left the small room where the rest of his and Wren's lives had been determined by a brutal roll of the dice.

When he reached their large bedchamber, he laid the now unconscious Wren down gently on the blue and gold sleeping furs. Wren stirred briefly and then relaxed, rolling on his side, which gave Haven a chance to catalogue his novice's injuries.

There was the bruised cheekbone and cut lip that Wren had sustained while H'rak questioned him. And there was a dark mark on his other cheek where Haven had slapped him and the raw, capital H on his inner pelvis where Haven had cut him.

Seeing Wren's wounds, Haven felt a rush of shame. He wanted to take a moment to heal Wren using the power of the Light but at the same time, he wanted badly to get both of them off the Tiberion warship. He decided reluctantly to find the Gowan ambassador first, who was probably mad with worry that the mediation hadn't started at the proper time, and let him know his planet was safe. Then he would return for Wren and get him onto the pod and away from the Tiberions and all their barbaric nonsense as fast as he could. Once they were in deep space, he could take as much time as he wanted to heal Wren's injuries. It would probably be the last time he was allowed to touch his novice or indeed, get anywhere near him, but Haven tried not to think about that. For now, he had business to attend to.

Wren stirred sleepily as he opened the door to go out.

"Master?" His pale amber eyes were half lidded with sleep. "Where are you going?"

"Hush, Wren." Haven went back to stroke his forehead, tousling the golden-brown spikes of his novice's hair gently as he spoke. "I'm going to find the Gowan ambassador and then we're going to get out of here. Do you think you're up to packing our things?"

"Certainly, Master." Wren sat up on the bed, rubbing his eyes and yawning. "It will be a relief to put on my clothes again -- or any clothes for that matter. But what about these?" He held out his wrists, showing the heavy inhibitor manacles that were still locked around them.

"I'm glad you said something about those, I almost forgot them." Haven shook his head at his own forgetfulness.

"Don't worry about it, Master. I'll call B'orl and tell him you said to come release me while you find the Gowans. By the time you come back, I'll have everything packed and ready to go."

"Excellent, Novice. Don't be long -- I want to get out of here."

"I won't, Master." Wren looked down for a moment, his large eyes shadowed. "Master," he murmured softly. "Is it…is the reason you want to leave because of what happened here between us?"

"Oh, Wren..." Haven went back for a moment and drew the young man into his arms. Wren came willingly, flowing to him and molding his still naked body against Haven's side. "I can never regret what happened between us while we were here," he whispered into his novice's soft hair. "Never, Wren. No matter how much I regret the consequences of our actions, I can never regret the actions themselves."

"I don't regret it either, Master. Even...even if they separate us and we never see each other again, at least we had this one special time together."

"That's true, my Wren." Haven sighed and smoothed back the unruly hair to plant a kiss on his novice's high forehead. "And now, I must go. Be ready when I come back."

"Yes, Master." Wren pressed closer for a moment and then placed a shy kiss on Haven's cheek. "I'll be ready."

* * *

Finding and explaining things to the Gowan minister turned out to be a more lengthy process than Haven had anticipated. First, the furry diplomat demanded to know how he could be certain that the peace treaty was binding, and then he wanted to know how Haven had obtained it. Haven wasn't about to tell him exactly how much had been sacrificed to win his planet's freedom and he left him and his erotically shaved courtesan/slave girl with the rolled piece of parchment and a puzzled look on his fuzzy face.

On the way back down the hallway to the bedchamber he and Wren were sharing, he met B'orl.

"Ah, Master Haven, good day to you." The assistant to the minister of the wardrobe smiled and bowed, looking very like a frog when he performed the awkward gesture.

"Good day, B'orl." Haven nodded tersely. "Have you finished removing Wren's inhibitor manacles?"

B'orl gave him a blank look. "Why, no, Master Haven. I've just been fitting him for the genital bindings and restraining collar his new master ordered."

"New master?" Haven felt himself go cold all over. "What are you talking about? Who is supposed to be his new master?"

"Why, Minister H'rak, of course." B'orl's protuberant eyes popped wide, surprised. "He was already in the room when I got there -- he said you'd sold young Wren to him just this morning. I must say I was a bit surprised since I know how attached you are to him but I --"

But Haven was already running down the hall as fast as he could, hoping to catch the Tiberion minister of war before it was too late. He didn't even like to imagine what the bastard would do to Wren if he had enough time with him. "*Wren?*" he called as he ran. "*Wren -- where are you?*" There was no reply over their link and when he thought of it, Haven realized he hadn't heard anything from his novice in some time. It wasn't like this morning when Wren had been blocking him either -- this time there was a blank silence where the young man he loved should have been. A silence that made Haven's heart go cold.

"You'll not find him that way," B'orl called out after him as he rushed down the corridor to the bedchamber.

"Why not?" Haven skidded to a stop in front of the empty room, looking for any clue as to where his novice had gone.

"Because H'rak's taking him home to Tiber on his own private ship along with that other slave he bought from the minister of finance." B'orl arrived behind him, puffing with exertion. "He said…he said he wanted time alone with them. Both of them," he explained, still trying to catch his breath.

Haven felt the cold that had started in his heart spread to the rest of his body. "Was Wren even awake when you saw him?" he demanded, turning to the stocky Tiberion.

"Why…why, no, Master Haven." B'orl shook his head. "He was already out. It's easier to transport slaves when they're unconscious, you know. I just assumed that Minister H'rak had already drugged him for the journey. He lives in the capital city near the god-emperor's palace, may he live forever, and that's on the far side of Tiber. It's a fair piece to travel with an unruly slave."

"Especially one who doesn't belong to you," Haven snarled. "How long ago did H'rak leave?"

B'orl shrugged. "Maybe thirty standard minutes ago. I spent some time tidying up the costumes we'd given you and young Wren to wear after they went so I --"

He was left talking to the empty air. Haven was already racing to the docking bay where the pod was waiting. He had to catch H'rak before something horrible happened to Wren or he would never forgive himself.

Chapter Twelve

"Master?" Wren opened his eyes groggily to a bright light. His head was pounding and there was a funny taste at the back of his throat -- bitter and sweet at the same time. Had he fallen asleep? He dimly remembered that he was supposed to be packing their things so that they could leave the Tiberion warship, but the small bright room he was in looked nothing like the big gloomy bedchamber he and Haven had been sharing. There was something tight around his neck, some new kind of slave collar that cut into his skin when he moved his head. Wren wanted to take it off, but when he tried to move his arms, something held him back.

Looking up, he saw that both his wrists were still encased in the inhibitor manacles, which in turn were chained to the ends of a black metal bar above his head. That didn't seem right -- he was certain the game of Pain or Pleasure that he and Haven had been playing had ended. And anyway, his arms had been chained to golden posts, not a black metal bar. So what was he doing in a small, brightly lit room instead of the large bedchamber they had been assigned? He tried to think what he had been doing before he had fallen asleep, but the last thing he remembered was bending over the bed and then a sharp, pinching pain in the back of his neck.

Looking to his right, he saw something even more disturbing. The slave girl who had been deflowered at the Grande Promenade the night before was chained naked beside him. She was slumped, unconscious, hanging by the chains that held her upright and there was a fresh brand on the pale pink skin of her pelvis. A capital H.

She has an H on her. Same as me. H for Haven, Wren thought. But staring at the initial burned into the girl's tender flesh, Wren realized blearily that his mark and the slave girl's were nothing alike. The small thin cuts his master had made on his skin were already scabbed over and on their way to being healed and the lines were so fine and thin they could barely be seen. The mark on the slave girl's skin was made of thick bands of seared flesh, forming a scar that would never fade. Where had he seen a mark like that before?

Suddenly it came to him in a sickening rush -- he'd seen a capital H brand like that on Minister H'rak's male slave, the Gowan he had shaved and forced to wear the strange, tightly wound leather straps around his shaft. Looking down at his own naked body, Wren saw the same configuration of black leather thongs wound around his own rigid sex. His bindings were torturously tight and his cock throbbed within their confining limits, aching with a pain that had nothing to do with pleasure.

"Do you like your genital cuff, young Servant of the Light? You'll need a penile piercing to complete the look, of course, but that can easily be taken care of." The grating voice rang in Wren's ears, interrupting his panicky self-inspection. He looked up and saw the flat, scaly face and glowing purple eyes of Minister H'rak looking back at him.

"Where are you taking me? Where is my master?" Wren tried to keep the fear out of his voice but it was difficult indeed.

"Interestingly enough, the answers to those two questions are related." H'rak gave him a hard, humorless smile that chilled Wren's bones. "I'm taking you home -- your new home, you understand. The home of your new master. Who just happens to be me." He grinned at Wren, a baring of teeth with no humor in it whatsoever.

"You're not my master. Where is Master Haven?" Wren demanded, trying to still the rising tide of panic within him.

"Back aboard the ship, I imagine." H'rak laughed, a harsh barking that sounded like he was trying to cough up a bone he'd swallowed. "We have quite a head start on him, young Wren. By the time he realizes that you're gone, we'll be into Tiberion air space and his claim to you will be invalidated."

"You won't get away with this, H'rak." Wren struggled uselessly against the manacles that held him in place. "The Order of the Light will never stand to see one of their own enslaved."

"Oh? Even one who has broken his vows of chastity with his own master, no less?" H'rak grinned evilly. "I think once they see the way you and Haven ensured the Gowans' freedom and cheated me of my vengeance, they may change their mind about wanting either one of you back."

"But the Council of Wisdom --"

"Will be receiving a transmission I sent them of your performance with your master very shortly," H'rak finished for him. "I recorded everything from start to finish. It should make some very interesting viewing."

Wren felt himself go cold all over. The Council of Wisdom would indeed be set against both him and Haven once they saw exactly what had happened between them. And without either himself or Haven there to explain the situation and beg for clemency, there was no telling what might happen. But he still had one hope left.

"Haven is my true master," he said, lifting his chin defiantly. "He will never rest until he finds you and reclaims me."

H'rak shrugged his broad shoulders, obviously unconcerned with Wren's threat. "Let him come," he said, turning from Wren and busying himself with a small heating unit in the corner of the room which appeared to be responsible for the bright light. "If he can get past my guards, I'll have him arrested for trying to steal another man's slave -- it's an offense punishable by death on Tiber, you know, slaves being as valuable as they are. Especially well-trained pleasure slaves. Of course..." He turned and there was a long black iron rod in his hand that glowed dull red at one end. "I'll have to mark you first. Can't let you enter Tiberion space without my brand on you."

* * *

"*Master! Master, are you there?*"

The faint call through their private link brought Haven immediate and immeasurable relief. It was so soft he could barely hear it but it was definitely Wren.

"*Wren?*" he sent back at once, as strongly as he could. "*Wren, I can barely hear you. Are you all right?*"

"*For now.*" There was a quiver of suppressed pain in his novice's mind-voice that made Haven's stomach clench. "*H'rak's gone to get something but he may be back any moment.*"

"*Gone to get something?*" Haven didn't think he wanted to know what but he had to ask anyway. "*What has he gone to get, Wren?*"

"*A...a bigger brand.*" The fear in Wren's mind-voice couldn't be hidden anymore. "*He said...said that the one he had on hand was too small. He needs to cover the mark you made on me when you cut me earlier so he can...so he can claim me as his own.*"

Haven felt sick. The idea of his novice, the man he loved being tied down and burned -- branded -- by the huge, cruel H'rak was too much to bear. "*Be strong, Wren!*" he sent. "*I know where H'rak is headed and I'm coming as fast as I can.*"

"*Unless you can get here in the next five minutes and somehow board H'rak's ship, I think it's going to be too late. To stop him from branding me, anyway.*" Wren's mental voice was fainter than ever but also surprisingly steady despite the fear in it. Obviously he had resigned himself to his fate.

"*Don't just let him do it, Wren. Fight back!*" Haven sent fiercely. For the fiftieth time, he cursed the slow propulsion drive of the pod he was piloting. If only it would move a little faster he could catch up to H'rak's ship. But the Temple of Light wasn't known for keeping the fastest or flashiest ships for its servants to use so the pod wasn't exactly built for racing.

"*I don't see how, Master. I'm chained in place and I can't call a Light weapon like you can.*"

"*You can -- I'll help you. Focus, Novice. Concentrate on the power of the living Light that surrounds you. Can you feel it?*"

"*Yes, Master, I always feel it.*"

"*Then call it. Draw it into you and shape it between your hands. Imagine what you want to form and the Light will do as you will.*" Haven hoped that Wren was ready to do as he instructed. Most novices weren't able to call a Light weapon into being until after their final trials when the full power of the Light was invested in them by the Council of Wisdom. But Wren had always been special, full of the Light's beauty and power from the moment Haven had found him on Rigel Six.

"*I don't know, Master... I just can't quite...*"

"*You're upset, Novice. You must calm yourself,*" Haven sent. He stared blindly at the black field of space dotted with far off stars that flowed by on the pod's view-screen as he tried to project peaceful, relaxing emotions through their link. If Wren was too distressed and fearful to concentrate, he would never be able to pull this off. "*Let the fear drift away from you,*" he instructed. "*And concentrate on the shape you need the Light to take.*"

"*I feel it, Master. The power flowing into me!*" Wren's mind-voice was excited, a little stronger. "*I think I'll be able to do it if I just have a few more min* --" His words were cut off abruptly, replaced by a pain so sharp and strong it nearly brought Haven to his knees. Suddenly the view-screen in front of him flickered, signaling an incoming call. Without thinking, Haven reached out and flicked the switch to accept it.

"Well, well, Master Haven, I see you're hot on my trail." Minister H'rak's flat, ugly face suddenly filled the view-screen.

"What have you done to Wren?" Haven asked, clenching his hands into fists. "I felt his pain. If you've injured him…"

"You felt the pain of the restraining collar I took the precaution of fitting him with." H'rak stepped back and the view-screen showed the room behind him. Wren was chained to a long metal bar and completely naked except for the bindings around his shaft and a black, metal studded collar. "The collar keeps him from getting up to the same kind of tricks you tried at our inquest this morning," H'rak said, stepping back so he was standing behind Wren. "I'm assured that once it's been on a few hours, such tricks will no longer be possible even when the collar is removed."

Haven stared, speechless with horror. So that was why Wren's mind-voice had been so faint! He had heard of such devices -- they blocked the area of the psyche that was able to sense and use the power of the Light. If left on for long, they could cause permanent damage by burning out the Light-sensitive part of the person wearing the collar forever.

"It causes young Wren here pain any time he tries anything," H'rak continued with an evil smile. "But not as much as I'm about to cause him. I think it's time he found out that I'm not quite as easy on my slaves as you are. And he *is* my slave, Haven. Or he will be as soon as I brand him properly." Reaching behind him, he pulled out a long metal rod with a glowing red H at one end. Haven saw Wren go white with fear, but he set his lips and refused to beg or cry.

"If you dare to do this, I'll kill you with my own hands." Haven heard the tremor of rage in his voice, but there was nothing he could do about it. Nothing he could do about any of it -- Wren was about to be hurt worse than the old, fat slaver Dungbar had ever hurt him, and Haven was powerless to stop it. Deep down at the bottom of his rational mind he knew that his training and the vows he had taken forbade him to kill, even in the service of the Light, but he didn't care anymore. The man he loved was being threatened and a red haze of anger clouded his thoughts.

"Do you really expect me to believe you'd break your vows, Light Bringer?" H'rak smirked at him and twirled the hot branding iron in one large scaly hand. "But even if you intend to, we're entering Tiberion space right now. Wren is my slave and he will be branded with my mark."

"Your god-emperor won't stand for this," Haven said through gritted teeth. "You'll be an outlaw on your home world."

"The god-emperor?" H'rak laughed. "Who do you think told me to take Wren in the first place? Rudgez the Fourth told me he tried to buy the boy and you wouldn't sell. But don't worry, Light Bringer -- the god-emperor won't lay a hand on your little slave boy himself. He'd much rather watch me use Wren. I'm quite good at putting on a show -- almost as good as you are yourself. Speaking of which, don't think you can call on your precious Order of the Light to help you -- I sent them a transmission of Wren's deflowering. Ask him if it isn't so."

"*It's true, Master,*" Wren sent weakly. His eyes were fixed on the branding iron but he still refused to show any emotion. "*The Council of Wisdom is probably ready to throw us both out by now.*"

"*I don't care about that, Wren. I'm coming for you, just hold on to that!*" Haven sent. Aloud, he asked H'rak, "Why are you doing this? There must be thousands of boys you could have had with no trouble at all. Why take Wren?"

"You cheated me of my vengeance and now I'm taking what's most precious to you in the universe." H'rak ran a long finger down Wren's cheek, making him flinch, though he still refused to say a word out loud.

"Vengeance? You mean on the Gowans? The god-emperor said something about your niece. What did he mean?" Haven was desperate to stop or at least delay the inevitable, and he had an idea that if he could get H'rak talking, keep him boasting, that he might be able to do just that.

"Ah yes, my niece." H'rak's muddy complexion darkened. "She was more than that, you know. I'd raised her from the time her father -- my brother -- died. From the moment she came of age, I knew she was the right female to give me an heir."

"What?" Haven felt sick. Was the Tiberion minister of war actually saying what he thought he was saying?

"You need not look so shocked, Light Bringer," H'rak grated. "I was her guardian, so by Tiberion law she was mine to do with as I chose. If my choice was to father a child on her, a son to come after me and inherit my estate and title, then no one would have thought it strange or wrong."

"No one on Tiber, I'm sure," Haven said, still feeling sick. "But I don't understand -- what does your niece have to do with the Gowans?"

H'rak scowled. "She ran away with one of my servants -- the captain of my personal guard and they sought refuge on Gow gi Nef. I demanded that they extradite the two of them to me but the fools refused." He laughed. "Of course, when I threatened them with the force of the Tiberion fleet, each ship equipped with an annihilator strong enough to obliterate an entire planet, they changed their tune. I was going to take both T'rilla and that idiot of a captain back to my estate and make examples of them."

"Why didn't you?" Haven asked, trying to keep the conversation going. He had begun to feel a small spark of hope. As they reached Tiberion air space, H'rak's ship was slowing down, preparing for reentry into the massive planet's atmosphere. As a consequence, Haven's pod was gaining steadily.

If he could just keep the Tiberion minister of war talking a little longer, he might get close enough to use the latcher cable on the pod to form a connection between the two space vessels. After that, it was just a matter of pulling close enough to dock his smaller ship with the larger one and opening the airlock to get to H'rak and Wren. Of course, without the airlock combination that should have been impossible. But a Sword of Brilliance would cut through anything, even the superhardened alloy that made up the skin of H'rak's ship. It would cut through his scaly neck too, Haven thought grimly. But he pushed the thought aside and tried to concentrate on keeping the big Tiberion talking.

"I would have made examples of them both. I planned to torture the captain of the guard to death and use T'rilla repeatedly until she was with child." H'rak described his intentions almost dreamily, as though recounting a secret and cherished fantasy. "Once my son was born, I would give it to a nurse to raise and kill T'rilla as well. I was going to make her death a long and painful one -- I wanted to teach her a lesson for daring to leave in the first place."

"Did the Gowans give her back?" Slowly, keeping his hands out of the view-screen's range, Haven pushed the blue button on the pod's console that launched the latcher cable.

H'rak scowled again. "They tried, Light Bringer, but once the ship they'd put her on reached the space around their planet it was attacked by pirates."

"And they took the captain of the guard and your niece away with them?" Haven guessed as his pod was slowly drawn toward H'rak's ship. The minister of war was caught up in his story now and didn't appear to notice the proximity warning flashing on the wall console behind him.

"No -- they killed the both of them at once." H'rak's grating voice was filled with rage. "A laser blast to the back of the head and they were dead before they knew it."

"But what do the Gowans have to do with it?" A glance at the pod's console showed that he was within docking distance of H'rak's larger ship. *Almost there*, Haven thought and sent to his novice, "*Hang in there, Wren. I'm coming for you.*"

"*Yes, Master.*" Wren's mind-voice was barely a whisper now as the collar continued to take effect. His novice took his eyes from the branding iron and fixed them on Haven instead. H'rak, who had his back to Wren's chained form, didn't notice.

"What did it have to do with the Gowans?" he sputtered angrily. "Why, if Gow gi Nef weren't a refuge for pirates and outlaws and space scum of all kinds, the attack never would have happened. If they'd had the guts to have some weaponry to defend their air space, the pirates wouldn't have dared to come so close and attack T'rilla's ship."

"But you were planning to kill her and her lover anyway, weren't you?" Haven asked. Closer…*closer*…The smaller pod drifted alongside H'rak's larger ship.

"I was planning on killing them both slowly and painfully. Thanks to the Gowans, both of them got a clean, easy death courtesy of the pirates they were too weak to defend themselves and their air space against," H'rak thundered.

"I see." Haven nodded but his eyes were on the console in front of him. The proximity light had been flashing for the last fifteen seconds and now it was a steady, dull red. There was a slight shiver and a dull clang as his pod kissed the side of H'rak's larger ship. Now he had only minutes to get in, get Wren, and get out of Tiberion air space before both ships entered the huge planet's atmosphere. "*I'm coming now, Wren!*" he sent as he ran.

"What was that?" H'rak turned to the wall console behind him but Haven was already charging toward the airlock, a Sword of Brilliance taking shape between his hands. The outer door to the pod opened with a sucking sound, and he was out into the short folding umbilicus that connected his ship to H'rak's in an instant. The sword in his hand was nearly three feet long -- its tightly focused blade so bright not even Haven could stand to stare directly at it. He swung it in a careful arc, cutting through the hardened alloy of the other airlock door while being careful not to puncture the umbilicus. The blade sliced into the alloy as easily as though he was carving through soft cheese. As soon as Haven had carved out the locking mechanism, he lifted his foot and kicked the door in. It bounced against the inner wall with a deafening clank of metal on metal and he was into the ship.

"*Wren,*" he sent urgently. "*Wren, where are you?*"

"*I don't know, Master!*" Wren's mind-voice was so faint now that Haven could barely hear it. "*I'm in a small room with the bright lights. The other slave, the one from the deflowering is here too. Be careful, H'rak knows you're here, I think. He's getting the iron hot again.*"

"*Don't worry about him. Just stay calm -- I'm coming!*" Following the weak sound of his novice's mind-voice, Haven ran through the ship, leading with the sword made of the living Light he had called. H'rak's ship was much bigger on the inside than he had guessed and the maze of corridors he found himself in was confusing. Still, he could feel Wren's presence through their link and knew he was getting closer.

"Over here, Light Bringer." H'rak's voice interrupted his intense concentration.

Haven turned to see the Tiberion minister standing in the doorway of a small, brilliantly lit room with the branding iron still in his hand. "Drop it, H'rak." He gestured with the sword, flicking its brilliant tip at H'rak's face. The minister of war didn't even flinch.

"Do you really expect me to believe you will break your vow not to kill in the service of the Light?" He sounded amused. "I know about your order, Haven. I know what you are sworn not to do."

"I have broken every other vow I made while I was on your warship, H'rak." Haven made his voice dangerously soft. "And I will break this one too if you dare to hurt my Wren. Now, *drop the iron.*"

"I think not, Master Haven. You're too late." In one swift motion Haven could see but not stop, H'rak turned and pressed the cherry red branding iron against the skin of Wren's pelvis, completely obliterating the small capital H Haven had carved into his novice's skin earlier that day.

"Master!" Wren's voice was a breathless shout. Through their link, Haven could feel the searing pain as Wren's tender flesh crisped and blackened under the red-hot iron. His novice's agony blinded him with rage and he swept the dazzling blade through H'rak's leathery neck, sweeping his ugly head from his broad shoulders. The superheated blade, hotter than the surface of a yellow sun, cauterized the wound even as Haven inflicted it. There was a surprised look on H'rak's flat face as his head rolled on the floor by Haven's feet. It was as though he had believed up until the last that Haven was making an idle threat.

"Wren!" Haven ran past the tall Tiberion's body as it sank slowly to its knees and knelt beside his novice. The sickening smell of scorched flesh assaulted his nostrils and turned his stomach.

"I'm all right, Master." Silent tears filled Wren's large amber eyes but his voice was calm. "Let's just get out of here."

"That's exactly what we're going to do," Haven promised, using the Sword of Brilliance to slice through the chains holding Wren captive. "I'll get you out of those manacles and the collar in just a minute. Let me see..." Turning back to H'rak's headless body, he searched with great distaste through the pockets of the Tiberion minister's rich robes until he found a set of optical keys. "These should do the trick. I'm glad he had them on him -- I wouldn't want to risk cutting so close to your neck with a Knife of Radiance." He tossed the keys to Wren who used them on his wrists and neck as Haven cut down the pink-skinned slave girl. He threw her across one broad shoulder before turning back to his novice. "We only have minutes before we enter the Tiberion atmosphere. Can you walk?" he asked, eyeing the evil-looking burn on Wren's skin doubtfully.

"I can make it, Master. Let's just go." Hobbling painfully, Wren stumbled along at his side as Haven carried the unconscious slave girl back toward the airlock. They got back to the pod not a moment too soon. As soon as Haven had disengaged from the larger vessel and took steps to pull out of orbit, H'rak's ship took an unpiloted dive into the Tiberion atmosphere and burst into flames.

Haven left the unconscious slave girl at the back of the pod and set a course for Radiant. Then he turned to his novice. "Wren," he murmured, pulling the young man close. "I was so afraid I'd never see you again."

Wren gave him a trembling smile. “I never doubted for an instant that you would come for me. I love you, Master.”

Then his eyes fluttered closed and he fainted bonelessly in Haven’s arms.

Chapter Thirteen

The light and dark were interchangeable. He couldn't feel anything except the pain in his hip, a horrible burning that wouldn't go away. The warming power that had filled him from the moment of his birth was gone. Wren might have been able to keep going without it, but the one he loved most in the world was gone too. Each time he opened his eyes, he hoped to see the familiar face with its deep blue eyes but it was never there. *He* was never there, and since Wren no longer had the Light within him, he no longer had a link to the man he loved. Haven was gone and he wasn't coming back.

Eventually Wren stopped opening his eyes at all and simply waited to die.

* * *

"The boy is dying." The master healer's voice pierced through the dull gray layer of grief that Haven had been wearing like a funeral shroud since the moment his pod had touched down on Radiant and Wren had been taken away from him.

"What?" He stood up, forgetting that he was in the council room and strode across to the master healer. "What do you mean he's dying?" he demanded, taking the man by his dark green tunic and shaking him. "His wounds weren't that bad. Are you so incompetent that you can't even heal a simple burn?"

"Master Haven, please -- control yourself!" The head of the council, Mistress Tegbreth, rapped her bony knuckles sharply on the plain wooden table where she and the other two council members sat. One of them was Master Langos, a withered man who nevertheless held the power of the Light strong within his crippled body, and the other was Master Serin, Haven's own master from the days when he had been a novice.

Haven was officially in disgrace and the Council of Wisdom had been waiting to conduct this inquiry into his misbehavior until Wren was well enough to testify. They had been waiting an Earth-standard month now, and Haven hadn't been allowed to see his novice in that entire time. Only that morning he had received an order to appear before the council and had come eagerly, hoping to see the young man he loved, even from across the room. But Wren wasn't here -- just the master healer telling Haven news that couldn't be true.

"He can't be dying," Haven whispered, forcing himself to release the master healer's tunic. "He can't be. He was well only a month ago."

"The restraining collar was in place too long." The master healer straightened his tunic with dignity and glared at Haven. "I cannot heal him with the power of the Light because the Light inside him has gone out. And anyway, Master Haven," he continued, giving Haven a pitying look. "It isn't the burn on his hip that is killing him, it's my opinion he's dying for lack of the Light. I've seen it happen once or twice before -- if one who has been a vessel for the Light all of their lives is suddenly cut off from it and has no one and nothing else to hold on to, they often just fade away." He shrugged his shoulders. "It's sad but what is one to do?"

"Let me see him," Haven said, turning toward the council. "Please, Masters, Mistress, let me see him." He stood in the middle of the circular council room, pleading with his eyes, appealing to the three who sat on a raised dais above him.

"Why, Master Haven, so you can corrupt him further?" Mistress Tegbreth glared down at him with small, beady brown eyes.

"It was never my intention to corrupt Wren." Haven bowed his head for a moment, almost overcome by the shame and pain he felt. "I love him."

"Yes, but Haven, you do not love him with a love that is proper between a Master and novice." Master Langos's voice was surprisingly strong coming from his aged, crippled body.

"That's true." Haven raised his head and faced the council. "I cannot deny my shame, Masters, Mistress. I love him as more than my novice. More than the ragged little slave boy I found on Rigel Six so many years ago. And though I know it is wrong, I desire him as well."

There was a moment of disapproving silence from the three on the Council of Wisdom and then Haven's old master, Serin, spoke.

"Haven, my boy, I am certain you didn't mean to let your relationship with Wren degenerate as it did on your mission to the Tiberions and the Gowans." His faded blue eyes were full of sympathy for his former novice as he spoke. "And we on the council will be the first to admit there were extenuating circumstances. You did what you had to do -- even when you killed Minister H'rak. The council is prepared to forgive you that indiscretion, at least."

"Thank you, Master. We did do what we had to. *I* did," Haven amended. "I knew the things I was doing with Wren were wrong and yet I couldn't see an entire planet blown to bits because I refused to break my vows."

"And we understand that, Haven," Master Langos said. "What we do not understand or condone is the fact that you openly admit to enjoying what you had to do to Wren. And Wren, when he has been able to talk, has said the same. Is that not right, Master Healer?"

The master healer cleared his throat. "I'm afraid so, Master Langos. The boy talks of nothing but how he misses his master's touch. It's all most improper."

"You think I enjoyed it?" Haven asked, his deep voice cracking. "Parading him around like some kind of animal? Carving my name in his flesh? Taking him in front of that sadistic god-emperor and his minister of war -- the sadistic jackal that nearly took Wren from me forever? You think I enjoyed those things?"

"Calm yourself, Haven." Master Serin's voice was soft. "Of course we don't believe you wanted to do all the things you were forced to do to your novice. And if you had come to us and told us as much and promised never to touch Wren inappropriately again, we might have considered letting you stay at the Temple and allowing him to stay on as your novice -- after a period of retraining for you both, of course. Such urges as you have both admitted to must be eradicated completely for the sake of decency."

"But you come to us telling us that you still want him -- still desire to have improper relations with him." Mistress Tegbreth's lips were compressed into a narrow line of disapproval. "How do you expect us to react to such a statement, Master Haven? You have abused and distorted the most sacred relationship among us. You were meant to be Wren's teacher and mentor -- not his lover."

Haven raised his chin. "It's true that the time we spent aboard the Tiberion warship changed my relationship with Wren. But I don't think that what happened between us was entirely due to our last mission. There is something between Wren and I, a seed that was planted years ago when I first saw him, that was meant to sprout and grow. I know in my heart we are supposed to be together, however wrong and improper it may seem. I cannot and will not deny that I love him with all of my heart and mind and soul. And my body as well."

"Haven, listen to what you are saying," Serin chided, frowning. "Can you find no shame within yourself for the laws of the Light you have transgressed?"

Haven sighed. "I am sorry I transgressed, Master. But Wren…he is like a part of me. Being separated from him for this last month has been like an amputation of the most painful nature. And so I beg you, let me see him. Let me try to heal him myself since the master healer has failed."

"How do you plan to heal him, Master Haven?" Master Langos sounded genuinely interested. "You heard the master healer -- he cannot be reached by the power of the Light."

"No, Master Langos. But perhaps he may be reached by the power of love," Haven said earnestly.

"Banishment is the punishment for the crime you have committed and yet you beg for leniency instead." Mistress Tegbreth frowned warningly and Haven felt his heart drop into his boots.

"I will accept my punishment without complaint, Mistress, only let me see Wren once before I go." Haven bowed his head. "If he dies despite my efforts, I will leave the Temple in disgrace and never set foot on Radiant again. And if he lives, I will still leave to give him time to recover."

"Well, Haven, it is most unusual." Master Serin frowned, his faded blue eyes uncertain.

"Please, Master, only let me try. Give me some time to try and restore Wren to himself. At the very least if I am successful, he is young enough to be rehabilitated and you won't lose two Servants of the Light at once." Haven pleaded with his eyes, knowing his old master would have more sympathy for him than the other two on the council.

"Is what Master Haven is proposing to do even possible? Could he bring the boy back by the power of his, uh, feelings for Wren?" Master Langos looked questioningly at the

Master Healer. "It seems to me I had read of a case in the archives --"

"Absolutely not." The master healer shook his head firmly. "There *are* some rare cases in the Healing Archives, but the records are ancient and most likely inaccurate. In my professional opinion, the Light has left the boy so their teaching link is severed irrevocably. Under no circumstances can Master Haven heal Wren, no matter what he says."

Master Serin arched an eyebrow at Haven. "You have heard the expert opinion, Haven. Do you still wish to try in this hopeless enterprise?"

"I do." Haven nodded firmly. "I believe there is more to the link between Wren and myself than meets the eye -- even the trained eye of the master healer."

"Let us put it to a vote then," Mistress Tegbreth said at last. "Those in favor?" She looked at the masters on either side of her.

"Aye." Master Langos raised his hand and nodded.

"Nay." Mistress Tegbreth frowned, keeping her own hands firmly on the wooden tabletop before her.

Haven looked breathlessly at his old master. At last, Master Serin sighed and raised his hand as well.

"Aye. I hope you know what you're doing my boy," he added, speaking to Haven. "And I hope that if you cannot save the boy, you can at least let him go gracefully. I can see you truly love him."

"Thank you, Masters, Mistress." Haven bowed deeply, trying to keep the joy out of his voice. It wasn't much, but at least he would be allowed to see his Wren one more time before he left Radiant and The Order of the Light forever.

* * *

Haven followed the master healer down the long, winding corridors of the temple to the healing compound in the east wing. The Temple of Light was an ancient structure that had been on the shores of Radiant's golden sea for generations. It had grown in a very haphazard fashion until its interior was like a complex maze that could take years to learn. It seemed to take forever, but at last they were standing in front of the simple wooden door that led to Wren's room.

"You have half an hour." The master healer gave Haven a sour expression. "See that you don't overstay your time."

"Thank you, Master Healer." Haven nodded his head and then let himself into the room, too eager to see his novice to be upset about the time limit he had been given.

He didn't know what he had expected to see, but the cold, pale face lying on the white pillow was so different from the old, vibrant Wren that Haven almost didn't recognize him. The figure in the narrow cot was so still that at first he was afraid the master healer's dire prediction had already come to pass and Wren was dead. But then he saw the white sheet that covered his novice's narrow chest rising and falling slowly and a surge of relief filled him -- Wren was still alive. At least for now.

"Wren," he whispered, dropping to one knee beside the cot and bending over the young man he loved so much. "My Wren, can you hear me?"

"Master?" Wren's eyes fluttered open slowly, their once beautiful amber depths dull with pain. "Master, is it really you after all this time?"

"I'm sorry, Wren. I wanted to come to you sooner but they wouldn't let me." Haven took the young man's cold, waxy hand between both of his own and tried to warm it with gentle friction. "They say you're not feeling too well."

"The Light has left me." Wren closed his eyes for a moment with a deep sigh. There were bruised looking hollows beneath both eyes as though he hadn't been sleeping.

"Wren, I'm so sorry, I blame myself." Haven brought the thin hand to his mouth and kissed it lightly. "I should have gotten the restrictor collar off you sooner."

"Not your fault. You came for me as soon as you could." Wren sighed and turned his head to the side, staring at the wall. "The master healer told me the Light had left me as a punishment for what you and I had done. He said…he said I would die since he couldn't heal me with the Light and it was all my fault."

"The master healer is an idiot!" Haven exclaimed, not caring who might be listening behind the door. "Come on, Novice, I've never known you to just give up this way before. Where is the brave Wren I've come to love and cherish?"

"He's gone." Wren tried to smile and failed. "He left when they separated us, Master. I…I can't live without you in my life. So if I can't be with you, I'd rather just let go."

"My Wren, you can have me. I'm here for you." Haven gathered the young man into his arms, alarmed at how very light Wren felt. He didn't have the heart to tell his novice that he didn't have Haven for very long -- time enough for that sad fact later after Wren was healed. And Haven did believe he could heal him -- he couldn't tell exactly how but he somehow knew it was possible.

"Oh, Master, how I've missed you." With a trembling sigh, Wren melted against him, pressing his thin cheek to Haven's broad chest with longing. Haven held him tightly, as though afraid that he might escape somehow. He wished he could hold Wren close forever but he knew it wasn't possible.

"I've missed you too, my Wren," he murmured, tilting the young man's chin up so he could look into Wren's eyes. "You don't know how much. I missed holding you like this, missed the scent of your skin, the taste of your lips." Hardly knowing what he was doing, he leaned down and pressed a gentle kiss to his novice's pale lips. To his surprise and pleasure, Wren kissed him back with fervor.

"Master," he whispered when at last they broke the passionate kiss for air. "I missed feeling your arms around me almost as much as I missed having you in my mind. But our link is gone now that the Light has left me."

"I don't believe that the Light ever truly leaves one of its servants," Haven said, looking into his novice's eyes. "It may go into hiding for a while, but it will come back out eventually." "*I believe in you, Novice*," he sent, trying to make their old mind-link work. But it was like sending his thoughts to a brick wall, a dead end. He couldn't feel Wren anymore, he realized. Still, he refused to give up. "I love you, Wren," he whispered into the spiky golden brown of his novice's hair. "I love you and I believe you can be healed."

Wren gave a shaky laugh. "Maybe you can do a better job than the master healer. He hasn't even been able to get rid of the scar on my hip."

Haven felt a pang of guilt when he thought of how the scar had gotten there. "May I see it?" he asked softly, looking at Wren.

"Yes, Master. Only…" Wren blushed a pale pink beneath his faded tan. "Only I don't have any clothes on under the sheet."

"Like I haven't seen you naked before?" Haven laughed softly and stroked his novice's thin cheek. "Come, Wren, don't be ashamed to show me. If anything, I should be ashamed to look."

"Why?" Wren looked at him curiously even as he pulled back the plain white sheet that covered his slender body.

"Because it's my fault. H'rak branded you to mark out my initial. I…" Haven trailed off as the twisted, pinkish scar shaped like a capital H appeared. The wound had healed well, he could see, but the evidence of what had happened to Wren remained, right there between his hip bone and the flaccid shaft of his cock.

"It's still your initial, Master," Wren whispered, breaking his train of thought. "In fact, I have a confession. Maybe the master healer can't heal me because I don't want him to. I like to wear your mark on me."

"Wren, don't speak so." Haven frowned, but his eyes kept returning to the letter burned into his novice's skin. "May I touch it?" he asked.

"Master, you know you need not ask me that." Wren's voice was faintly chiding. "Didn't I tell you that you own me body and soul?"

"You did, my Wren," Haven breathed, planting another gentle kiss on his novice's sweet lips. "But it's been so long I wasn't sure you still felt that way." Carefully, he traced the raised lines of the scar with one finger as he spoke.

"Of course I still feel that way." Wren nodded down between his legs. "Can't you tell, Master?"

Haven looked and saw that his novice's long, slender shaft was already half hard even though he hadn't gone anywhere near it. He had a sudden urge to bend down and take it into his mouth, sucking Wren to show him how much he loved and cared for him. But that was the kind of improper desire that had gotten them separated in the first place. Instead, he leaned forward and pressed his lips to the capital H that decorated Wren's pale flesh. He felt his novice stiffen under him and then sigh and relax. It reminded him so much of the way Wren had submitted to him when Haven had been forced to take him during the game of Pain or Pleasure that Haven's own cock began hardening in his pants.

"Master," Wren murmured as Haven traced the twisting scar with his tongue. "It feels so good to have your mouth on me. So good and so very right..."

Haven felt the same sense of rightness his novice described flowing through him as he continued to trace

Wren's scar. A warm, pulsing kind of power, a feeling so familiar that he almost didn't notice it was flowing through him.

"Master…" Wren said again and his clear tenor voice was slightly breathless now. "I feel…the place where you're touching me, licking me…it tingles."

Haven looked up for a moment. "Do you feel the Light, Wren?" he asked, searching his novice's golden eyes anxiously. "Do you feel it flowing at all?"

"Not now, I don't." Wren frowned in concentration. "But just a moment ago, when you were touching me…and before that when you were kissing me I thought I did, but it was so faint I thought I was imagining it."

"That wasn't your imagination, Novice. It was the living Light trying to flow from me to you. If we can make a connection…" Haven trailed off, thinking. "Wren, would you let me try something?"

"Anything you want, Master. As long as it doesn't involve a branding iron." Wren tried to smile and Haven smiled back. Just the fact that his novice was trying to make a joke gave him hope. He could see the old teasing Wren somewhere in the thin, pale face before him, he just had to find him and bring him forward.

"Lay back, my Wren," he murmured, caressing the hollow cheek gently with the back of his hand. "I'm going to try and love you back into the Light."

"Yes, Master." Without a word of question or protest, Wren lay back on the narrow cot and relaxed, opening himself for whatever it was that Haven wanted to try. Seeing the absolute trust Wren placed in him and the total submission he offered touched Haven to the core. Taking a deep breath, he leaned down and grasped Wren's half hard shaft in his fist. Wren moaned and arched his back, spreading his legs for his master, giving himself without a word.

"*My Wren*," Haven sent and this time he felt something like a twinge at the other end of what had been their old link. Then he bent his head and lapped gently at the head of Wren's cock. The tiny droplets of precum that had already gathered at the slit burst across his tongue, sweet and salty at once, and wholly delicious. Wren moaned softly and pressed up, seeking the heat of his master's mouth. In answer, Haven took him deeper, sucking the entire slender shaft into his mouth and savoring Wren's salty flavor with delight.

He didn't care anymore that what he was doing with his novice was wrong -- it didn't *feel* wrong at all. In fact, Haven had never felt anything more right in his life. He could feel the living Light flowing through him at the point where he and Wren were joined, could feel it seeping back into the young man he was loving with his mouth slowly but surely as he lapped and sucked. With every moan and gasp from Wren's full lips, he grew closer to being filled with the Light again and Haven wasn't going to stop until he was.

"Master…oh, Master…" Wren's voice was a breathless gasp as he writhed under Haven's restraining hands and hot mouth. He bucked up into the wet warmth that bathed his cock, moaning and digging his fingers into Haven's broad shoulders as Haven sucked him. "Master," he moaned. "It's too much. If you don't stop, I think I'm going to…"

"*Come, then, Wren,*" Haven sent, never taking his mouth from his novice's hard cock. He got the distinct impression that Wren heard him, even though he couldn't answer in kind. But they were close, so very close to a breakthrough that he didn't dare to stop and analyze things. He just had to keep going, keep the connection between them open so the Light could flow.

"Master! Oh!" Wren gasped, writhing under him.

"*Come, Wren,*" Haven commanded through their link. "*Come now. Come for me and come back into the Light.*"

"Gods, Master, coming so hard!" Wren groaned. Suddenly, Haven felt the shaft that was sliding between his lips and pressing against the back of his throat grow even harder. Then the trickle of precum became a river, then a flood as Wren submitted to his master's intimate kiss and allowed himself to let go completely. Haven swallowed the salty jets gratefully, taking pleasure in the sexual release of the young man he was sucking, enjoying the sensation of finally loving Wren to completion with his mouth.

At last Wren was finished, and Haven allowed the rapidly softening shaft to slide from between his lips. He looked up, smiling as he licked his lips.

"*Not bad, Novice. For a young man on death's door.*"

"*Master, that was…incredible.*" Wren smiled at him tentatively, reaching out to touch Haven's blue-black hair with one hand. "*I can't believe you did that.*"

"*Why? You did it to me, Novice. Besides, it worked, didn't it? Just listen to yourself.*"

Wren's amber eyes opened wide as he realized that he was using their old link again. "Master," he burst out. "It's back -- the Light is back, I can feel it in me. And look, my scar is gone." He pointed down to the place where the brand mark had been.

Haven looked at it critically. "Well, mostly gone, anyway," he said, frowning. For though the twisted mass of scar tissue that had disfigured Wren's pale golden flesh had disappeared, there was still a faint, white tracing of lines that spelled the letter H where the brand had been.

Wren laughed. "*Don't you see, Master? That's the original scar, the one you put there when you signed your name on me with the god-emperor's knife. I wouldn't want to lose that one -- how would anyone tell who I belonged to without it? Besides, it reminds me of how you feel about me.*"

"*Worthless novice.*" Haven ruffled his hair affectionately. "*You don't need a scar to remind you that I love you. I'll tell you every day for the rest of our lives if you want me to.*" Then he stopped abruptly, remembering his promise to the Council of Wisdom.

"*Master, what is it?*" Wren touched his shoulder lightly, worry written on his beautiful face.

"*It's just that I promised I'd leave here, Wren.*" Haven had to blink back tears suddenly. He took a deep breath and continued. "*They wanted to banish me anyway for the things we had done. Not because we'd done them, but because I refused to say I was sorry for what had happened between us.*"

Wren's response was fierce and immediate. "*I'm not sorry either, Master. We were meant to be together, no matter what the council says. If you leave Radiant, I'm going with you.*"

Haven sighed and cupped his novice's cheek. "I am sorry, my Wren, but I gave my word. Besides, now that the Light flows through you again, I can't ask you to give up your promising future as a master in the Order to follow me into exile."

"I don't care about that -- any of it." Wren's long lashes were spiky with sudden tears. "Light or no Light, if you leave here without me I'll die, Master. I know it."

"You won't die, Wren," Haven said softly, although secretly he felt the same way. Felt that if he was separated from the young man who had become so much more than his novice his heart would stop beating in his chest the moment he left Radiant's orbit.

"Master, please! I know how you value your word and that you don't give it lightly, but just this once, put our love above your honor. Take me with you!" Wren was begging now, and Haven felt like an invisible hand was tearing at his heart as he looked into the wide, wet amber eyes.

"Wren, I --" he began, but suddenly a heavy hand was on his shoulder.

"Time's up, Haven," the booming voice of one of the temple guards rang in his ears. "Master healer says you're to leave at once -- there's a ship waiting to take you off planet." He was seized on both sides by large, muscular men.

"Master, no!" Wren clutched at his tunic, but Haven was dragged backward, the guards' relentless momentum breaking his novice's tenuous hold on the fabric of his clothes.

"I love you, my Wren," he said, raising his voice to be heard as the guards dragged him out the door. "Never forget that. I love you."

"*Master, I love you too*!" The heartbreaking anguish in Wren's mental tone was enough to bring tears to Haven's eyes. Then he was dragged around a corner and out of his lover's life forever.

Chapter Fourteen

"Time to get up, young Wren." The cheerful voice of the master healer's head nurse, Berra, spiked through Wren's head like a Knife of Radiance. He had a monstrous headache from trying to contact Haven all night. But though the Light now flowed through him more strongly than ever before, he was unable to speak to his master through their link. That was because in the three days since Haven had been dragged from his bedside he had put a wall between them -- a barrier so high and wide Wren could find no way to scale it. Not that he wasn't trying.

* * *

"*Master,*" he had sent as Haven disappeared from view. "*Master, please, tell me you'll come back for me. I'll wait for you as long as it takes -- please!*"

"*Wren, you must not talk so. You have your whole future ahead of you and just because it no longer includes me doesn't mean it won't be glorious.*" Haven's mind-voice was sad but firm. "*I can't let you sacrifice your own prospects to go wandering the galaxy with me.*"

"*It would be my privilege and joy to wander free with you wherever you go,*" Wren had protested.

"*You think so now but you're young yet. Young enough to be given to another master for training before you take your trials.*"

Another master? Just the thought made Wren feel sick to his stomach. "*I don't want anyone but you,*" he sent fiercely. "*I love you, Master, with all my heart. I could never feel so for another. Come and get me and let me show you -- please!*"

"*No, Wren, we must say no more on the subject. In fact, I think it best if we say no more at all. You must release your fear and anger and need into the Light, just as I have always taught you. And I must let you go for your own good, for the good of the future that might yet be.*"

Wren had felt the barrier going up at that moment and he fought it -- fought it with all his might. But Haven had been a full-fledged servant of the Light for years longer than his novice, and Haven's will had prevailed. Wren could feel his sorrow but under that, also a feeling that he was doing the best thing for Wren. That he was saving Wren's future by leaving him and closing off their bond. Desperate to communicate, Wren tried one last time.

"*Master, if you leave me here without you, it will be the death of me!*" he sent around the rapidly growing barrier.

"*I love you, My Wren.*" His master's voice was little more than the ghost of a sigh in his mind. "*And that is why I must leave you. Try to understand and don't hate me too much, little one.*"

"*I could never hate you, I love you!*" Wren sent, but he was talking to a blank wall. Haven had cut himself off completely and there was nothing Wren could do about it, though he had been trying day and night for the last three days.

* * *

"Come now, sleepyhead. As I said, the council awaits. We must make you presentable." Berra smiled at him cheerfully as she stripped the sheets away from him in a no-nonsense kind of way. Not for the first time, Wren thought how awful it was to be cared for by someone who was so relentlessly practical. Berra didn't care to hear about his broken heart or the way he would die without his master. No matter what Wren said to her, she still forced him to get up and walk in the sunny paths that surrounded the temple daily. At first Wren had gone eagerly, hopeful that he might somehow find Haven. But the feeling he got through their walled-off link, however faint, was unmistakable -- Haven had left Radiant. He was gone and Wren could wander forever and never find him in the sun dappled paths around the Temple of Light.

And now Berra was saying something about the council -- likely they were going to assign him to a new master. Wren shivered at the thought and then squared his shoulders. Well, why should he care? He wouldn't be here much longer, so they could do what they liked. Last night after trying to contact Haven until he felt like his head was filled with broken pottery shards, Wren had decided what to do. If he couldn't have the future he wanted with his master, he would have no future at all. There was no easy means of suicide available at the Temple of Light, but he was bright and resourceful and knew he would find something. If nothing else, he would simply stop eating. Indeed, it would be easy enough since he had no appetite since his master had gone away without him.

He allowed Berra to chase him out of bed and dress him in the clean, neatly pressed tunic and trousers she had brought with her, but his mind was far away, wondering what Haven was doing. What he was thinking. If he was feeling half as much pain as Wren was.

Twice as much. The answer came to him unbidden, and for a moment Wren looked around hopefully. Had that been Haven's mind-voice he heard? But the solid barrier that still remained between them assured him it was all his imagination. Sighing heavily, he followed the master healer from the dormitories of the Healing Complex and out into the labyrinth-like halls of the temple. The master healer had been in to examine him only the day before and when he had seen how the twisted knot of scar tissue had disappeared from Wren's hip, leaving only the faint white lines of Haven's H, he'd seemed quite excited. Wren didn't know why and he hadn't cared enough to ask. He had simply lain in bed, his face to the wall, and let the master healer do as he wished. He was too tired and distraught to do anything else.

Soon enough, they reached the circular council chamber, the same place where his master had been tried, no doubt, Wren thought. It was decorated simply, in earth tones, as was the rest of the temple, but the beauty of the handwoven tapestry on the wall or the well-crafted wooden table the Council of Wisdom sat behind was lost on Wren. He simply didn't care anymore.

The master healer came to a halt and indicated that Wren must stand before the three at the table, which he did. He studied the faces of the council dispassionately. These were the three who had parted him from his master. Master Langos, Mistress Tegbreth, and Haven's own old master, Master Serin. He wondered if they knew they had signed his death warrant when they banished Haven from Radiant. He wondered if they cared.

Master Serin cleared his throat. "Council is now in session. This is regarding a rather unusual matter between a master who has left our Order, Master D'Lon Haven, and his novice, Wren."

"Really, Serin, is this necessary?" Mistress Tegbreth looked like she'd been eating unripe fruit, so pinched and pursed was her thin-lipped mouth.

"I believe that it is or I would not have called a session of the council, Mistress Tegbreth," Serin said mildly. "The master healer has new evidence to display."

"Well, let him display it, then." Master Langos made a motion with one twisted hand. "Although I fear I must agree with Mistress Tegbreth here, Serin. The case is clear enough -- Master Haven and his novice transgressed and broke their vows not to get involved in a sexual relationship. What can the master healer possibly have to say that can mitigate these circumstances?"

"It is not what I have to say, but what I have to show." The master healer sounded perplexed. "If you will all examine this holo-scan..." He made a motion with a small, pen-like silver instrument, a projector, Wren realized. And then a life-size holo-image of his own pelvis appeared, rotating in front of the council's eyes. He knew it was his because of the twisted lump of burn tissue that formed a crooked H on his hip.

"What is this?" Mistress Tegbreth looked scandalized despite the fact that Wren's genitals had been tastefully blurred out.

"This, Mistress, is an image taken on the first day Wren arrived back at the Temple. See the distinctive branding scar there?" The master healer pointed at the ugly mark on Wren's hip.

"One can hardly help seeing it, Master Healer," Master Langos said dryly. "What of it?"

"It's not there anymore." The master healer manipulated the small silver projector and the image changed. "I examined the boy yesterday and found this instead."

A new image of Wren's pelvis flashed up before them. It was clear that this was a later image because the twisted lines of H'rak's scar had been replaced by the clean, faint white marks of Haven's H.

"The scar shows much improvement, true," Master Langos acknowledged. "How was it accomplished?"

"Did you call us here simply to explain a new healing technique?" Mistress Tegbreth glared at the master healer. "Because, however impressive, it does not strike me as the best use of this council's time."

"No, Mistress Tegbreth -- this is not my work." The master healer shook his head emphatically. "Though I healed the flesh and stopped the infection that had set in, I was unable to remove the scar tissue. I believe the boy's master did this before he left. And it was not only Wren's scar that he healed, but the psychic wound inflicted by the restrictor collar as well. Wren has been brought back into the Light."

"What?"

"Impossible -- how?" Master Langos and Mistress Tegbreth exclaimed at the same time.

"Master, Mistress, if you will permit me…" Master Serin nodded at both of them courteously and they gave him their attention. "Ever since we sent Master Haven away from the temple and from Radiant itself, I have been plagued with doubts," he began, steepling his long fingers in front of him. "I have known Haven since before he was Wren's age and never have I found the taint of Darkness in his soul."

"Never until he seduced his novice," Mistress Tegbreth muttered. Master Serin raised an eyebrow at her silently and she subsided, allowing him to continue.

"As I was saying, it bothered me. I began searching through the archives, looking for something -- what I could hardly say. But something to explain the bond I felt between Haven and young Wren here. Late last night, I found something and when the master healer came to me with this…" He gestured to the holo-image of Wren's pelvis still floating in front of them. "I knew I had the answer."

"Well, if you would be so kind as to share it with us, I have other things to do this morning," Mistress Tegbreth said acidly.

"Yes, do share, Serin." Master Langos looked genuinely interested.

Serin took a deep breath and looked at Wren, who was beginning to have an interest in the proceedings after all. What exactly was Master Serin saying?

"The bond between Haven and his novice, Wren, goes well beyond the normal teaching link shared by a master and his novice," Serin said, smiling slightly. "It is, in fact, something that has not been seen in this temple for more than eight hundred years -- so long that we of the Order have forgotten it existed."

"A bond no one knew existed? What nonsense is this?" Mistress Tegbreth exclaimed.

Master Serin continued quietly, unfazed by her outburst.

"The connection between Haven and Wren is a genuine love bond -- grown in the presence of and nurtured by the living Light that surrounds us all." He looked at the other two council members gravely. "Haven was right when he said there was a seed planted between him and Wren that was meant to sprout -- it was the love bond. That is the only way Haven could have healed a scar not even the master healer could touch and brought young Wren back into the Light."

"But…but then, you're saying…" Master Langos looked confused.

"That Haven was right. He and Wren are actually *meant* to be together -- the Light *put* them together. You will both remember that Haven found young Wren on Rigel Six and recognized his aptitude for the Light at once," Serin said.

"Yes, but that is hardly a reason to condone the type of behavior that has been going on between the two of them!" Mistress Tegbreth exploded.

"I'm afraid that it is, Mistress Tegbreth," Master Langos said thoughtfully. "If Serin is right -- and I believe that he is -- the living Light actually put these two together. They are two halves of one whole, incomplete without each other."

"Exactly." Serin nodded. "And once Wren has passed his trials, they will be a formidable team -- two masters bonded by love and Light such as this temple has not seen for eight hundred years." Serin sounded triumphant and Wren felt his heart give a little skip in his chest. Could it really be true? He was meant to be with his master? He had always known it in his heart, but to hear it said openly by the Council of Wisdom was something else entirely.

"I don't believe it." Mistress Tegbreth's sour words punctured his happiness before it could even begin to grow. "If Haven's love for the boy healed him so thoroughly, why is his mark still on Wren's…er, hip?" She gestured vaguely at the rotating holo-image, obviously embarrassed to look at it too openly.

"Please, Masters, Mistress," Wren heard himself say as he took a step toward the raised dais where the Council of Wisdom sat. "I didn't want that mark to fade. It is my master's mark, you see. And it's all I have left of him."

"Not anymore." The deep, familiar voice came from outside the council chamber but it was followed immediately by the person Wren wished most to see in the universe.

"Master!" He threw himself happily into Haven's strong arms and his master caught him and squeezed him in a bear hug so tight Wren could scarcely breathe. Not that he cared -- who needed to breathe when his master was back?

"I came as soon as I got your message," Haven said, speaking to his old master, as he continued to hold Wren close.

"I only sent it this morning -- that was fast flying you did, Haven," Master Serin said dryly.

"I couldn't bear to leave orbit around Radiant," Haven admitted. "Every mile further away from my Wren felt like another mile away from my heart."

"Master, I felt the same. I wanted to tell you -- why did you block me?" Wren looked up into his master's deep blue eyes pleadingly, searching for an explanation.

Haven sighed. "I thought I was doing what was best for your future. Will you forgive me, Wren? I can see now how wrong I was and I promise we will never be separated again."

"That depends on the will of this council, Haven," Mistress Tegbreth said sharply. "You have not been reinstated as a master of the Order of Light, nor is it certain that you will be."

"Reinstated or not, I won't be parted from Wren a second time." Haven faced the council resolutely, his deep voice quiet but decisive. "I beg your pardon, Masters, Mistress, but Wren and I need each other and if we can't be together in the Order, we will be together elsewhere. I will fight to the death anyone who tries to take him from me."

"There's no need for that, Haven," Master Langos said hastily. "I think we can *all* see" -- he gave Mistress Tegbreth a hard look -- "that the bond between you and your novice is, er, special. And now that we know it is a..."

"A love bond," Master Serin supplied quietly.

"Right, a love bond, I see no reason why the two of you should not be reinstated in the Order at once. After all, it would be a shame to lose both our best negotiator and such a promising young novice at the same time. Don't you agree, Mistress Tegbreth?"

Mistress Tegbreth looked more sour than ever but finally she nodded. "I suppose in light of the new evidence…"

"Good, then it's settled." Master Serin clapped his hands, clearly pleased with the outcome. He smiled at Haven. "Haven, my boy, I can't tell you how happy I am. You were right all along -- you and the boy belong together. Congratulations." He smiled at them both, nodding as he and the other council members left the raised dais.

At last, there was no one left in the circular council room but Wren and his Master. Wren was so happy he was afraid -- could this really be true? Could he really be back with his master for good?

"Master, can it be? We're never to be parted again?" Wren could scarcely believe it. He clung close to Haven's side, resting his head on his master's broad chest, afraid that if he took his hands and eyes off Haven for even an instant, the older man would disappear.

"Never again, my Wren." Haven lifted his chin and planted a soft kiss full of promise on Wren's lips. "Never again. We will live and love together and grow old together, me faster than you, no doubt," he added with a wry twist of his lips. "And as soon as you pass your trials, we will be master and novice no longer, but equals." He sighed. "I guess I'll have to think of something else to call you then since

'Novice' won't be appropriate. And you can call me D'Lon or Haven, whichever suits you best."

"Neither suits me." Wren cuddled even closer to him, putting his arms around Haven's neck with a contented sigh. He felt like his heart might burst with happiness, but he knew he would die happy if it did. "I shall always call you Master because that is what you are to me -- the master of my heart. Just as inside, no matter where we go or what we do, I will always be your slave boy."

Haven laughed and hugged him tight. "*Well then, I love you, slave boy. Are you ready to go out into the wide universe and seek some new adventures -- this time as equals?*"

"*I'll go anywhere with you, Master,*" Wren sent, planting a soft kiss on Haven's lips. "*Just lead the way.*"

THE END

Evangeline Anderson

Evangeline Anderson is a registered MRI tech who would rather be writing. And yes, she is nerdy enough to have a bumper sticker that reads "I'd rather be writing." Honk if you see her! She is thirty-something and lives in Florida with a husband, a son, and two cats. She had been writing erotic fiction for her own gratification for a number of years before it occurred to her to try and get paid for it. To her delight, she found that it was actually possible to get money for having a dirty mind and she has been writing paranormal and Sci-fi erotica steadily ever since.

See what Evangeline's been up to by checking out her website at http://www.evangelineanderson.com.

TITLES AVAILABLE In Print from Loose Id®

COURTESAN
Louisa Trent

DANGEROUS CRAVINGS
Evangeline Anderson

DARK ELVES: TAKEN
Jet Mykles

DAUGHTERS OF TERRA:
THE TA'E'SHA CHRONICLES, BOOK ONE
Theolyn Boese

DINAH'S DARK DESIRE
Mechele Armstrong

FORGOTTEN SONG
Ally Blue

HEAVEN SENT: HELL & PURGATORY
Jet Mykles

INTERSTELLAR SERVICE & DISCIPLINE:
VICTORIOUS STAR
Morgan Hawke

SHARDS OF THE MIND:
THE TA'E'SHA CHRONICLES, BOOK TWO
Theolyn Boese

STRENGTH IN NUMBERS
Rachel Bo

THE ASSIGNMENT
Evangeline Anderson

THE TIN STAR
J. L. Langley

THEIR ONE AND ONLY
Trista Ann Michaels

VETERANS 1: THROUGH THE FIRE
Rachel Bo and Liz Andrews

VETERANS 2: NOTHING TO LOSE
Mechele Armstrong and Bobby Michaels

Publisher's Note: The print titles listed above were previously released in e-book format by Loose Id®.

Non-Fiction by ***ANGELA KNIGHT***
PASSIONATE INK: A GUIDE TO WRITING EROTIC ROMANCE

LaVergne, TN USA
14 September 2009
157759LV00002B/1/P